Spruced Up

Rupert Hudson

Copyright © 2022 Rupert Hudson
All rights reserved.
ISBN-13:

*When a great ship is in harbour and
moored, it is safe, there can be no doubt.
But that is not what great ships are built for.*

--Clarissa Pinkola Estes

Chapter 1 - Martin's Miserable Morning

"Good morning, this is Richmond Lake dispatch with your AM weather report. Today we've got widespread precipitation, with potential thunder showers and a moderate fire danger level. Tomorrow's danger level will start up-trending quite..."

"Oh shut up," Martin grumbled, silencing the radio with one fell swoop of his swollen left hand. He was having a rough day so far, as evidenced by the gloomy shadows of depression that lingered on his weathered face. The rain this morning had leaked into his bed, awakening him with a sopping wet knee and subsequent shivers that lasted for approximately thirty-seven minutes. He urged his sore body out of his comfortable mattress, wondering momentarily why his body was always so rigid in the mornings. This thought morphed into pure rage as he peered out of his window and noticed that the rabbits had gotten into his garden. His indignation redoubled as he noticed that the number of rabbits had similarly increased twofold since the day before.

"This is not a 'tell all your friends party garden', Bugs." He yelled out of the window while doubts filled his mind about this action, due to the fact that these rabbits definitely didn't speak English. "This is *my* garden and if you dig under the fence and eat my kale again, I'm going to find your bunny hole and eat your family."

Bugs stared back nonchalantly, seemed to shrug its tiny shoulders and the two rabbits hopped off underneath Martin's small cabin.

Martin shrugged as well, attempting to push away the burning anger that he was feeling in his forehead. He threw on a hodgepodge outfit, walked swiftly outside, and started to bury his emotions in the hole that the rabbits had dug under his fence. While doing so he managed to catch his shirt on the sharp part of the fence and rip up a good ol' hole on the sleeve.

"My favourite gardening shirt," he quietly said to himself with a slight tear in his eye. He looked around to make sure Bugs didn't see his betrayal of emotions but there was no sign of life. All of a sudden he felt lonely and incredibly disappointed in himself for scaring off the bunny, but he ignored those thoughts and continued digging his hole, distracting himself with cartoon images of the delicious peanut butter and banana sandwich that he was going to consume for breakfast. The day before, he had convinced himself to drive to the nearest town to get some treats for himself, which included organic peanut butter ("much too expensive," he grumbled to a cardboard cutout of the store manager), perfectly ripe bananas ("I hope they're not bad by tomorrow," he spat at the shopkeeper), and fresh-baked bread ("it had better not be stale when I get home," he silently screamed at no one at all).

As he was finishing the hole, Martin's mind had started to convince him that something was going to be wrong when he got back inside. That someone would have snuck into his cabin and stolen his precious food. Or worse, *eaten it* right there in his kitchen. Here is what played out in his head,

Martin enters his kitchen to find a plump teenager with peanut butter all over his face (including over his left eye, which he is unable to open)

Teenager: I didn't do it! I didn't do it!

Martin: Do what?

Teenager: Eat your peanut butter and banana sandwiches!

Martin: No one said you did.

Teenager: Oh...yeah...

Martin: Though I believe the proof is written all over your desperate, chubby face.

Teenager: You're the chubby one!

Teenager pulls a photo out of his pocket and shows it to Martin - it's of a chubby, young boy.

Martin: Where did you get that?

Teenager (*reading the back of the photo*): Martin Bushnell, age 12.

Martin: So what?! I was 12.

Teenager: Maybe you still are.

Martin looks in the mirror and sees the same chubby 12 year old and screams.

Martin woke up from his imaginary horror movie, yelling a little. He looked around again to make sure that no one was looking and finished up the hole. His forehead was sweaty, despite the coolness of the moist air and he grunted with discomfort, quietly longing for a body that never experienced sweat. He threw down the shovel and went back inside, walking with a quicker-than-average pace that alluded to his unacknowledged fear that he would be confronting his teenage self when he entered the room. To his dismay ("shouldn't I feel relief?" he thought) there was no one in his cabin. He started to feel a bit queasy due to his especially wavering mind but proceeded to prepare the delicious sandwich nonetheless. Alas, after his first bite, he was fairly disappointed, grumbling, "too sticky" to the line of dead horseflies along his windowsills. Nevertheless, he finished the oozing sandwich and felt a small jolt of energy that inspired him to continue with his day, despite the strange start. He took a look at his calendar and groaned, releasing a small segment of half-chewed peanut that tumbled down through gravity onto his spotless (now not-so) floor.

<u>May 20</u>
Do laundry **and** bathe.

"Why did I do that to myself?" he thought. Bathing **and** laundry on the same damn day. Furthermore, due to his flippant disregard for holding all his food firmly in his mouth, he would also have to clean the floors for the fourth day running. He had no running water in his cabin so all of these tasks were time-consuming and strenuous. His rampant mind kicked forward a memory in order to distract himself from any negative thoughts that these tasks might bring forth.

When he was in town yesterday, one of the women in the grocery store struck up a conversation with him.

"I don't see you around very often," she said, with what may have been a question mark at the end.

"I live *off the grid*," Martin said.

"Ohh, how sweet. I watched an Amazon documentary about that!"

Martin found her pretty and wanted to watch an Amazon documentary with her but he would not allow himself to show any vulnerability.

"I don't have a TV," he said with false pride.

"Shame. It's nice to be distracted by a story once in a while. Do you have running water?" Her eyes were full of curiosity. His eyes were full of fear. She blinked slowly. He blinked rapidly.

"No. I fill up jugs for drinking in town and use rainwater to bathe and wash clothes," he stated plainly.

"Wow. I'm impressed. That must be difficult."

Martin shrugged and said, "I'm used to it." His eyes darted around, logging all of the nearest exits.

"Don't you get bored out there? Or lonely?"

Beads of sweat began to develop on his forehead, despite the forceful air conditioning that the grocery store so gracefully provided though he blamed it on their shameless use of fluorescent lighting. Due to the sweaty distraction, he forgot to respond to her question. She looked at him, waiting patiently, and then said,

"Well, if you do ever need a friend, you can call me."

She proceeded to take out a notepad and pen out of her prismacolor purse to write her number upon. This was getting a little too overwhelming for Martin.

"I don't have a phone either," Martin shyly mumbled. He focused on the (extortionate) organic peanut butter in his basket and slowly made his way out of both the conversation and the store. The sky outside was full of streaky cirrus clouds that, to an imaginative observer, could have looked like deities or spirits. However, Martin barely noticed as he was distracted by the unconscious act of suppressing his emotions and the conscious act of getting home. He got in his dirty, baby blue truck and drove off, looking over his shoulder slightly to see if the woman was still at the store exit. To his quiet dismay, he could only see the automatic doors, which were waiting for another human to pause near its sensor so it could fulfil its sole function with robotic joy.

"I hate robots," Martin said to pass the time.

As Martin's dislike for automation brought him back to the present, he once again realized that it was time for him to bathe *and* do laundry. Though when she had asked him about its difficulty he had shrugged it off, it was actually a pretty arduous task, involving a lot of time and a number of different buckets.

Bucket 1 - soapy water for clothes
Bucket 2 - clean rinse water for clothes
Bucket 3 - soapy water for human
Bucket 4 - clean water for human
Bucket 5 - large bucket to stand in so he could dump Bucket 3 and 4 overtop of his sweaty head

While Martin collected all of these buckets, he noticed the tiny sun-crusted rabbit pellets smiling up at him from his stone pathway. A memory from his childhood flashed into his mind, involving Looney Tunes, a mouse, and a yelling mother. He stopped for a moment to try to see this memory but then quickly proceeded to ignore it. He *never* thought about his past. There was no point. It was over and done with.

Be here now. Moment by moment. He had to be strong. He was an outcast from society. He was swimming up the stream. He was different, unique, powerful!

After pumping himself up for a good thirty seconds, he forgot about the rabbit pellets and started to fill his buckets from the outdoor rain barrel he had once set up. His hand slipped a little when he turned on the already-rusted spout and the water started spraying everywhere, getting the bottom half of his left pant leg quite damp. He yelled,

"NO!"

The anger persisted for some time, despite the fact that he was about to get those pants wet anyway in Bucket 1 *and* 2. He did not notice this inconsistency. In fact, only the osprey flying overhead had any awareness of what was really happening. To calm this agitated man down, the osprey uttered a great, "**you are loved**!" but the man seemed to ignore this friendly gesture. This appeared to happen every single time the osprey tried to share compassion with a human being. For some reason, they steadfastly ignored him. One man had even pointed an exploding stick at him. However, he still persisted ostentatiously, as he *was* the world's most compassionate osprey. He flew off towards a nearby herd of elk, planning to land right in the midst of their herd and hold a discourse on the connectivity of nature, the importance of loving-kindness, and quantum non-locality. Fortunately, with the elk, he was rather successful and joined their herd for the next three years.

In the time in which the Osprey's Great Discourse was uttered, Martin had successfully managed to trip over at least three out of five of the buckets, and ended up scrunching into Bucket 5, limbs splayed in all directions. Out of despair and irritation, he dumped the contents of the rest of the buckets (soap, water, clothing) into Bucket 5 and ended up bathing with his clothes. He was actually rather satisfied with this outcome and thought about how he might share this story with the woman in the store next time he went to town. These thoughts were quickly discarded as he knew how important it was for him to remain in solitude. As he cleansed himself in the dirty bath water, he imagined that with every wipe of his ragged bath cloth, another dirty piece of society was wiping off him. For just a moment, Martin was peaceful.

Once he had wrung out, hung up, and dried off the clothes and himself, he realized that the whole ordeal had taken him a better part of an hour.

"That's an hour I'm never getting back," he mumbled to himself, not really sure of what that phrase meant as well as forgetting the moment of peace he had felt during that "hour he was never getting back".

A nearby butterfly thought to ask him, "what would you do if you got that hour back?" but shyness got the better of her and she ended up just fluttering near the sleeve of a hanging t-shirt. A droplet of water from the clothing dropped on her left wing, causing her a slight imbalance, as well as a gorgeous, glistening effect that may have made Martin's left eye erupt in a single tear if he had been paying any attention whatsoever to the magical world around him. However, he was still complaining to himself about the bathing and laundry ordeal.

"That's the last time I schedule those on the **same day**," he growled. He thought to go to his calendar and split apart the subsequent laundry and bathing days, but realized that he would have to swap around his entire routine schedule, which was definitely not scheduled for that day and would take him at least half an hour. He glanced at his calendar, noticing May 23 had an open half hour, and wrote down "change calendar". He smiled, proud of his routine, from which he rarely wavered. In fact, on the bottom of the page on the calendar, he had written "don't stray far from this schedule, or there will be HTP".

HTP = Hell To Pay.

Without taking a breather after his intense bathing session, he looked at the next thing scheduled.

10am - Clean and Fix Solar Panel

"Great," he whispered ironically. This was another job that Martin was dreading. As the dismay flooded his nervous system, he allowed it to grow by adding:

10:23am - Thoroughly clean all floors...again

One may ask, was there anything on Martin's calendar that he would not complain and/or worry about? You can probably figure out the answer to that one yourself.

When Martin had put up the solar panel, he was rather impressed with himself. The solar panel was a grand, shiny, tall structure that stood in front of his quaint cabin. He used it to power his fridge, radio, and the outlets in his home. Having a solar panel made him feel like he was on the cutting edge of society, but whenever that thought came in he immediately threw it in the garbage can at the bottom of his mind. He wanted to be *out of society*, not on the edge of it. Unfortunately, soon after he built this majestic suncatcher, he realized that it required regular maintenance and cleaning, which added another lengthy task to his already gargantuan list. Living off the grid was not easy.

"But it's worth it," he weakly convinced himself.

His solar-panel cleaning outfit was hanging on the clothesline, still sopping wet and absolutely unwearable.

"How could I not have thought of that when I put a solar panel cleaning and laundry on the same day?" he chastised himself, tensing up his body and grinding his teeth. He solemnly put on his alternative solar-panel cleaning outfit, which was exactly the same as the other, just slightly newer-looking. He then took his ladder out of the shed and got to work. On the top right panel, there was a large pile-up of bird poo. He looked around for the culprit, thought he saw something far up in the sky, and yelled "IF YOU DO THAT AGAIN I AM GOING TO COME UP THERE AND STEAL YOUR EYES." Unfortunately, what he had seen in the sky was a Boeing-737, which typically does not have eyes. The delinquent bird who had splattered the bird poo onto the panel was actually sitting on a branch to the right of Martin, watching the poor man stress out his body and mind yelling at an unreachable airplane. The little robin realized what he had done and felt a profound sense of guilt. He was not aiming for the panel, it had just slipped out as he was flying away from a large osprey. He had not been able to discern if the osprey was trying to eat or embrace him so he had fearfully made an escape, unfortunately emptying his bowels along the way. He made an attempt to apologize but the sensation of guilt was so strong in his fluffy red chest that his apology was nothing more than a whispery whistle.

Martin was unaware of this incredible incident happening to his right. Once he finished cleaning the panels, he made his way to the back of the structure, holding up a panel where a loose wire needed reconnection.

"Your own mind has a lot of these loose wires that could use some reconnecting," he thought. This thought startled him as it seemed rather out of character and he dropped the panel back into place with a heavy bang. His left hand seemed to have been left behind in the left side of the panel when it had slammed shut. Martin shrieked so loudly that a nearby colony of bees decided it was time for them to find a new hive. He pulled his hand out of the panel, ran back into his cabin, and dipped his throbbing digits in the unemptied brownish Bucket 5 bath water. This soothed him and he calmed down ever so slightly. His hand was already purple and swollen. This day was turning out to be one of the most difficult days he had ever experienced.

"You have had many days worse than this," his mind mentioned, but the pain in his left hand caused him to disregard these troubling thoughts.

"Good morning, this is Richmond Lake dispatch with your AM weather report. Today we've got rain showers across the district, with potential thunder showers and a moderate fire danger level. Tomorrow things will change quite..."

"Oh shut up," Martin instructed and shut off the ridiculous rambling radio.

The morning was almost over and Martin felt like he had done nothing at all. He looked around his cabin, rather disgruntled by the chaos of the place. Cleaning was on his schedule every day but he never felt like it was enough. It could never be the way he really wanted it to be. He wasn't exactly sure what that was, but this wasn't it. However, at the same moment that Martin was judging his surroundings with pure negativity, a little bumblebee peeked her head in through the window on her way to a new hive. As she observed the small cabin she thought, "wow, I hope our new hive is as clean as this place!" She was quite taken by the three cast iron pans hanging above the sink in a size-related order as well as the soft touch of a pile of rose petals in the middle of the coffee table. She jotted down some notes on her left wing regarding her future room décor and bumbled off in the direction of her new home, feeling newly inspired.

At this point, all Martin wanted to do was lay down for a moment and read a novel. However, he made an effort never to put his nose in a book that was not completely based on fact. If anyone right then would have asked him why, he would have said that by reading fiction you are completely ignoring the truth of the world around you. You are allowing yourself to distractedly disappear, little by little.

"But haven't you been distracted all morning? You have been dreaming of your breakfast, complaining about all your tasks, and harshly judging the world around you while ignoring the beauty of everything you are a part of," his mind suggested.

Martin almost jumped out of his skin. He *never* had thoughts like this. His mind was usually supportive of him. He would look at his schedule, see the task to be done, and do it. No questions asked. For some strange reason, on this miserable morning, his mind was acting like an orangutan on the loose from the Bronx Zoo. He was going to have to do something about this. He looked at the calendar for the month of May. On the page was a picture of one of those lookout towers that people worked in to pretend they were living off-grid for a summer.

"You try *actually* living off grid," Martin boasted towards the picture.

As he looked at the picture a little more, he noticed some writing in the bottom left-hand corner about Farm Equipment Fires. He just about looked away due to the fact that he *already knew* how to deal with farm equipment fires when he saw a little phrase at the bottom,

'**Be aware of your surroundings,** *friction on rocks can cause sparks in fields and roadways*.'

Martin knew there was something important about this phrase but couldn't figure out what. "Friction on rocks..." he muttered. "Fields and roadways?"

Suddenly, a spark lit up a dusty lightbulb in his mind.

"I know how to deal with this pesky mind!" he almost exclaimed.

Shrugging into his thick red and white jacket and adding some finger-padded gloves, he grabbed his keys and pulled out a large rifle from the closet nearest his front door. He gently caressed the rifle with his swollen hand, slung it over his back, ran out the door, got on his ATV and started driving down his favourite path. The noise of the ATV frightened off all the animals in the vicinity so no-one was there to see the crazed look in Martin's eyes. He was going hunting.

Chapter 2 - The Bear

    A continuous low layer of stratus clouds buffeted the sky that day. The sun had attempted to shine through earlier that morning, but the atmosphere was much too heavy so it had decided not to waste its energy. The groundhogs were buried deep and warm in their holes, finishing up their studies of the blueprints of a nearby organic farm. Last year they had managed to nick enough chard, squash, and radishes to feed half an army. Luckily, their army was good with rationing so they had had enough to last them the winter. Unfortunately, as they noticed the writer of this novel writing about their secretive lives, they politely asked him to leave, and closed their tiny, brass-plated door. Thus, the story returns to Martin.

    The black and gold-striped ATV was crashing its way through a small cut line amongst the myriad of birch, aspen, and spruce. The beige birch's skin was slowly peeling, the trembling aspens' leaves had just fully emerged, and the black spruce trees were dropping their scaly cones. However, Martin was driving at almost the speed of light (or so it seemed in his head), so he was, once again, unable to be aware of his surroundings. His mind had stopped spouting nonsense for the time being and was instead focused on his destination. There was a large, secluded lake (Martin had proudly named it Large Lake) about 5km from his house that hosted a variety of wildlife who came there to quench their thirst and gossip about the rest of the ecosystem.

    Currently on the east side of Large Lake there was a moose named Elliot along with Beatrice, an otter, and Salty the sparrow. They were all looking at a pile of excellent sticks on the ground.

"Don't you guys get it? If you leave them here, those sticks are going to be decomposed and subsequently turn into your food," Elliot suggested.

"You're not making any sense, buddy. Those sticks are literally *only* for nest-building material and we're taking them with us," Salty the sparrow retorted saltily.

Beatrice wasn't having any of this.

"These sticks are mine. I saw them first. My siblings and I are playing the most epic underwater fighting game at the moment and these could be used as my weapons for round 2."

Beatrice proceeded to go for the sticks.

"WAIT," Elliot cried. "You can't just disrupt the ecosystem like that. You're messing with the karma of the forest."

"Oh. My. God. Elliot, you always do this. You bring spiritual nonsense into the picture and make us all feel bad about everything," said Salty.

"I don't feel bad. I just want to triple-flip stab my brothers with these things. I'd invite you guys but...you can't breathe underwater," Beatrice dramatically rolled her eyes. She probably would not have invited them even if they could breathe underwater. Beatrice went to snatch the sticks once more but as her slimy hand caressed the first of the sticks, a massive "BOOM" came from the cutline.

Salty was startled out of her skin.

"That maniac is back!!!" the now skinless sparrow cried.

As they started to run away, Elliot paused.

"Wait," the majestic moose said. "Remember last time he came here? He set that pile of sticks over there on fire. Now they're gone. I hate to say this, but we've got to take them with us."

In her panic, Beatrice was starting to feel slightly more generous.

"Okay, we each take a third of them, but quickly."

They each grabbed their third of the sticks and ran, swam, and flew off into their respective hideouts. Elliot delicately buried his sticks by a patch of wood-loving mushrooms, Salty added a third story to her palatial nest, and Beatrice was able to win both the second and third rounds of The Otter Odyssey.

Martin felt happy for the first time that day. The roar of the ATV, coupled with the landscape whizzing past him and the dreams of shooting a large elk or bear were distracting him from all of his troubles. His mind was no longer telling him what to do or how to think. He was in control. He revved the engine, causing the exhaust pipe to make a large "BOOM."

"ARE YOU SERIOUS?!" he yelled, realizing that his to-do for 1pm that day was to look into fixing the exhaust on the ATV. It had been spouting fumes like crazy while leaking oil in its wake. It could completely fall apart on him at any point but he pretended not to care. He was going hunting whether the ATV liked it or not.

He ripped his way to Large Lake, exploding through the trees like a crazed Formula 1 racer, spun out in a donut-like formation ("I meant to do that," he thought) and shut off the ATV. He pulled out his binoculars and set to observing the lake. Normally he did not enter this area in such a dramatic fashion. The animals tended to get quite frightened when large bursts of sound echoed through their forests, but today was different, he was on a rampage. He impatiently waited for an animal to enter the view of his binos and, as luck would have it, he found something. A lone male caribou peacefully lapping up the water with its tongue.

"A caribou?" Martin thought. "Those are rare birds. I'm not sure how it didn't hear me but I'll take it."

Well, the reason why Lapzig, the lone caribou, had not heard Martin crashing through the trees was because he was mostly deaf. On an unfortunate afternoon while he was in his teenage years, he had been alone in the woods practicing a new dance move called the Beautifly. It was a move that he had invented himself, modelled after the way the tiny blue butterflies by his home would flap their wings. As Lapzig did not have wings he was patiently attempting to move his antlers in the same fashion but they wouldn't budge. With his eyes crossed and his jaw tight, he concentrated with all his might.

"Come on, come on," he pleaded. "This is the only way that Anastasia will be your mate."

At the same time that he felt that they were just about to start flapping, he heard a crashing through the trees. Startled, he turned around to determine the location of the noise and saw a plump, moustachioed human with a bright orange jacket.

"Ahhh, my prayers have been answered," he said to the ferns. "I have always wanted to ask one of these how to grow one of those hair balls under my nose."

The man had not noticed him so Lapzig crept up close. He knew that humans were quite frightened of all types of wildlife so he moved slowly and quietly. He had learnt some stealth tactics from his pal, Leon, who proclaimed that he was a cougar but was more like a bobcat. The orange man's back was turned and he was holding something in his hand that Lapzig could not see. He managed to end up right behind the man.

"Excuse me," he said as politely as possible. "I just wanted to know..."

Before he could unveil his moustachioed question, the moustachioed man screeched, turned a full 180 degrees as rapidly as his plump moustachioed body could let him, and fired his shot gun directly next to Lapzig's right ear. Lapzig bolted through the trees, his ears ringing loudly. From this day forth, he was fully deaf in his right ear, and mostly deaf in the left, though he was more upset that he was no closer to learning the secret of bushy hair underneath the nose. For this reason, he had not heard our dear, malicious Martin, who was now making his way towards the precious caribou with a nasty look in his eyes.

Though he would not admit it if you asked him, Martin was not a very good hunter. He hadn't ever killed an animal with his gun, but had once sideswiped a deer by mistake in his ATV and counted that as a "hunting kill" in his hunting journal. His lack of hunting skills came from the fact that he was distracted rather easily by anything that came up, both internally and externally. As he was attempting to make a sneaky manoeuvre to the other side of the lake, he saw a large trout swimming around near the shore.

"I bet I could catch that trout with my bare hands," he said to himself with all the false masculinity that he could muster.

"Do it then," he retorted.

He threw down his weapon, pulled off his Guns 'n' Roses shirt, and dived into the water. The ripples from the dive made their way over to Lapzig's lapping tongue. Since becoming mostly deaf, his other senses had developed dramatically, and as the tiny ripple brushed against his outstretched tongue, he was able to sense, "human". He looked up and saw what looked like a man attempting to catch a trout with his bare hands.

"Only a bear can catch a trout with its bare hands!" he shouted to Martin. "Believe me, I've tried." This last part was uttered rather forlornly as his most recent attempt to woo Anastasia had involved him showing her how his newly improved sense sphere would help him catch fish with his hooves. He was not successful and she was, as always, unimpressed.

Martin was just as unsuccessful and returned to the shore a dripping mess, disappointed in himself and upset about the dampness of his hunting trousers. Lapzig, having noticed that the human did not wear a moustache, was uninterested and wandered back into the forest, attempting to use his improved eyesight to see into the bellies of the surrounding trees. Perhaps he was successful, but unfortunately the story must return to Martin so this shall never be revealed. Exhausted by the trout wrestling, Martin lay back on the cool rocks surrounding the lake, breathing heavily with his eyes closed. He had forgotten about the caribou and wanted nothing more than to be at home, with a blanket wrapped around him and a log fire burning.

"Perhaps I ought to take a week off of everything," he suggested to himself, though this was immediately met with a retort. "But who's going to fix the ATV? Who's going to take care of the garden? Who's going to be accountable for the relentless responsibilities associated with living 'off grid'?

Martin felt stuck. He started to question why he even made this decision in the first place.

"What led me to be here?" he questioned daringly. This was territory he rarely ventured into. His fortified mind would usually stop him going to any kind of depth, but today, he was tired, and his fortress was vulnerable.

"Looks like someone needs help remembering," uttered a gruff voice from behind his head.

Martin jumped straight up to his feet, like a cat landing from jumping off a tall building, but in re-wind. He turned rapidly and there, sitting comfortably on an oval-shaped boulder at the edge of the forest, was a large black bear. Its long fur glistened in the sunlight and its eyes were curious but piercing. It stared directly at Martin who stared back. He tried to keep one eye on the bear while another scanned the surroundings for his rifle. However, moving the eyes in two different directions is a rare feat, which Martin was unable to perform. He momentarily broke eye contact with the bear to see that the gun was nowhere to be found.

"Ahh, your weapon? I threw it over to Beatrice for the third round. Luckily she hasn't figured out how to actually use it, though I imagine those things don't function very well underwater."

This bear was talking to Martin. In English. Martin was flabbergasted.

"Have I gone crazy?" Martin said half to himself and half to this seated creature.

"Well, yes. That's why I'm here."

"What do you mean by that?" Martin was noticing that the bear's mouth was starting to crinkle upward into a knowing, patient smile.

"Well, listen, my friend. When you moved here into these woods a few years back, the elders who manage this forest were unimpressed and determined to get rid of you as quickly as you came in. We have seen what capacity humans have to rip apart an ecosystem in a matter of weeks. However, there have been a great number of you, mostly many years ago, who worked with our forests, quietly and patiently, and helped them flourish. For this reason, I was able to convince the rest of the elders that you may not do us any damage and we left you alone."

"...I just don't understand how you are talking to me right now." Martin was not really listening to what the bear was saying. He had fully convinced himself of his own lunacy and was afraid of what was going to happen next. Was he going to have to go to an institution? He couldn't bear the thought. He had always been fine. Just going from one task to the next. Never stopping to think, just moving along. Sure, he would get stressed out sometimes but he never thought he was losing it. Perhaps all that isolation really did mess a person up.

"Hey, Martin, you're not listening to me. If you just stand there in disbelief, we're never going to get anywhere in our first session, and the first one is the most important."

"Session?"

"I told you, I am here to help you remember. I have seen how you spend your time. You are constantly busying yourself with menial tasks to try to forget the traumas of your past. You have convinced yourself that this "off the grid" life is the perfect, ideal way to be, though you have not thought about your real motives for doing it. Are they wholesome? Are you doing this for the right reasons? Do you even want to be living here?"

"Of course I do," Martin spat. "The world out there is a mess. Everything is full of negativity and suffering and the best thing that I can do is to remove myself completely. It is the only way I am going to live a happy life."

"Dear Martin. I have run into many others of your kind in these woods. Some come to look at the trees or forage for fungi, or to take a slight respite from their busy lives and, despite the fact that they typically live amongst other humans, quite a few of these people seem pretty happy to me. In fact, you are one of the most unhappy humans I have ever come across."

Martin had had enough. His forehead was aching, the sky was darkening, and he was *talking to a bloody bear.*

"Listen, *bear.*"

"My name is Spruce Engelmann, or Dr. Spruce."

"Okay then, Dr. Spruce. Listen." Martin paused for dramatic effect.

"Yep, listening."

"I'm lovin' this whole thing that we've got going on here," he said sarcastically. "I get it. You're a bear therapist, a bearapist, har har, and I'm in mental trouble and you're here to help me and whatnot but I've got a lot going on back home so it's time for me to go."

Martin was trying his best to sound confident when in fact he had a tender feeling in his sternum coupled with a shakiness that spread throughout his lower body. Dr. Spruce took notice of this. The first session had gone well.

"Okay, Martin, you can go."

"Thanks Bruce."

"Spruce."

"Yep."

Martin picked up his t-shirt, tugging it over his body with his back turned to Dr. Spruce. He knew that when he turned around there would be nothing there. He knew that he was okay. He just needed to get home. He just needed to change the oil in his generator or check his propane levels or organize the rocks near his garden. Everything was going to be fine. He breathed a sigh of relief, looking over the rippling lake, and turned back around. Dr. Spruce was still there. He had a beautiful, curious smile on his face now that made the tenderness in Martin's sternum open up a little bit more. For just a moment, he felt like a 12-year old boy. He wasn't sure exactly what being a 12-year old boy had felt like but, for that moment, that was all he knew. He quickly composed himself, and attempted to block out the maddening thoughts of a potential mental breakdown that imposed themselves upon his mind like the dark, towering cumulus clouds that were forming above his head.

"When you need me again, you'll find me," said Dr. Spruce. He jumped off the rock like an Olympic high diver, landed softly on all fours, laughed gently, and padded off into the forest. When his large bear bottom was no more than a speck in the trees, Martin broke loose of the stunned state that he had settled in and rushed towards his ATV. He rammed the keys in the keyhole, turning them too quickly and causing the engine to rev and sputter without starting.

"No no no no no!" Martin yelled at the ATV, kicked it hard in its middle, and attempted the keys once more. The exhaust spouted black smoke, which rose up quickly and joined the forming storm clouds but, alas, the ATV did not start. Oil was slowly leaking out onto the smooth rocks of the lakeside, which seemed to make their pale pastel colours a little more pronounced. Martin actually took notice of this and the tender feeling in his sternum was apparent once more. He ignored this quickly, but not as instantly as he may have done that morning, and gave the engine a massive kick with his CSA-approved steel-toed boots. The engine clunked and groaned, as if it had been woken up from a dream about electric sheep, and he turned the keys a little more delicately than the first time. The engine woke up with a "BOOM" and Martin was on his way. He drove more carefully than on his trip in as he was still in a bit of shock. The trees passed by him slower than before and he managed to see the peeling back of the skin of the yellow birch that he had previously missed. He had just about convinced himself to stop the ATV and take a quick look when he heard a massive roar of thunder from directly behind him.

"Uh uh, I ain't having this," he said, while pressing his foot on the pedal and letting the speed increase.

He hated thunderstorms. For some reason, thunderstorms always caused him to have darker thoughts and descend into unwanted territories. He wasn't going to allow himself to go there today. He raced along the cutline until the world around him became a green and brown blur. He could hear nothing but the roar of the engine and, once again, his thoughts slipped away from him. He began to relax. Perhaps he had just seen a regular ol' bear and had a panic attack. Yes, maybe that was it. Panic attacks cause hallucinations, don't they? Everyone has a panic attack once in a while. He had had a stressful morning and the trout wrestling had not made things any better. He had just been a bit scared and his imagination got the best of him. As he relaxed even further, the rain started to pour down on his head. He saw a flash of lightning to the east and the rapid roar of thunder showed that this storm was directly over him. The ground was quickly turning into a slushy muddy river and his ATV was out of control. Despite this, he continued to increase his speed, desperate to get home and away from all of this mess.

The rain was falling so hard that he could barely see in front of him. He knew that the turn into his property was somewhere close by but he could not make it out. Perhaps he had already turned into it. Yes, that was it, he was close to his home now, he was sure of it. He started to dream once more about the peanut butter that he was going to finish very soon after setting up a small log fire. His visions of peanut butter became ever more distracting while the rain fell harder and harder. He thought he could make out the clearing of his property up ahead and upped his speed just a little more.

"One more minute, one more minute," he repeated to himself like a mantra.

As he reached the clearing, he saw a pair of lights up ahead and thought, "strange, I must have left the generator on. I don't usually do that."

He got a bit closer to the lights and realized that this wasn't his house. Once he heard the loud honk coming from the truck directly in front of him, he fully knew that was the case. He managed to pull himself quickly off of the road, sideswiping the truck's right headlight, jumping the ATV directly into a ditch and right into a large white spruce tree. As Martin collided with the tree, he blacked out.

Chapter 3 - Martin Is Rescued

Martin found himself surrounded by storm clouds, the thick, black cumulonimbus pressing down on him from all sides. He looked upwards and saw that he was standing right beneath the eye of the storm. However, this was a literal eye that was poking its way through a hole between the clouds. Light from above streamed through the eye like a prism, shooting a dazzling rainbow in all directions that seemed to be protecting Martin from the storm. The eye started to spin like a pinwheel, speeding up rapidly until its pace was maddening and all of the colours had melded into a solid mass. Martin's feet suddenly rose from the ground and he was drawn towards the rotating eyeball. For some reason, he felt like he needed to get there, to be close to it, to be within it. However, the closer he seemed to get to it, the further it spun away from him.

"Stop," cried Martin. "I can't keep up."

The prismacolor eyeball stopped rotating and stared directly at him once again.

"I stopped many years ago," it spoke, in a voice familiar to Martin. "Now, why don't you?"

Martin felt that deep tenderness in his sternum that reminded him of a bear he once met. He suddenly remembered headlights on a rainy road and the battered ATV tumbling over a ditch into an unsuspecting tree.

"I'm dead," Martin thought.

"I AM DEAD." Martin screamed with fear.

"You're not dead, big guy, just badly bruised and a little concussed," said a woman's voice from afar. He knew her voice. It was the voice of peanut butter.

Martin realized his eyes were closed. He could no longer see any prismacolor eyeballs, just darkness with small lights flickering within it. He tried to open his eyes but the pain was overwhelming. He left them closed, and let his eyeballs rest on the little stars behind his eyelids.

"Where am I? Why can't I open my eyes?" His voice was weak and full of pain.

"You hit your head on a tree. I'm amazed you survived. I was out walking through the trees when the storm hit. You must have been doing the same. I was driving my truck back home when your ATV came careening out of the woods. You're lucky I was driving slowly! Any other day, this wouldn't have turned out as well as it did. Adding to your stroke of luck, I am a doctor." The voice that Martin heard was excited and kind. He knew that the voice was familiar, but did not understand why.

"My ATV?..."

"Ooh, I'm sorry to say that it's looking worse than you are. I left it crushed up against the tree and saved you instead. Would you have preferred me to nurse it back to health instead?"

He ignored the joking response. "Who are you? I know your voice."

"My name is Evaline. We have talked in the grocery store a number of times, though you never really seemed to want to talk to me."

"It's not that...it's just..."

A phone in another room rang loudly.

"Sorry, hold on a second," said Evaline sweetly. Martin could feel her lightly touch his arm as she left his side.

She picked up the phone and he heard, "oh no, that's not good. Okay, I'll be there as soon as I can. I've got to get a cab as my right headlight was completely smashed in."

Martin's sternum began to hurt with a strange sense of guilt.

"You're just down the street from me?" she continued. "Okay, thanks dear, I'll tell you what happened when you get me. See you soon."

She walked softly over to Martin's side. He attempted to open his eyes to look at her but the pain began to swell as soon as he thought about performing this action.

"Looks like you're not the only one causing crashes today. I'm needed at the hospital, there has been another crash a few kilometres down the road from where we collided. Just rest as much as you can. That's what you really need. If you manage to get up, help yourself to anything in the kitchen. There is a delicious miso soup on the stove, chocolate chips in all of the cupboards, and berries of all sizes! I'll be back in a few hours."

He started to say that he did not like miso soup but managed to stop himself. Evaline left the room and a few minutes later he heard the door shut. He wanted to open his eyes, to get up and go home, but his body wouldn't let him. He lay still, trying to recall that day's events, but to no avail. He could feel tiredness seeping throughout his body and he was unable to do anything but succumb to it. Sleep found him once again and he embraced it.

Martin awoke to the sound of a gas stove being lit, china bowls being clinked around, and someone humming a song. Along with this, a tantalizing smell crept towards his average-sized nostrils. As he breathed it in, his crusty eyes started to open, little by little, until he could half-see his surroundings. He noticed that his right hand was bandaged and he thought he could see another bandage on his thigh. Panicky thoughts of not being able to do work on his house floated around his head, which also had a large wrapping around it. His breath became shorter and his eyes started to flicker around the room as he felt fear and panic wrap around the rest of his body. The solar panel is going to fall apart, the garden is going to get ravished by rabbits, I am never going to succeed in living off the grid and no one will respect me. These thoughts and many more were starting to whirl around his head like a prismatic spinning eyeball.

He realized that Evaline had noticed him and was coming towards him with two bowls of soup. The sight of her soothed him slightly. She had her hair back in a ponytail and was still wearing what he imagined to be her work uniform. The steam from the soup was rising lazily around her wholesome face. She placed down one of the bowls and sat next to him, taking a spoonful of the soup and bringing it towards Martin's mouth. He kept his mouth closed.

"I don't want it."

"Martin, you must relax and have something to eat. I understand that this must be quite a shock to you, being in a stranger's home, covered in bandages, being force fed soup." She giggled a little after saying this. Martin's panic subsided a little more.

"I'm just not a big fan of..."

Luckily, he didn't get a chance to finish this ungrateful sentence as Evaline had stuffed a spoonful of soup into his mouth and the ingredients ravished his tongue. His initial reaction was disgust until he noticed that the taste of the soup had transported his tastebuds to a place they had never been. The flavours in the soup were numerous and resulted in a soothing feeling that spread throughout his body. Something crispy was in amongst the liquid and he bit down on it, enjoying the texture of this mysterious entity.

"It's good, eh? Want more?"

Martin was slightly too enraptured by the soup to respond with words, but Evaline already knew the answer. She had been developing the recipe for years and had never had a single person reject her crafty concoction. The crispy fried tofu, combined with the savoury, salty taste of the soup and a smooth, calming dollop of tahini created a "Soup For All The Senses," as Evaline had titled the recipe.

The shame that Martin felt from being hand fed soup was counteracted by the taste and warmth that filled him up. He finished the bowl rather quickly, hoping for another round.

"I'll get you more but I need to finish my own bowl first." Evaline grabbed her soup and hungrily enjoyed her meal with as much pleasure as if it were the first time she had made the recipe. "It has been a *looooooong* day," she said between mouthfuls.

Martin wasn't really sure what to say so he kept quiet and closed his eyes. He had started to feel a flickering nervousness and didn't know how to respond to it. Usually when he got this feeling he immediately left the situation, not recognizing the sensations but rather reacting blindly to these tingly nerves. However, there was no way he could leave right now, as his body would not allow it. After Evaline finished her soup, she grabbed him another bowl and helped him through the process of eating it. Once the bowl was depleted, Martin felt satisfied and slightly energized. His eyes were open once again and he was hoping that Evaline would say something. She did.

"So, Martin. I can see that you're starting to recover slightly and I hope that you will be willing to have a friendly conversation with me. You see, I'm pretty interested in the way you choose to live your life but whenever I try to get any details from you, you seem to get nervous and run away. Why is that?"

"I'm not nervous," Martin said nervously.

"It's okay, man, we all get nervous sometimes. That's what the world does to us, but it's how we work with it that defines us."

"Are you some kind of therapist?" he said with more distaste than he meant to. Some awful picture of a bear with glasses and a lab coat was appearing in his head but it quickly vanished.

"Oh no, I don't have the composure for that kind of job," Evaline laughed. Her laugh was patient and kind. Martin knew from the way she laughed that she could be a good therapist if she wanted to. This thought seemed a bit too soft for Martin's liking and he ignored it. She continued, "I actually work in an ER where I spend a lot of time talking to patients at their bedside. I'd say I'm getting pretty good at it." She winked at Martin and he retreated into his nervousness.

"What about you?" Evaline asked. "How do you like to spend your days?"

"Uh, well, I have a pretty scheduled day but it's all pretty boring stuff and I don't think you would really care about any of it."

"Go for it. How about you tell me about what you did this morning? What led you to driving a small vehicle onto the highway like a maniac?"

Martin gulped with shame, but decided that he would comply with her wishes. He was having difficulty himself remembering what had happened that day and thought this might help.

"Um, well, I'm having a bit of trouble remembering."

"Yes, that makes sense. Just do your best."

"There were two rabbits who were raining on my bed. No, sorry, those were two different things. Two rabbits. Rain on my bed. Yes, that's right. Ok, then there was this teenage boy who was eating my peanut butter and he showed me a picture of myself as a fat child..." he paused, slightly confused.

"Do you have a son?"

"Uh, no, no." He smacked his hand against his forehead, which caused him a significant amount of pain. A storm was rumbling in his hand and he hated that he couldn't remember the events of that morning. "I think it might have been a dream."

"OK, good." Evaline leaned in a little closer. She smelled like a mixture of miso soup and roses. Martin's left arm went tingly as she got closer towards him. "Keep going."

"I think, in reality, it was me who was eating peanut butter."

"The jar you had in your basket at the grocery store? That stuff is delicious albeit rather expensive."

"I agree. It was a treat."

"Good, we should all treat ourselves once in a while. So, you were eating peanut butter but imagining yourself as a chubby teenager? Geez, if I *were* a therapist, we would go down that rabbit hole, but let's just stay on the surface. What did you do after your meal?"

"It was something to do with the sun, the sun was broken, no no no, that doesn't make any sense, um, the sonar panel! Sorry, the solar panel. I had to fix it and that's how I hurt my left hand because it fell on me."

"The entire panel fell on you?"

"No, I don't think so, just a little part of it. I can't remember anything that happened afterward. I'm trying hard but it feels like something is in the way."

"Well, it sounds like you had one of those mornings where everything falls apart all at the same time." The soft tone of Evaline's voice was comforting to Martin but the many walls of his mind were still there, which wouldn't allow him to respond to or return her compassion for the time being.

"Yeah."

There was a pause. Neither of them knew what to say. She noticed how tense he was and started to fear that she was the one causing him to tense up. She moved back and sat down in a chair next to

Martin. Her withdrawal upset Martin but also made him feel slightly more relaxed. For the first time, he noticed that he was lying in a bed, with red and gold sheets pushed to the side. On the bedside table was a small alarm clock turned towards the wall, a leopard print lamp, and one of those squares to put your drink upon. As he noticed this, he started to feel rather thirsty, despite the mountains of soup that the masses of bacteria were comfortably digesting in his gut. Evaline was very perceptive, due to her many bedside conversations, and stood up.

"Let me get you some tea. I'll bring us out some dessert as well. In the meantime, try your best to remember the rest of the events of the day."

She started to walk away and then paused and looked back.

"I hope I'm not making you feel uncomfortable with all of this prying. Although it's definitely an important exercise to help your mind settle back to normal, part of it is due to my own self-interest. You're an interesting guy, Martin."

"Interesting?" he thought to himself. "She's just being nice because she's a doctor and she does this to everyone. She can't find me interesting. I don't need people to find me interesting. I just want to go home and finish my work."

Martin's regular spiral was starting to form once again, but he actually managed to stop himself momentarily. The lack of memory from the day was gnawing at him. He knew that something important had happened. The ATV was a clue. Where would he have gone on the ATV? Suddenly it came to him. Large Lake. He went out hunting! As part of the memory started to return to him, Evaline walked back into the room.

"The tea is steeping." She noticed the excited expression on his face. "What is it? Why do you look so excited?"

"I went out hunting!"

"Oh, you like to do that?" She had a disappointed tone in her voice and looked slightly away from him. He couldn't grasp the reason why. Behind her head, he noticed a poster on the wall that seemed as if it had been around for many years. The title was "<u>Returning Home</u> - Nurtured By Nature" and painted a colourful display of a river beside the trees, sporting a number of fish. Her head was in the way of the bottom right corner of the poster, but as he saw this, he realized that perhaps she was a bit upset that he was a hunter.

"Well, I've never actually killed anything."

"But you would want to?"

"I don't know."

Martin was starting to feel a sensitivity in his sternum once more, but it felt a little more like tiny toothpicks sticking him in that raw space. He was disappointed in himself but couldn't understand why. Evaline stood up once more.

"Let me get the tea."

As Evaline left, Martin looked back at the poster. The bottom right corner, which her head had been covering, featured a large black bear who seemed to be looking directly at him. As he saw this, the memories of Dr. Spruce came flooding back towards him. The trout he never caught, the bear who spoke to him, and the unbelievable storm that appear out of nowhere. Panic spread through his body and once more, the fear of his own lunacy clouded his mind. It wasn't safe for him to be here. He could never tell Evaline about this. She would despise him both for being a hallucinating crazed lunatic and a reckless hunter.

Evaline entered the room as his panic was reaching its pinnacle. She had two cups of tea in one hand as well as a plate in the other. She set the plate and one of the mugs down on the dresser near the door once she noticed the fearful look in Martin's eyes. She brought the tea close to Martin's nose.

"Smell this."

"I can't, I have to go, Evaline."

"Just smell the tea."

His nostrils, constricted from the stress chemicals that were being released throughout his body, opened ever so slightly to let a calming aroma tickle his nose hairs, enabling the nostrils to open a little bit wider in order to let the aroma reach further up. He sat there for some time, just breathing.

"What is this?"

"It's a combination of calming herbs and leaves that I collected in the woods near where we crashed earlier. Have a sip."

She brought the cup gently up to his mouth and he slowly sipped the tea. The flavour was even more profound than its odour and he found himself finishing the cup in less than a minute. Another treat for the senses appeared afterwards as Evaline brought the plate of dessert over, which Evaline called a "Billion Dollar Brownie." The mixture of brownie and tea had toned down his anxiety in a way that he had never been able to do himself. As he lay there satisfied, and rather sleepy, he allowed his eyes to close softly.

"Martin, I apologize for making you panic." Evaline's voice came from the space beyond the darkness of his closed eyes.

"No, you didn't... it was the..."

He was unable to finish the sentence.

"I didn't mean to judge you for enjoying hunting. Who am I to tell you what to enjoy? My expectations for others run a bit high sometimes. I'm really sorry."

Something Martin hadn't felt for a long time was starting to develop inside him. It was a feeling of trust. This unfamiliar old friend greeted him with a gentle push that forced a little piece of the brick wall in his mind to crumble.

"Evaline, you didn't make me upset. You have been nothing but good to me. I was panicking because I remembered what I had seen earlier this morning."

Evaline looked up with curiosity. Her eyes were asking him to tell her what had happened and despite the nagging insecurities, he let the truth spill out.

"I was upset and manic because of the terrible morning that I was having and I wanted a release. I thought that driving at breakneck speeds to Large Lake, my favourite hunting ground, would make me feel better, so I raced through the trees to the lake, where I saw a caribou who somehow didn't seem to notice the noise that I was making. As I made my way towards the caribou, I noticed a large trout flapping around in the water and thought that if I caught it with my bare hands it would make everything that I had failed at that morning disappear. However, I failed at this as well. When I got out of the water, there was a *huge* bear sitting right next to my clothes."

"That's why you ran away so quickly? I would have thought you'd get used to seeing bears living out in those woods."

"It wasn't that. Evaline, I think I'm losing my mind. I was already acting in a perverse way earlier that morning, but I think something happened here that broke the camel's back. I have to tell you this, as I have to tell somebody, but I want you to take me straight to some sort of...institution after this, and leave me there. I don't think I'm safe to be around anyone, not even myself."

Evaline remained quiet, giving Martin enough time to muster up the courage to explain to her what he had seen.

"The bear... he spoke to me. He asked me questions about myself as if he was some sort of human mental health expert. He told me his name was Dr. Spruce and said that we were having a successful first session. As I was leaving, he said that we would see each other again when I needed him most. This is why I was driving away with such ferocity. I knew I was losing my mind. I was afraid, and I still am. I'm sorry you have to have someone like me here. I shouldn't be here. I shouldn't be allowed in society. This is why I live off the grid, but even that is causing me to be a lunatic. I need to be put away."

There was a very long pause. Martin was almost to the point of tears and every inch of his body felt sore and tight. He was more afraid than he had been in a very long time.

"Martin, I'm not going to take you anywhere." Evaline said quietly. "I have spent enough time in nature to know that the most incredible things can happen out there. What if what you saw actually happened?"

"What? You don't think I'm crazy?"

"No, I think you saw something very profound. Good fortune is coming your way. Now rest, you need it."

Unfortunately, the majority of this conversation, which happened after Martin had closed his eyes having eaten the Billion Dollar Brownie, had been taking place solely in his own mind. As he had drifted off, that unexplainable space between sleep and dream had allowed this imaginary, honest exchange with Evaline to take place. She had noticed him drift into this realm and had begun to make her way out of the room, when she heard him mumbling some of the conversation out loud. Her curiosity brought her closer to him, where she heard him whispering a strange confession about a therapist who looked like a bear, an admission of his lunacy, and a parable about trout wrestling. She peered at his sleeping face, wishing to know more about this strange man and his conversations with nature, but decided to keep any further questions for the morning.

Chapter 4 - A Big Reaction

Martin awoke from slumber covered in sweat with his blankets on the floor and pillow nowhere to be found. He had that special untethered feeling after a deep sleep when you have no idea where you are, spending seconds or even minutes in an uncontrollable fugue state. For Martin, those five minutes were confusing, panicky, but surprisingly relieving at the same time. He had been living such a routine life for so long: waking up and falling asleep in the exact same place, doing the exact same thing, with the exact same mindset. Being awoken in a foreign place without any idea where it was made him feel a little more alive than normal. As he attempted to process his surroundings, his dreams flooded back to him, making his forehead begin a second round of heavy perspiration.

He had been shackled to a stone wall in a dark, gloomy space. Although there seemed to be a twinkle of light coming from an undiscoverable location, his weary eyes refused to adjust to the darkness. The shackles were tight around his wrists and he could see that underneath the rusty, silver cuffs they were bloody and scarred. He gleaned from this that he had been attached to this wall for a long time. He was aware that he was wearing nothing but a small pair of shorts or underpants and he could feel inches of grimy hair protruding from his cheeks.

"Hello?" he called out to the dark, hearing his own raspy voice echo around him, his throat screaming with pain and thirst as the words passed through. "I'm so thirsty."

He heard a familiar sound that reminded him of the type of noises that would come from a kitchen.

"Help me, I am chained to a wall!" he shouted out to nowhere, his voice getting weaker with every syllable.

"Would you like some soup?" a familiar voice echoed throughout the darkness.

"Evaline? Yes. Please. Yes." He was desperate and empty.

The sounds of footsteps coming towards him brought him much-needed relief. His shackles started to feel looser and the thought of having another bowl of that delicious soup was filling up his depleted jar of hope. The footsteps were close.

"But it's miso soup. You *hate* miso soup."

"No, I don't, I was wrong, I love it, it's amazing soup, please, I'm so thirsty."

"Open wide!" A cackle of laughter oozed from all sides and Martin could suddenly discern a preposterously large bowl of steaming liquid held between two cracked, grey hands. The holder of the soup came closer into Martin's field of vision and he could see that it was all at once both Evaline and *not* Evaline. This version of her was dried up and old, with most of her teeth missing and one bulging eyelid that would not open. Her skin was saggy and discoloured. She began to laugh once more as she poured the large bowl of boiling hot soup over Martin's head. Sensations of burning and pain clouded his vision and he could feel a piece of hot seaweed sizzling the skin of his shoulder straight down to the bone. He tried to scream but as soon as his mouth was open the soup poured in and he could no longer breathe. He was drowning in the hot, savoury liquid. As he started to lose consciousness, he heard the woman scream, "you're all mine, Martin, all mine!"

As memories of the dream passed through his mind, the events of the previous day crowded amongst these horrifying images. He slowly propped himself up on his forearms, his head and back sticking slightly to the soaking sheets beneath him. His body felt sore, but at least he could move. He attempted to wake up his legs and, stiff as they were, he found himself able to bring them over to the side of the bed. He picked his Guns 'n' Roses shirt off the floor and gingerly put it on, trying to make as little noise as possible. With his unbandaged left hand he gently turned the alarm clock on the bedside table towards him. It was early. With a mighty will, he stood up and moved towards the attached bathroom. He flicked on the light and a monster looked back at him in the mirror. He had a bandage wrapped around the majority of his head, with a small blood stain on the right side. His right eye was purple and bulgy with more puffiness below. He looked worn out and felt like a pile of desiccated coconut shreds. He couldn't stand it. He quickly turned off the light and left the bathroom. Quietly, he opened the bedroom door and stepped out into the dimly lit living space, holding his breath so as to not make any unnecessary noise.

Her apartment was clean and collected, with a number of interesting artifacts hanging on the walls. Part of him longed to look around and see the things that she enjoyed. However, he knew he had to go. He clumsily found the front door and, with a sad look towards Evaline's bedroom door, he left. Slowly, he helped his sore body find its way down three flights of stairs and exited the building into the brisk, morning air. The sun had just begun to peek its way out of the horizon, daubing the low altocumulus clouds with faint tinges of orange and pink. Martin took a powerful moment to observe these colours and felt as if he had never seen anything like this. He felt a deep sadness in his chest, and his eyes held onto a small collection of salty water, which mirrored the dew on the surrounding grass.

"What is going on with me?"

He felt as if he were losing a familiar part of himself. He wanted it back but he could not fathom how this could occur. The only possibility was to return to his home, to his routine, to something he could control. But how was he going to get home? He lived a 40 minute drive out of town to the north, which meant there was no way he could walk, especially with his messed up body. One idea popped into his head but he threw it away as quickly as it came. He distracted himself with thoughts of stealing a parked car ("but I have no idea how to do that"), finding a bicycle ("you're not riding that far with these injuries") or hitchhiking ("at 5am to a place that no one ever goes? Yeah right") and eventually came back to that same idea that popped into his head before: Connor.

Connor was a young man who lived in town and often volunteered at the thrift store where Martin would shamefully purchase clothes once in a while. While Martin had dreams of being completely self-sufficient in all aspects of his life, he was having trouble teaching himself to sew, and eventually had had to succumb to going to the store. He always tried to find times where there would be no one in the shop, which always happened to be the times when Connor was working the cash machine. The boy had regularly attempted to strike up a conversation with Martin and, through his persistence, had managed to glean a few facts about Martin that had piqued his interest.

"I have always wanted to see a full-on solar panel close up! I have read about them but no-one in this town has anything of the like. I would love to come over to see your way of life. Perhaps it would inspire me to do something the same."

Though most people would have been taken by Connor's charming personality and honest curiosity, Martin would typically say something like "my way of life isn't for most people" and walk out the door. The last time that Martin had been there, after having a similar conversation and making his way out of the door, Connor stopped him and said:

"Listen. I understand that you do what you do because you don't want to be involved with this problematic society. I get it, absolutely. However, I think you and I feel the same about many of the ways that this world functions and perhaps we could be friends if we gave it a shot."

Martin was not really listening to this, distracted by the fact that he was running a few minutes over schedule, but through a hole in his distraction he managed to catch this last sentence.

"If you ever want to try it out, I live at 454 Cunningham Avenue, come by anytime."

For some reason, this address had stuck in Martin's head and though he couldn't bear the thought of having another conversation with Connor, he knew it might be the only way he would get home. Martin took a moment to get a bearing of where he was in town and realized that Cunningham Avenue was just about a 10 minute walk from his present location. His body mustered up the will to walk the distance and he went onwards, with a strong feeling of foreboding, towards Cunningham Avenue.

*   *   *   *   *   *   *   *   *

Although it was early, Connor had been awake for hours. In fact, at the moment that a muffled knock had rattled his front door, he had been fastidiously brushing his teeth, the final step in his morning routine that allowed him to break free into whatever the day held for him. His focus on the teeth brushing was strong and mindful, so the knocking on the door brought him such a shock that he swallowed a bit of toothpaste, leaving the minty chemical taste lingering in his throat for a bit too long.

The mindfulness that Connor had been applying to his tooth brushing was inspired by the fact that he had just signed up for an upcoming Vipassana meditation course. He was rather terrified about the fact that he was going to have to spend 10 days in silence while learning some ancient therapeutic practice and was attempting to 'practice mindfulness' with his daily activities, from teeth brushing to sweeping the floor, in order to get a leg-up for the course.

He gargled his throat quickly, though as he headed towards the knocked door he could still feel the remnants of that painfully fresh mint flavouring lodged in there. As he got closer to the door, he distracted himself by wondering who this early morning visitor could be. Perhaps it would be his future lover; a French woman who happened to find herself in a small town in the middle of nowhere in desperate need of breakfast and directions. As this dream materialised, he fretted for a moment about which delicious breakfast would win her over.

"French toast? Croissants?" he thought, but quickly dismissed those ideas, labeling them much too cliché and downright offensive. Then he remembered the tasty jar of peanut butter he had picked up the night before and settled on peanut butter and banana sandwiches. Being French, she probably would have never tried this delectable treat, though once that thought came up, it was also dismissed as 'highly discriminatory'. Who was he to assume what the French do or do not eat?

This fantasy that Connor was creating was becoming clearer by the minute, but he quickly had to stop and remind himself that this was just one of many possibilities. Over his life, he had learnt that expectations can be quite dangerous. He had the tendency to dream up big stories, only to have them crash down in front of him when the truth was harsher than the dream. He tried his best to be open as he slowly opened the door with anticipation. What he saw in front of him was both more terrifying and exciting than he could have possibly imagined.

*   *   *   *   *   *   *   *   *

Martin found his walk to Cunningham Avenue to be rather successful. The walls inside his mind were starting to build themselves back up, convincing him that although Evaline had treated him with kindness, there was no need for him to see her again or even thank her. All he wanted was to return to the regularity of his life and the only way he could do that was to ask for help from an irritating young man. He knew that he could easily convince Connor to give him a lift back home by suggesting a look at his solar panel. In fact, perhaps he would get Connor to give it a good clean! His maliciously manipulative mind was starting to take front seat, and the open, trusting, emotional side of himself was crawling back into his chest. This innocent prisoner had been allowed out of its cell for the first time in many years, only to be wrongly accused once again and sentenced to another indefinite spell in its gloomy, tight jail cell.

As he stepped onto Cunningham Avenue, the sun had ascended above the horizon and only a few remnants of cloud remained in the sky. The light from the sun shone onto the cracked pavement, lighting up small specks of quartz that lay within the cement, which made the road seem like a path of diamonds. This was the only day of the year that this happened on Cunningham Avenue, due to the fortunate placement of the sun's location and rotation of the earth. This gorgeous confluence was lost on Martin, as per usual, as all he was concerned about was getting home. The small sparrows that lived in the trees lining the sides of the road were singing to Martin, hoping that he would see the beauty that they were witnessing.

"See, even human-made things can be pretty sometimes," sang one of the sparrows in a deep baritone voice.

"Gee, Mr. Human if you look down, diamonds you'll find," belted the second sparrow, a tenor.

"Please, take a moment from the thoughts that doth envelop your mind," sang the youngest sparrow, in a rather high-pitched voice.

None of these attempts would bring Martin to the present moment as he stumbled through the avenue focusing on his search for house number 454. About three-quarters of the way down the street, he found it. It was a small bungalow, painted pastel brown and yellow, with green shutters, and a wooden door that looked like a door you might find on a large tree trunk. Connor had inherited the house from his father, who had been a huge fan of The Hobbit, and made an effort to have a house that looked as similar to Bag's End as possible. He had even attempted to grow grass on the roof of the house, but quickly had to remove it, due to sheep from a nearby farm regularly finding their way on top to chew on the succulent greenery.

The first day that this had happened had been Christmas Day when Connor was 7. His parents had taken this opportunity to explain excitedly to Connor that the noise above their heads came from none other than Santa's reindeers in sheep's clothing. However, as the 'reindeers' began to come every day, without missing a bleat, it became more difficult and confusing for the family to keep up this lie, especially since Connor now expected presents every time he heard their hooves. Eventually, the grass was removed and from that day onwards Connor stopped believing in Santa Claus.

The profusion of flowers in the front garden fearfully peered at Martin as he stomped over to the house, shaking with the worry that this bandaged monster may stomp upon their newly opened heads. Luckily, he narrowly missed the blossoms, despite his sore, wounded body not exactly moving in a normal fashion. As he wandered towards the door, the jailed mouse in his chest prison managed to speak up momentarily.

"Be nice," it said, and was quickly stuffed back down.

He knocked on the door and waited.

As Connor slowly opened the door and saw Martin, a large smile appeared upon his fresh, glowing face, though upon noticing the many bandages wrapped around the man, he expressed deep concern.

"Martin, you came! What happened to you?"

"There's no time for that. It's not too early, is it?" Martin did not stop to allow him to respond to his question. "Listen, I need you to take me to my house... well, no, I mean, would you like to come and look at my solar panel?"

"Yes."

There was a pause. Connor seemed to be trying to make a decision.

"But there is something very, very important to do first. You have to come in."

Martin didn't feel like he had time for this but, after all, this was the only way he was going to get home, so he cautiously stepped through the front door. The inside of the house was rustic and alive, full of plants placed perfectly on the house's many clean surfaces, along with dried herbs hanging from the ceiling and doorways. The smell of fresh black tea entered Martin's nostrils, which brought his guard down slightly. The scent brought him back to a memory that he could not quite remember. Something colourful, fragrant, and alive. To his own surprise, he sat down on a comfortable-looking chair and allowed his body to rest. Connor looked at him and smiled gently.

"Yes, relax yourself. Give me about... three minutes and I will be back with something very special."

Martin looked about the room. The exigency of having to rush back to his own home had diminished slightly. There was some kind of calming energy in this place that forced him to relax a little and observe the world around him. He actually kind of liked the way that this house was set up and started to jot down ideas in his mental notepad for future additions to his own house. He had always struggled with finding the right method for drying the plants and mushrooms that he sometimes foraged for in the forest, but this house seemed to have a perfect structure for that kind of task. It was a web of interwoven sticks, held together by yellow twine, which hung from little ceiling hooks at each corner. Two layers of plastic screening were placed on the sticks, where the plants could easily dry. He noticed that Connor had morel mushrooms drying up in the rack, a delicacy that Martin took pride in finding every spring. He stood up to observe the structure a little more as Connor came back into the room.

"Ah, you're interested in the morels, eh? I picked them up from a burn patch on my way back home yesterday. Take a few with you if you'd like."

"Uh, no, that's okay." Martin felt abashed at having someone see his curiosity. He sat back down on the chair.

"Here, eat this." Connor thrust a plate into his hands, which featured two large slices of sourdough bread, slathered with peanut butter, and garnished with a hefty amount of sliced bananas. Martin's stomach rumbled loudly upon seeing the extravagant breakfast laid out before him.

"Hungry, eh?" Connor said with his mouth full and a dollop of peanut butter resting patiently on his chin.

Martin looked away, mortified that his noisy stomach had betrayed his secret feelings of craving and desire. For a small moment, gratitude entered his system, and he began to think how lucky he was for being given this satisfying meal. However, gratitude was a stranger to Martin so he slammed the door on this new visitor as soon as it had arrived. He scarfed down the sandwich without looking at his host and stared at his empty plate like a desperately hungry greyhound. There was a hefty amount of peanut butter left on the plate and though Martin wanted nothing more than to lick the plate from top to bottom, he was frozen by heavy thoughts of embarrassment. If he was in his own home he would have been able to do this! He silently hoped that Connor would leave the room so he could allow that last droplet of gooey blended peanuts to enter his mouth and make its way into his digestion factory.

"Man, that's such an incredible treat." Connor said with satisfaction, after having finished his own sandwich about a minute after Martin. "I'd be down for another half-wich, you wanna share one with me?"

"Uh, OK." Martin definitely had space for more in his belly, but his main reason for affirming Connor's offer was to get him out of the room. Connor could see what was going on and licked his own plate before getting up to head to the kitchen, as if to say to Martin, "it's okay, go for it." Once he was preparing the next sandwich, Martin brought the plate up to his face, tilted it upwards and prepared his tongue for the licking of a lifetime. However, the peanut butter that Connor had bought was of very good quality, with a fair amount of oil, which caused the orangey brown clump of nut butter to slide off of the plate and fall directly onto the top-right side of Martin's trousers.

Without a moment of hesitation, Martin grabbed the pillow that was resting behind his back and yelled into it. Connor did not notice, or if he had, he didn't care. When he returned into the room with a sandwich-for-two, Martin had unsatisfyingly transferred the peanut butter from his pants into his mouth and was now attempting to clean off the oil stain. Connor put down the plate and got a damp cloth.

"Here, it needs to be rubbed off quickly before it soaks into the fabric."

Connor attempted to rub off the stain but as soon as he got close to Martin, the cloth was torn out of his hand.

"I will do it myself," Martin said threateningly.

"OK, man," Connor backed away with his hands up. "I wasn't tryin'a hurt you or anything."

Martin furiously rubbed the oil out of his pants until he achieved some sort of satisfaction, then the two of them sat there quietly finishing their halves of the sandwich-for-two. Martin's mind was rather agitated now, making him extra careful with this second round, doing everything in his power to make one of the messiest sandwiches of all time not to be messy at all. He was actually rather successful this time around. As they finished their sandwiches, a fluffy, white cat entered the room and rubbed up against Martin's pants. He flinched and automatically kicked the cat away but composed himself quickly, hoping that Connor didn't notice.

"Oh, don't worry, that's my cat Redbird. She's harmless."

"I wasn't worried." Martin shut the conversation down completely with that one sentence.

Redbird found this new human rather curious. Normally, she could rub up against the legs of anyone who came into the house and she would immediately get belly rubs, ear scratches, and kind cooing sounds. This time she was getting nothing, so she tried harder. She took both sides of her face and rubbed them on both sides of both of his feet. She looked up at him with the cutest eyes she could muster and said, "don't be mean, I'm just trying to cuddle a bit." He just looked back at her with a weird kind of fear in his eyes. She had never seen anything like it so she decided to sit down and stare at him some more.

Both Connor and Martin watched Redbird for some time.

"I've never seen her stare at someone like that. Maybe she likes you."

Martin grunted and stood up, subtly pushing the cat away with his right leg.

"We ought to go. I've got a busy morning ahead of me."

Connor stood up, stretched with one of those satisfying stretching sounds, and grabbed Martin's plate.

"Sure, man. I'll clean up, make us a couple of matcha teas to go, and we'll be on our way."

Martin had never tried a matcha but hated the colour of it. He almost told Connor not to make it but something stopped him. Perhaps he remembered his desire to refuse the miso soup, which turned out being one of the best meals he had ever had. Or perhaps he was just distracted by Redbird's piercing eyes. She made a strange sound that was almost like a bird chirping. As Martin attempted to avoid her gaze, he started to daydream about Evaline and the kind way he had been treated by her. The soft, cozy bed and the attentive way she took care of him were starting to make his legs, stomach, and groin feel warm and uncomfortable. He tried to shut her out of his mind and although he was successful with scooting away those memories, the warmth still lingered. It felt as if something was alive, gently caressing his full tummy. He looked down and saw that Redbird had curled deeply into his lap without him noticing. The scoundrel!!! He was about to throw her to the other side of the room when Connor walked into the room with two thermos cups and a smile that lasted from one ear to the other.

"What a beautiful sight to see. I'm sorry that you both have to part ways. Do you want to bring her along for the ride?"

"No!" Martin shouted insensitively. "Um... no, it's a dangerous place that I live and she could be eaten by a cougar."

Connor picked Redbird off Martin's lap and held her up to his face, kissing her gently on her tiny nose.

"Take care of the house, Redbird. Please don't eat my morels this time. There are enough mice in the basement for you to fill yourself up fifty times over."

As if she understood his words, she immediately darted to the basement to play "Tom and Jerry" with the mice downstairs. Before she went through the door, she turned round and gave Martin a loving stare, waiting for him to say goodbye to her.

"...goodbye cat."

Satisfied, Redbird made her way to the basement, while Connor and Martin found their way into the garage. The car that Connor had them get into was a gorgeous yellow convertible. Martin felt a slight excitement when getting in the car and hoped that Connor would put the roof down while they were driving, but didn't really want to say it. As they drove out of the garage, Connor closed the door and asked,

"Do you mind if we put the roof down? It's a beautiful day."

"I don't care," Martin grunted, while a few butterflies fluttered around his chest with joy.

Connor handed him his thermos and off they went through the quiet town. The morning was still young and the residents of Cunningham Avenue were just starting to emerge from their slumbers into the unknown of the day to come. As they passed the home of Thomas Kimbe, he was pulling on his almost too comfortable arm and leg bands, which would be his final piece of costume for his morning run. In a pale blue home a few doors down, Cindy was trying to brush the teeth of her dog, her son, and herself all at the same time. Surprisingly, she passed this difficult test with flying colours, forcing a delicate rainbow into existence just behind her home. As the yellow convertible flew by what Connor called "the castle on the hill", which was a large house at the end of the street, Raj and Bhavna were just waking up to find that a raccoon had snuck into their house and crawled up between them in their bed overnight. They immediately named the raccoon Lucky and adopted it into their family.

Though the brilliance of the neighbourhood was lost on the passenger of the yellow convertible, the driver was aware that today was a special day. Connor was feeling fresh and enthusiastic, making an effort to wave at anyone who he passed. He was driving rather slowly, taking in the beautiful summer's day and listening to a couple of ravens in the distance who were trying to figure out how to share a loaf of bread they had found. Martin was irritated by the slow driving while a scratchy feeling was forming in his throat. The plethora of peanut butter that he had ingested that morning had given him quite a thirst, so much so that he couldn't resist taking a sip of the awfully coloured tea that Connor had made. The taste caused his mouth buds to tingle, his throat feel slightly soothed, and his fatigue to drift away. He had another sip, and another, enjoying it more with every slurp.

"It's good stuff, eh? I have a friend in Japan who sends me over the good stuff. It's all organic and superior grade."

"Tastes like plants," Martin offered, though a small bit of gratitude was riding on those three words, which gave Connor a little lift in his heart, and allowed him the confidence to ask the question he had been waiting to ask.

"So," since the top was down, Connor had to speak significantly louder than normal, "what's with all the bandages?"

"I dressed up as a mummy for Halloween and forgot to take off the costume."

Connor, who had been sipping his tea, spurted a small fountain of the green goodness over his steering wheel in a tiny fit of surprised laughter. Martin, too, was flabbergasted. He had just told a joke. He never told jokes. The buzz he was feeling from the tea had lifted up a few layers of his psyche. It made him uncomfortable and he quickly retreated back into himself. There was silence for a minute or two, when Martin realized that Connor was waiting for him to actually answer the question.

"I was in an accident yesterday. Bad weather and I couldn't see the road." Normally with something like this, Martin would have lied to place the fault on someone else, but he felt as if he couldn't do that. He didn't want to do that to Evaline.

This was enough conversation for him and he quickly proceeded to distract himself with another sip of tea. He hoped that Connor wouldn't ask too much more about the events of the previous day as he was doing his absolute best to forget it. He didn't ask and they drove mostly in silence, with Connor attempting to practice 'mindful driving' and Martin angsting about getting back finally to the normalcy of home.

Chapter 5 - Doesn't Feel Like Home Anymore

"Oh, my, god," Martin exclaimed as they drove up his quiet driveway. The storm had been more dramatic than he had realized, causing him three major complications upon arriving:

1) Some of the panels on the solar panels had been pulled open, revealing the wires within.
2) Half of the fence in his garden had been blown over to join the fence on the other side. The majority of his vegetables had been eaten. One of the rabbits was a few meters away, still chewing, looking rather plump.
3) His front door had been blown open. He didn't even want to look at the debris inside.

"Whoa, man, this place is amazing!" Connor's eyes were full of joy. For a few years, he had been dreaming about living in this type of way. Although his father had done his best to make their home feel like it was out in the 'Shire', Connor never truly felt like it was the natural home that he had always dreamt about. He knew that Martin had been attempting a life like this and had always wanted to see what was possible. This place defied his expectations. Despite the destruction caused by the storm, the place was gorgeous. The grass was short and clean, the house was meticulously painted pale turquoise, and he didn't even want to get started on the allure of the surrounding forest. He started to dream about the foraging that he could do if he lived like this. The mushrooms, the lichens, the berries! As his mind explored this more-real-than-ever dream, he noticed Martin's disappointment and sadness.

"Are you okay? Aren't you happy to be home?"

"It doesn't feel like home when it's such a mess."

"Aw, come on, I'll give you a hand and we'll get it back together."

Normally Martin would have shoved Connor away, making some sort of excuse so that he could have the place to himself and start on his daily routine, but this amount of mess was disastrous. He hated to say it (so he didn't) but he really needed help. Connor parked the yellow convertible near the side of the house, imagining that this was his home, and hopped out of the car. He pulled a screwdriver out of his pocket and shot a toothy grin at Martin.

"I'll take care of the solar panel and the garden. You go sort out the inside."

Martin's machismo wanted to step in the way of this comment as those two jobs were the more 'manly', difficult jobs, but his distress had caused a spike in his body pain, which blocked his testosterone-filled retort. As Connor almost-skipped towards the solar panel, with the screwdriver between his teeth and his sleeves rolled up, Martin hesitatingly carried his weary body towards his open front door to inspect the damage. As he reached the doorframe, he stifled a scream as a racoon darted through his legs from underneath his sofa. The racoon turned around towards Martin, who turned around towards it, and saw that it seemed to be giving him the most innocent look possible with upturned hands and doughy eyes. One of the hands had a familiar orange-brown dollop on it. Peanut butter.

"Get out of here, you filthy thief!!!" Martin shouted, spit flying out of his mouth and landing on the raccoon's soft head. "How could you do this?!"

Ma, the young raccoon, was so ashamed that he could not find the words to apologize to this man. He wanted to explain that it wasn't his fault but did not want to stay long enough to find out what this raging, red-faced human would do to him if he did. The truth was that Ma had just arrived. A few hours earlier, he had received a message from his squirrel buddy, Cynthia, that a human door had been left open and no one was there. Cynthia wanted to keep this newfound treasure mostly a secret and had only told a select handful of her trusted friends. When she told Ma, he had pleaded to her to call off the raid. He had lost a cousin a few years ago in a similar situation and vowed never to be involved in any of these criminal escapades from that day hence. Cynthia was obstinate and would not listen. He told her that if she did not come back within two hours, he would come looking for her, which is exactly what he had just done. He had found Cynthia neck-deep in a jar of peanut butter, yelling "HELP" in a muffled, sticky voice. He had managed to pull her out of the jar and wipe off her face when Martin had come to the door. Cynthia had snuck her way through a small hole behind the sofa, but Ma was not so lucky.

Martin ran inside and grabbed an antique baseball bat that he was planning to use to smash the raccoon's head in. When Ma noticed this, he knew that it was time to go. With his head hung low with shame, he departed, wishing that this man would forgive him and recognize that he was not to blame. Unfortunately, Martin was not aware of this backstory and spent a few minutes swearing at the raccoon with promises of complete annihilation the next time they met.

The disorder in the house was so overwhelming and he was utterly uncertain where to start. His whole body was aching, but he did not want to sit down for fear of some nasty animal virus lingering on the fabric of the sofa. He was paralyzed by his unrealized expectations. For hours now, all he had wanted was to be in his comfortable home. He had been dreaming of working in his orderly garden, cooking himself a meal, and mowing his lawn, but none of this was going to happen today. His whole day would be spent cleaning up a filthy unnatural mess. The thought was too much for him. He ended up just standing still, unable to move, like a tired dog with too many beds to choose from.

"How is everything in there? These panels are going back together quite easily. It doesn't look like anything was damaged in any bad way." Connor yelled from outside.

His voice shocked Martin out of his vegetative state and he managed to convince himself to just get started on one area of the house. He started slowly to pick up books that had been pushed to the floor, then moved on to giving the floor a proper sweep, and eventually found his way into the kitchen. This was the saddest part about the whole thing. That damn animal had basically finished the last of his expensive peanut butter. Furthermore, the bread had bite marks in it and a couple of the bananas had been broken into. He miserably threw away a substantial amount of food, shuddering at the sight of any sickly animal pellets, but eventually managed to make the kitchen a more reasonable place to be in. He looked around and realized that he had actually cleaned up the majority of his house, and had slightly enjoyed the process. He wasn't even sure how much time had passed and there was a tentative tenderness developing in his sternum once again. He immediately thought of Dr. Spruce and wondered if he would actually see him again, but shut that thought out as quickly as it had arrived.

"I must focus," he said to himself. "Get everything clean, get that boy out of here, and get back to my life."

A few minutes later, Connor stepped into the door frame with a few beads of sweat forming on his brow.

"The solar panel is a-OK and your fence is back in its right place. The vegetables, however, look like they need a bit of help. I was going to dig up the ones that look the worst and throw some more seeds in the ground, but I'm parched. Any chance I could get some water?"

He finished his little speech, most of which he had pre-planned, as he was hoping that Martin would give him the go ahead to continue working on the garden. He had always had a green thumb, but had never experienced working on a garden outside of the town. The soil looked like it was chock-full of nutrients and would support almost anything. The smell of it grounded him immediately and he wanted to spend the day digging his hands into its cool, wet crumbles.

"I'll deal with the garden," Martin grunted while pouring a glass of water from a large plastic jug. He handed it to Connor and said, "water."

Connor wasn't going to take no for an answer so quickly.

"I have a lot of experience in the garden and..."

"So do I." Martin interrupted him, giving him a look that made him quiet down and focus on quenching his thirst.

The insides of Martin were confusing him. The tender mouse in his sternum was telling him to have Connor stay for the day. To allow him to help out with the garden while Martin could rest his sore body and perhaps cook up a little grub for the two of them. Besides, Connor had treated him with the utmost kindness by providing him with a delicious breakfast and a ride home in a breezy convertible. On the other hand, Martin was sick of everything that had been happening. All of this was outside his normal routine and he just wanted things to be back to the way they used to be. This stubbornness was still the most prominent voice within him and did its best to force the little mouse back into its slumber. However, the tender part of him was stronger than before and let out,

"Thanks for your help."

Connor looked up from his water. He wasn't expecting this and it gave him a few tingles in his stomach. They were becoming friends!

"Anytime. Seriously." Connor said with a soft smile.

The mouse was still there and managed to push away Martin's typical reaction. Instead of making up an excuse to get Connor to go, he said quietly,

"I think I could use some time to myself. Do you mind heading home?"

"No worries at all. I just appreciate getting the chance to see this place and get to know you a little better. I'm feeling inspired and will go look around the woods a little bit. Any direction you recommend I go?"

Martin surprised himself by giving Connor the directions to Large Lake. Since its discovery, he had done his best to hide its location, taking pride in his secret hunting spot. As Connor kindly said his goodbyes, Martin felt a twinge of regret for making him leave, but brushed that aside. As the yellow convertible drove off, Martin opened the door to his bedroom, which had been left closed, and laid his body down on the comfortable bed.

"Finally alone, finally at home." Martin said, expecting to feel relieved. Unfortunately, this was not the case. He was feeling a nasty sickness in his stomach and his head felt both lighter and heavier than ever before. Something was wrong.

"I don't feel at home here anymore," he said with a tear in his eye. He didn't even know why he said it but once it came out, he knew it was the truth. Even with the house cleaned up and with things back to normal, it just didn't feel the same. He had a tight feeling in his chest and did not feel he could ever move again. Thus, he lay there for what seemed like hours, perturbed by an orchestra of distressing thoughts.

"If I'm not happy here, where will I be happy?" he thought. "Will I ever be happy again? Was I ever even happy in the first place?"

Thoughts like this and many more flew in and out of his mind like birds diving for flies on a sunny morning. He felt utterly depleted, depressed, and disgusted. How could he feel like this? He was living exactly the way he wanted to live. Away from everyone, on his own, doing whatever he wanted to do. But what was it that he wanted to do? Maybe he should... but he couldn't think of anything. Suddenly, a new thought slipped into his mind and he latched onto it.

"That's it!" Martin sat up with excitement, which greatly affected his achy body and he had to lie back down for another two minutes before he was able to tumble his way slowly out of the bed. He knew what he had to do. He just had to get back on schedule. Back to his routine. Then everything would be perfect again. He had a perfectly false smile on his face and shunted away any doubtful thoughts that arose, heading towards his calendar. He looked at the time. It was exactly 10am. He searched for the correct calendar date, placed his finger on it, and let it track its way down to 10am, where he found:

10am: Wash the ATV.

He felt as if some kind of spiritual knife had stabbed him in the throat. He looked around, half-expecting some kind of god or clown to be next to him who would say "GOTCHA!" and give him his real calendar back, which would offer him a task that didn't involve the one thing that had been destroyed the day before. But no, this was his calendar, and that was the task. He felt like the world around him was a ridiculing audience doing their very best to push him down to the lowest of low. He walked out of his front door, clutching his calendar in his unbandaged left hand and bellowed as loud as he could into the forest.

"AHHHHHHHHHHHHHHHHHHHHHHHH"

And it felt really good.

He tried it again.

"RAAAAAAAAAAAAAAAAAAWR"

That shout was more like the growl of a lion. He never expected a noise like this to exist inside him. His chest was beginning to loosen up and he dropped his calendar on the ground, stamping on it as an act of defiance. He needed more of this feeling, whatever it was. He decided he had to go deeper into the forest, far away from all of his belongings, his house, and anything at all. He knew of a place a few kilometres into the forest, where there was a slope, which led up to the top of a fairly steep hill that looked over the surrounding forest. He put on his wellingtons, a soft hat, which he had never worn before, and a sweatshirt that said "I'm An Off-The-Gridder" on it. He had a lot of excitement racing throughout his body. Something about this noise-venting experience was so cathartic! But how could it be so good? It wasn't part of any type of regular routine he had done in the past, which he had believed was the only way to actually feel good. He didn't care anymore, he just wanted to scream again, letting his voice explore as far across the forest as possible.

He raced through the trees, scaring all the bunnies, beetles, and bluebells as his large wellingtons stamped upon the ground. His body no longer hurt and he felt like he could run forever. Maybe he would run forever! He could holler at every interesting location, live off of the land and never see another human being again. Is that what he wanted? He didn't really know for he just wanted to scream. After about an hour, he made it to the top of the hill, and took a moment to catch his breath. The view from the top of the hill was stunning. Stands of mixed forest blew in the light breeze. The sun was dancing in and out of the puffy cumulus clouds. The leaves of the deciduous trees had just started to make their way out of their buds. Martin actually noticed all of this, amazed by what he was seeing. But before he could observe his surroundings any longer, a manic shriek emanated from his lips, causing spittle to exude from his open mouth, and the nearby birds to feel spooked enough to flutter in and out of their nests. The scream was powerful, immense, and echoed across the forest. Martin felt a true sense of relief. He smiled. A real smile. One of those smiles that just exists on the face without any effort whatsoever. He laid down on the grass, feeling pleasant sensations dart across his body. He didn't know what was happening, but he liked it.

"Ahh, I see you're ready for our next session," said a deep, grizzly voice from behind Martin's head.

Chapter 6 - Familiarity

A nervous feeling crept over Martin's arms, hands, and chest as he slowly turned to look in the direction of the voice. He knew who it was but he was having trouble coming to grips with the truth. He had actually managed to forget the previous day's interaction with Dr. Spruce and convince himself that it was nothing but a panic attack. However, once he turned and saw the large bear, this threw that hypothesis under the bus for the time being and, strangely, he was definitely not in a panicked state. In fact, this was the calmest he had felt in as long as he could remember.

"So... you're actually real?" Martin hesitatingly whispered.

"No need to whisper, young Martin. If you're capable of a scream like that, you can have a conversation in a real, strong voice." As Martin sat up and looked at the bear, he noticed that he was wearing a small pair of glasses this time.

"How did you... The glasses... Do you have a prescription?" He wasn't really sure what he was trying to ask with this question, he was just rather flabbergasted that a bear that spoke **and** wore glasses was actually sitting right in front of him.

Dr. Spruce laughed joyfully. The booming laugh echoed back to them a couple of times, before skipping away into the distance. He delicately took off the glasses with his large, furry hands.

"I think one of your kind dropped these in the forest. I found them this morning and am hoping that someone returns to the trees and notices me in their glasses. I'm sure it would give them quite a shock! Of course, I'll return them afterwards... though I am already rather attached to them. Would you like to try them on? They make things look rather different."

He handed over the glasses to Martin who shook his head. A quiet moment followed and lingered for some time. Dr. Spruce was gently contemplating Martin, who was doing his best to look away, pretending to be fascinated by the green grass.

"The grass is very pretty at this time of year", Dr. Spruce offered. Martin suddenly felt embarrassed and looked back at the bear who had put the glasses back on.

"So, Martin, this session is going to be longer and more in depth than our previous session. Are you okay with that?"

"I don't really understand what that means or why you're here," he stated obtusely. "I don't need any help."

"You're intelligent enough to know that what you just told me is a lie. Things have been a bit messy recently, haven't they?

"Only the last 24 hours and it's because of you. I raced away from you as fast as I could yesterday, which caused me to have an accident and led to everything falling apart."

"I'd say that things have been falling apart for a lot longer than that."

"You're wrong. I was happy. I was following my routine, day in and day out. Everything was going in the way that it was supposed to until yesterday. I just need to get things back on track and it will be okay."

"And your hypothesis is if you just scream all the time, this will get things back on track?"

Although his words were piercing Martin in places that made him uncomfortable, the tone of Dr. Spruce's voice was in no way harsh, just curious and understanding. Although most of Martin just wanted to run away from this altogether, he wasn't used to being talked to or treated in this way, which helped him to remain exactly where he was.

"...maybe."

"So let's talk about the screaming. How did that make you feel?"

"Like something horrible had come out of me and was gone for good."

"Good. That's very good. However, what if there is more in there that can't come out through just screaming?"

Martin didn't know how to respond to this and looked down. As he did, he noticed that his leg was twitching uncontrollably. He wasn't sure how long it had been doing this but he was unable to stop it. As he looked down at it, so did Dr. Spruce, who immediately smiled.

"Martin, we are going to go deeper into something that was perhaps underlying one of those screams. May I ask you a question?"

"You already have been."

"Ah, yes, you're right. What I want to know is why did you choose to live in such a way? Out in the middle of the forest, away from everyone else like you. I'm assuming you have family. Parents? Siblings?"

Martin paused. For some reason this question stumped him. "...I think so?"

"Mmhmm. And before you moved out here, you had friends?"

"I'm not sure." Martin responded confusedly. He never thought about these things.

Dr. Spruce removed his glasses and looked directly into Martin's eyes. He lingered there for about thirty seconds. Martin was unable to remove his own eyes from the bear's and felt as if those small beady eyes were digging around in a closet at the back of his head that had not been opened for years. It hurt and Martin wanted it to stop. As soon as he was about to say something, Dr. Spruce looked away slightly.

"Are you okay?" Dr. Spruce asked.

"What did you just do?"

"What was necessary to continue our journey together. Now, can you answer my question for me. Why did you choose to live like this?"

"It's the ideal life. Society is full of crooked people and suffering. By choosing to live out in the woods, on my own, I am fulfilling the real purpose of a human being." Martin said this proudly and mechanically, as if reading a script.

"As an... off-the-gridder?" The bear gestured to his sweatshirt.

Martin blushed a little bit but wasn't sure why.

"Listen, Martin, I don't need you to perform for me. I need you to tell me the truth."

"That was the truth. What else could it be?"

"What else indeed?"

A gust of wind blew between them, for a moment Martin thought that he heard a familiar fleeting piece of music being carried by the wind.

"Hm, did you hear that music? I don't think I've heard that song before. Do you know it?"

Martin was surprised. He had chalked it up to one of the many strange sounds of the wind. The wind blew by again and the song was slightly more pronounced. It was so familiar to Martin but he could not figure it out.

"It seems familiar but I'm not sure why."

"Why don't you close your eyes? Perhaps that will help you hear it better."

Martin closed his eyes hesitatingly. As he did, the wind became stronger and the music surrounded him. It was a song that he used to know. A song that he had sung many times. It reminded him of a place he used to live. Somewhere he hadn't thought about in years. All of a sudden, a scene flashed before him, filling him up with all kinds of strange forgotten sensations. Seven years ago, he had spent a year living in New York and as he remembered this, he was aware that it had been a very important time in his life but couldn't remember why. He tried to open his eyes, suddenly terrified, but his eyes would not open.

"Relax into it, Martin," said a soothing voice from somewhere outside. He couldn't remember who he had been with. The scene playing before him was becoming larger and more defined. He almost felt like he was in it, as if he had suddenly just plugged into some virtual reality game. As the scene enveloped him, he realized that he could do nothing but surrender and observe whatever was about to play before him.

Chapter 7 - Off To New York

Martin woke up from an odd dream about a bear wearing a lab coat and moccasins. He stretched out his legs, imagining that he could stretch them all the way to the nearest ocean, dipping his feet in the water then returning the cold toes to the comfort of the furry blanket in which he was enveloped. He smiled at the thought of this and then felt another's skin brush against him. He did his best to move as quietly as possible so as to not wake Rose up. She was a champion lucid dreamer and would get quite upset if Martin interrupted her while she was surfing around the rings of Uranus or trying to make herself 2D. He pressed the side button on his phone to check the time and when he did his eyes quickly scanned the myriad messages that he had received overnight. He was graduating from university today, resulting in many well wishes from his family and friends. Amongst those messages was something strange that he had to read more than twice to truly comprehend.

The night before, he had sent out a tweet to a famous actor and former wrestler named Alabar Stone. It was a half-serious message, mostly meant to make Rose laugh, in which he said, "Alabar Stone, tomorrow I am graduating from university and I wanted to say that you have been a huge inspiration to me on this journey. Thank you." It was simple, funny, and secretly honest. Alabar Stone had made an incredible transition from being a pro wrestler to starring in major films, in which he actually did a very good job. This had legitimately inspired Martin to recognize that life can be more malleable than most people thought, though he was rather embarrassed to admit this as Mr. Stone was a joke amongst his friends. Rose recognized this and, although Martin had presented this message being sent as an ironic joke, she knew very well that he was serious and hoping for a response. Well, that is exactly what he had received in the morning. It read:

Alabar Stone: Congratulations, my man. I am grateful you reached out to me on this important day and I wish you all the best in all that you decide to do in the future. #changeisinevitable

Martin's body flooded with excitement and he no longer cared where Rose was in her dream.

"ROSE! ROSE. Roooooooosssssssseeee."

She actually had been awake a little before Martin had triple-yelled her name. In her dream that night, she had managed to transform herself into a beaver with a little yellow waistcoat and had held a dance party for all the other animals in the forest in which she found herself. After dancing for a couple of hours, she was exhausted and knew it was time to return to the real world. As Martin had been stretching towards the ocean, she had also been waking up. She was always amazed by how these dreams actually affected her body. Her legs were stiff and sore from all the dancing, and she hoped that they weren't going to have to go to some post-graduation dance party. She turned to Martin as he began to yell her name and her face took the full brunt of his explosion of excitement.

"What?!" When he got excited, she knew it was going to be something good.

"LOOK." Martin passed her the phone and she read over the tweet, multiple times. A smile enveloped her face, brightening up her olive-coloured skin and causing Martin to melt momentarily.

"Oh. My. God." She threw down the phone and kissed him. They lay back down in the bed holding each other. Martin was looking up at the ceiling, his satisfied grin like half-wheel of cheese.

"This is going to be the best graduation day ever."

They lay there for a few minutes, enjoying the positive feelings and noticing the light start to pierce through the blinds, temporarily painting the walls with tiny lines of white light.

"Martin, I'm really going to miss you."

"It's going to be okay, Rose. Besides, I have no idea how long I'm going for and if it turns out to be a more permanent thing, you're going to come up and move there with me."

"Yeah, I guess so," Rose said with hesitation.

The day after graduating, Martin was moving up to New York. A couple of months prior, he had gone to a large music festival with four of his closest comrades. Four out of five of them had been working at the university radio station and had managed to convince the conference to give them press passes, and the fifth, Zach, had told the girl at the registration desk that he was from the band Arizona Graveyard, and she had immediately given him an artist pass. This fully convinced the others that Zach had some type of supernatural mind power, as he often did things like this. As members of the press plus a top artist, they decided to talk up their radio station as much as they could and managed to secure a number of interviews and acoustic sessions with high-profile acts. The managers of these bands, as well as the bands themselves, had all treated them with the utmost respect and, after each of these sessions, they giggled privately with each other as they knew that they were nowhere near as important as these people were treating them.

Furthermore, most of them were under the influence the majority of the time as it was their last year of university and they were at a free music festival where nobody knew them. The number of surprising, incredible, and important things that happened to them during this trip was astounding and, if this were a trilogy, they would be written about in further depth. But alas, this is only here to serve as context to explain Martin's decision to go to New York.

One of the interviews that they had managed to secure was with an up-and-coming musician named Roshi who performed under the name Lodgepole Pine. He was a young man from Japan, who had been living in the States for some time after meeting his manager and best friend Foggy Allen. Foggy was the type of guy who lived and breathed the music industry. He knew almost everyone who was anyone in the business, and those he didn't know he had scheduled meetings with. He and Roshi were on their way up. The music of Lodgepole Pine was mysterious, sexy, and smooth, which was everything that the industry was latching onto at the time and, due to Foggy's expertise amongst the industry folks, they had a number of labels grabbing at them with all types of alluring deals. However, Foggy and Roshi had decided at the beginning that they never wanted to "sell out". For as long as they could, they were going to try to do the majority of the work by themselves, and so far it had worked out. The nature of the times were such that having a strong presence on the internet was just as good as the promotion that a record label could do for an act and, by creating a number of viral campaigns, they had managed to pique the interest of thousands of fans.

Martin, through the work at the radio station, had reached out to Lodgepole Pine, who were very interested in doing an interview with them. They had set up the interview in a beautiful, wood-panelled room outside the venue in which Lodgepole Pine would be featured that evening. Martin's best friend Yadiel was to be the interviewer and they had worked hard on the questions that they would ask. With their interview questions, they wanted to stray from the typical, "who are your inspirations?" or "how did you come up with your band name?" and so they asked more absurd, but revealing questions. A few examples:

"If you could have an animal sidekick with two robotic modifications, what would it be?"

"Can you describe what the emotion love is to you and where it resides in the body?"

"If your music was a delicious meal, what would we be eating tonight?"

Many of the acts who they had interviewed before had kindly gone along with these questions, but had also looked at Martin and friends as if they were a little bit too silly for their liking. However, when Yadiel interviewed Roshi, it had clicked immediately. He was on board with all of the questions, even asking Yadiel some nonsensical questions himself. The interview was less like an interview and more like the beginning of a friendship, while the same thing happened between Martin and Foggy on the sidelines. Though everything about the interaction was overwhelmingly exciting for Martin, he had worked hard on being able to push those feelings aside and maintain his composure. He and Foggy managed to have one of those friendship-securing conversations without Martin seeming desperate or needy, which ended in Roshi and Foggy inviting the boys to their show at night as well as the afterparty that followed.

The rest of the week was full of instances where Martin would receive text messages from Foggy saying things like, "come to The Purple Sunflower at 7pm" or "I got you front row seats for the fashion show, wear your best frock". Martin and Yadiel would attend every single event that Foggy asked them to. The rest of the boys, Zach, Isaac, and Sigmund, would join them for some of these events, but also had a number of their own side adventures, which can be followed in the spinoff Netflix series that is bound to come after the success of this novel. Near the end of the week, as the boys were hardly functioning due to overexertion, Foggy took Martin aside while they were backstage at a 2 Chainz concert.

"Martin, move to New York. I'm pretty sure I need an assistant, at least for the summer. I'm not sure how much I can pay you, I'm not sure if it's going to be a long-term thing, but if you're okay with that, I think you'd have a good time."

The feeling in Martin's chest was strong and urgent. His heart felt like it had grown three sizes, his breath was rapid, and his sternum felt inflamed. This was everything he had been waiting for. He had always wanted something like this to happen and here it was. Without hesitation, he said,

"Yes, I'll come."

The two months following the festival had been a whirlwind of excitement as he was winding up school, getting ready for New York, and ended up meeting and immediately falling in love with Rose. This had complicated things slightly but he was still set on going to New York. It was his dream to work in the music industry, to rub shoulders with all of the famous musicians, and rise to the top of the top. Besides, Rose had said she would move up there if he ended up staying for a while. Or was it him that said she would move up there? He couldn't remember, but it didn't matter because he knew that it would all work out.

Rose and Martin spent the day of graduation enjoying themselves as fully as they could, trying their hardest not to think about the following day's goodbyes. Though their relationship had been short, they were completely taken by one another. Deep down, Rose felt angry and upset towards Martin for leaving, although she knew that there was no way he could not go. It was his dream, coming to life right in front of his eyes, how could she try to stop him? She wondered if he was doubting his decision to go at all, but she was too afraid to ask him as she didn't want to push anything. He was. He was terrified about the fact that he was moving to somewhere completely unknown, with only a slight idea of what he was going to be doing. Furthermore, Rose had entered his life and it had almost completely changed his mind, but he felt pulled to New York. He felt as if some kind of path had been laid before him and he would be a fool not to step upon it.

Their last night together was full of laughter and love. They went to a small house party where all of Martin's friends got together and wished him a beautiful farewell. A close friend of his, Isaac, who had joined them for the festival in Texas had decided to move up to New York with Martin, something for which Martin was extremely grateful. It made the whole idea of this new adventure much easier to grapple with. Isaac had family up in New York and had always wanted to stay with them for some time, but also was going up there to support his friend. As the party was ending, Martin and Isaac said goodbye to their friends with tears in their eyes. They headed out the front door, glancing carefully around at the quiet streets of their hometown, trying to take it all in before they left. While unlocking his bike, Isaac skillfully rolled himself a little cigarette, positioned it carefully in the right side of his mouth, and hopped on the saddle.

"I'll pick you up at 9," he said to Martin with a sad smile. He loved his hometown more than he could ever express but, like Martin, he couldn't turn down an adventure like this. Martin nodded at him and Isaac put his feet on the pedals.

"Isaac, I really appreciate that you're moving up there with me."

"I'm not doing it for you," he said to Martin with a wink and a smile. He pedalled off into the night, maneuvering his bicycle better than any professional could, with smoke trailing behind him from the lit cigarette. Rose came out of the front door.

"You ready? I feel like *I'm* leaving too! Everything is so emotional in there."

They walked back to Martin's apartment, hand-in-hand, making jokes about anything and everything, and relishing these last moments together. As they got to his room, they collapsed into each other's arms and fell asleep instantly. Normally, Martin was unable to have lucid dreams like Rose did. He would usually get too excited about it all and wake himself up. However, that night he had a dream that he was with Rose, wandering around in a colourful field full of wildflowers, laughing the night away. Rose had a dream that was very similar to his and when they discussed it upon waking, they were convinced that they had some sort of psychic connection, and promised to visit each other's dreams while they were apart.

Martin was a planner and a perfectionist, so he had packed many days prior, prepared meals for himself and Isaac, and had breakfast for him and Rose ready in the fridge. He was grateful for this, as it allowed them to have a little extra time together. After lying in bed, reminiscing and giggling about nothing, they slowly got up to bring Martin's things downstairs. They embraced and kissed and, as they did, Martin felt as if a lightning bolt struck him from head to toe. He felt as if pure love was radiating throughout his body and wondered if she felt the same. He was too afraid to ask and just let the sensation pass through him. They went downstairs and found Isaac already parked out front. Their other friend, a foreign exchange student from New Zealand, was in the car.

"Hey Martin. Jer decided last minute that he wanted to join us for the journey. He's going to spend a couple of weeks in New York then fly back to his little island. You cool with that?"

Martin was more than cool with that. Jer (short for Jerry short for Jeremiah) had been an incredible introduction to the friend group in the past few months. He was a soft-spoken, intelligent boy who had a quiet tendency to reveal a new hidden skill every week or two. At the party the night before, he had suddenly started to perform magic tricks, which had almost everyone at the party yelling at him with incredulity. He opened the back window, pulled up his sunglasses, and smiled kindly at Martin.

"Yes, of course. Nice to have you on board, Jer."

They threw his belongings into the back of the car. He had brought everything that he owned, including his record and CD collection, as it was possible that he was going forever, and he would need everything if that were the case. Before he got in the car, he turned to Rose. Isaac and Jer were standing on the other side of the car, giving them some space for their goodbye. Rose's eyes were already full of tears, the sight of which brought Martin to the same state.

"What if you just didn't go?" Rose bravely asked.

Martin choked on his feelings.

"I... Rose... you know I would love to... but..."

"Martin, you do not need to explain yourself. I wasn't trying to stop you. I just... I'm just going to miss you more than I've ever missed anyone."

Martin breathed through the emotions that were now lodged uncomfortably in his sternum. The doubt started to spread through his mind bringing him right to the edge of turning around and telling the boys to go without him. What if this was his only chance at love?

"But, you're gonna move up there in a couple of months once we sort everything out and then it'll all be fine." He said quite desperately.

"Yeah, I guess so." She looked away as if there was a lot more to say on that subject.

"Rose. I love you. Everything is going to work out."

"I love you. Now, go, you have a long drive ahead of you."

Neither of them wanted to move but clumsily embraced each other, allowing their sadness to touch momentarily and soothe their worries. The bond that they had formed felt strong and impenetrable, but as Martin got into the car he felt as if a small piece of that bond was fraying. He ignored it and waved to Rose as Isaac drove off and directed them towards the highway. As they turned the corner and Rose's image disappeared, he imagined her becoming a large red bird, following above them on their journey. He smiled sadly. Isaac looked at him.

"So, my dude, we're actually doing this. You feeling okay?"

Martin realized that the moment he had been preparing for over the last two months had finally arrived. A wave of panic seized his body, painting his stomach with pain and shortening his breath.

"Yeah, I'm fine," he lied. The uncertainty and fear that Rose had distracted him from was opening up in him and he was unable to hide. For the next few hours of the drive, he let Jer and Isaac be the conversationalists, remaining as quiet as he could without anyone noticing. Around midday they stopped at a beach to have lunch. Isaac and Martin shared theirs with Jer, who in return taught them how to do an incredible magic trick that involved matches, a cell phone, and a small statue of a beaver. Martin's unpleasant feelings were beginning to subside and be replaced with real excitement. He was going to New York, a place that he had dreamt about for years. He was going to work in the music industry! To work for a band who were about to be huge! Everything was going to work out.

He stepped away from Jer and Isaac to have a moment for himself and walked a little way down the white, sandy beach. The sun was shining with a dramatic purpose, lighting up the beach with more power than he had ever seen. A large crab was flipped upside down on his back about six feet away from the water with its legs dancing back and forth in an unsuccessful attempt to flip itself over. The tide was going out, which meant the water wasn't coming to save it. He stared at the crab for some time, too distracted by the thoughts of his current adventure to even think about flipping the crab back over.

"You just gonna stand there and stare at me or flip me over? That seagull has been eyeing me up for the past ten minutes and I ain't gonna be no food for no damn gull." The accent was thick and Brooklynish.

Martin was shocked back to reality. He looked to his left and saw a seagull hungrily licking its beak, poised as if ready to suck out the crab's innards as soon as Martin turned his back.

"Sorry, bud, of course."

He carefully flipped the large crustacean over, after which it shook its legs and directed its beady eyes up towards Martin.

"Appreciate it, champ. You headed up to New York?"

"Yeah... it seems that way." Martin said nervously.

"Oo, boy, you ain't gonna survive up there with frail innards like that. You're going to need to get a harder shell, like this one here." The crab tapped one of its claws on its shell, creating a little tapping noise, which made the nearby seagull angrily flap its wings. The crab peered over at the gull then back at Martin.

"Looks like it's a good time for me to scuttle outta here. Listen, you best be careful up there. There are many gulls looking to suck out your insides, if you know what I mean."

"Uh, not really."

"You'll find out in due time. Protect me from the bird as I sneak into the water."

As the crab crab-walked into the ocean, Martin walked sideways as well, standing with the crab between his two feet so as to protect him from the bird, whose eyes were now red with craving. As the crab touched the water's edge, he breathed a little sigh of relief.

"Appreciate it." He snapped his claws a couple of times as a sign of gratitude and disappeared into the vast ocean. The seagull was staring at Martin with desperation.

"Get outta here, bird. Go eat someone's french fries."

The bird said something vulgar that Martin could not really understand then flew up high, allowing itself to be blown in the wind towards a nearby café. Martin started to walk back to his friends, uncertain how to interpret the advice that the crab had given him. He wanted to discuss it with Isaac and Jer but did not tend to share his ability to talk to animals with others. The only person he had told was his little brother Hilroy, as he himself was able to communicate with waves, clouds, and other water-based natural phenomena. Neither of them were sure why they were able to do these things, but they had managed to integrate themselves happily into the world without revealing their secrets.

Martin was still thinking the crab's gull metaphor over as they drove on. Isaac had put on a Beach House record, which was bringing the vibe of the car to a sublime level of sweet relaxation.

"Hey Isaac?" Martin said, making sure to wait until track 7 was over to speak, as track 7 was Isaac's absolute favourite.

"Yeah, man."

"Is there any nature up in New York? I mean, will there be any animals around?"

Jer poked his head through the space between the two front seats.

"En't you seen Madagascar? There are all kinds. Penguin spies, egotistical lions, nervous giraffes, the lot."

"Uh, but Jer, they escaped from the zoo, remember? They went to Madagascar."

"Oh, right." He sat back in his seat.

Martin smiled. This wasn't the answer he was looking for but it was a good round of banter. Isaac forgot about the question that Martin had asked and settled back into the soothing music that was floating around them. The three of them found themselves feeling very calm, which subsequently allowed a more open conversation to arise.

"Guys, I'm pretty nervous about all of this," Martin said boldly.

"Dude, me too, but how can we know what's going to happen? Nothing to be nervous about as we haven't even experienced anything yet," Isaac proposed.

"If we dwell in the future, we'll never live in the present," Jer suggested.

Isaac stepped back in with, "just allow yourself to be nervous. That's what I'm doing. Just sit with it and let it pass through you. It'll eventually go away, all emotions do."

"Oo, I don't know man," said Jer. "I'm still pretty miffed that Australia chopped New Zealand in half a few years ago."

"Jer, that never happened." Martin said laughing.

"You en't from there, you know nothing."

They all laughed joyously, enjoying these silly conversations that distracted them from their collective nervousness. Isaac was the only one who had been to New York before but he had never actually *lived* in New York. The closest that Martin had been to New York was when he read and reread the novelization of Home Alone 2: Lost in New York City in Grade 5. He was convinced that his love for that novel was what had fueled his desire to live in New York. He had never actually seen the film, as Blockbuster had never had it in when he was young, and although the copy was eventually returned, by then he was rather attached to the irony that he had only read the book version. The banter continued and the excitement began to grow in the car. They saw a sign that said **New**

York City: 20 miles, which brought all types of feelings to all of them, which they chose not to discuss.

They drove on a little more and turned onto a ramp that took them onto a highway. As they reached the top of the ramp, a spectacle appeared in front of their eyes. It was the big city in all its majesty. The sun was shining on the windows of all the buildings and they stood there, tall and glittering, like a modern day version of the Giza pyramid complex, full of just as much mystery of those temples of old. Martin's heart leapt into his throat, butterflies flooded his gastrointestinal system, and tears made their way through his sinuses, welling up in the space between his eyeballs and the skin underneath. Isaac looked just as emotional but threw on his sunglasses to avoid any New Yorkers seeing him. Jer was busy drawing an almost perfect sketch of the scene that lay before them.

"You think I could make some money selling street art and doing magic here?" He asked the other two, holding up his spectacular drawing of the skyline.

"Paint yourself silver and you'll be a rich man," Isaac said smilingly. The rest of the drive was spent in a deep quiet awe. As they drove towards the city and allowed the buildings to get grander, they could do nothing but stare all around them. The car rolled onto a majestic bridge, held up by thick cables and strong pillars, which served as a fitting entry gate for the grandiose cityscape that lay before them. He had made it to New York.

Chapter 8 - Only In New York

Martin had sublet an apartment in Bushwick, a borough of Brooklyn that was the new "hotspot" of New York. He spent the first couple of days exploring and settling in, though he had only sublet this place for a month, due to the uncertainty of everything, so he made sure not to get too settled. As he walked around the chic neighbourhood, he gawked at the spectacular outfits that the residents wore. Everyone there looked like his friends back home! Back in South Carolina, his friend group had been on the fringe, due to their love of the arts and thrift-store fashion. The city that they lived in was known for its large fraternities and sororities, college football, and history of racism, which made Martin and his friends stand out alarmingly. Here in Bushwick, however, they would have easily slipped into the crowd of all the other fashionistas around. Surprisingly, Martin felt slightly disappointed, as he had rather enjoyed the attention he had received back home.

However, the disappointment did not last long, as his excitement to see the plethora of music venues, health food stores, and used bookstores in the area overwhelmed any negative feelings. He went in all of them, treating himself to a chocolate-covered artichoke and an old copy of Allen Ginsberg's Howl. He imagined that this was the former copy of Ginsberg himself and held it proudly in his hand, texting Isaac and Jer a picture of it, with the words "Future me?" Isaac quickly responded with "two days in and you're already a Brooklynite" and Jer followed up with an incredible picture of himself painted silver with a hat full of coins, bills, and what looked like a diamond. They had separated upon arriving to the city as Isaac was going to be living with his uncle and auntie up in the Bronx and Jer had decided to "sleep with the flowers in Central Park", but had quickly ended up meeting a beautiful, wealthy woman who invited him to stay with her in the Upper East Side. The next day was going to be Martin's first day working with Foggy and Roshi, after which Isaac was going to meet up with him to do some further exploration of the area.

Martin made his way back to his comfortable temporary home to settle in for the night. He called Rose, read her the majority of Howl, and went to bed early.

As he awoke, he had the most fluttery feeling in his sternum and felt as if this was truly the first day of the rest of his life. He didn't really know what that meant, but it just felt like that. He spent longer than usual picking out the day's outfit as he wanted to make sure he looked as "cool" as possible, as Foggy and Roshi were seriously stylish. He felt like he couldn't compete with them but did his best to find something suitable. Luckily, his mother was a professional clothes designer and had made him a few colourful, unique shirts to bring with him on the trip. He felt a little pride as he put on one of these shirts, as he knew that he would be the only one in the whole city to wear it. He stepped outside, allowing the sun to shine on his face for a full minute before getting on his way. However, as soon as he turned towards the subway he saw a young man with horn-rimmed glasses and a comfortable beard wearing the **exact same shirt as him**. He was flabbergasted. He tried to get the guy's attention.

"Excuse me, where did you get that shirt?" He asked politely. The young man ignored him completely then proceeded to put headphones in right at the moment that he walked past. Martin was hurt by this interaction but tried his best to stay level-headed. A little sparrow hopped up onto a steel fence next to Martin.

"You new here?" She said with a rough but compassionate voice.

"Yeah. I just moved here from South Carolina. Did you... did you see that guy just ignore me like that?"

She laughed in a singsong way. "You better get used to that. It's a tough place to live and easier for some to just ignore what's around them."

"But not everyone is like that, right?" he asked with a tremor of fear.

"Of course not, but you can't expect it to be like it was back home. Now where are you off to?"

He showed her Foggy's address on his phone. It was still in Brooklyn but further west towards Manhattan.

"Ah, are you in a hurry?"

He looked at his watch.

"I have about 40 minutes."

"Good, follow me."

Instead of taking Martin on the subway, she led him through the neighbourhood, passing through small parks and a quiet graveyard. As he passed through these peaceful places, he made a note of them in his head, hoping to return to them with Isaac later. They ended up at a rather fancy, homogenous apartment building.

"Wow, this is his place? Thanks so much for bringing me here, I imagine that was quite a lot more interesting than the subway is."

"You're very welcome, young man," tweeted the sparrow. "Nature is always here to help. Remember that." She flew away, settling herself on an upward draft of air, quickly flying towards the clear skies above.

The journey with the sparrow had helped Martin forget about any nervousness that he may have been feeling about the first day of his new job. However, as soon as he went to ring the buzzer for apartment 223, those familiar feelings tiptoed through his body. For just a moment, he felt completely alone. The last time that he had been in a new situation like this was the first day of university, though this seemed more terrifying. The university life was more like a training ground for whatever was to come next and Martin was not sure if he had been aptly trained. He was rather fearful of social situations, despite having an innate ability to hold conversations with most people that he met. Due to this fear, he often found himself planning a conversation beforehand, though it never panned out in the way that the script in his mind suggested. He pushed through all of these fearful thoughts and rang the buzzer.

"Martin?" Foggy's voice rang clear through the speakerphone.

"Mr. Martini!" Roshi's singsong voice came from the background, making Martin smile. Foggy and Roshi were perfect complements for each other. Foggy was the more serious, business type, speaking with clear, calculated words that showcased the significant intelligence that the man brandished. Roshi, though also very intelligent, was silly and full of love on the outside. If Martin had been asked to describe the perfect manager-artist duo before meeting these two, his answer would have come pretty close to describing their relationship. He thought about this as he stepped through the door and into the elevator, feeling their kindness fill up the lonely space inside of him.

He stepped onto the second floor and heard the familiar sound of R. Kelly floating through the hallway, hoping that it was coming from his destination. Fortunately, it was. The door was slightly ajar and he found Roshi and Foggy in the middle of some conversation.

"This is a **big deal,** Roshi. I want you to promise me that you aren't going to run away for the next few months. I need you here. I need you to finish all of these projects."

"I can say that I will, but I never really know where things are going to take me. What if I meet a woman who invites me to go to the bottom of the Marianas Trench?!"

"Then you're bringing me with you."

Martin stepped through the door quietly, not wanting to interrupt the conversation but secretly hoping that they would also invite him to the bottom of the ocean.

Roshi saw him and without even saying hello ran off to a room in the apartment. Foggy embraced him wholeheartedly and smiled. Foggy was about six inches shorter than Martin, though his presence was large and warm. Beneath his serious nature, he was compassionate and likeable. During the festival in Texas, Martin had been taken by how kindly Foggy spoke to everyone that he had a conversation with. Early on, Martin had realized that in order to get anywhere in the entertainment industry, one must have a talent for schmoozing. Foggy had that skill on lock, but there was also a significant amount of genuineness behind all of his attempts to forge strong partnerships with others. Perhaps this was why Lodgepole Pine had risen up in the industry so quickly. The excitement in Martin's stomach rose like a hot air balloon up into his head. He was going to learn from this man! He smiled back at Foggy.

"Want a coffee? Breakfast?" Foggy generously offered.

"Sure." Martin said nonchalantly, trying to sound a little bit like he didn't care. Foggy looked at him strangely. "Oh, I mean, absolutely, yes. Thank you."

"That's better."

Martin nearly jumped out of his skin when he felt something furry and heavy land on his shoulders. He realized that a large fur coat had been put on him by Roshi.

"Ooo, man, lookin' good! You're going to need to be looking best for the party tonight." Roshi embraced the fur-wrapped Martin and gave him a kiss on the forehead. "Good to have you on the team."

"The team?" Martin thought. "I'm on the team?!" This was almost too much for little Martin. He felt the fur coat warm his body, while the words warmed his heart, and relaxed into it a little.

"There's a party tonight? I was going to spend the night hanging with Isaac, but I guess I can cancel."

Foggy turned from breakfast that he was preparing. "Isaac can come, you've got a plus one."

Martin felt a twinge of relief. The thought of cancelling on Isaac had bothered him as he held a huge space of gratitude for Isaac for driving him up here and moving with him. To have at least one close friend around was a big deal to him as everything else was so new. However, things were already starting to feel easier as he was with two of the coolest people he had ever met, being fed breakfast, and was on the list for his first New York party. He and Roshi sat down on the island in the kitchen and Foggy brought them frothy lattes and an oatmeal bowl that was covered in all types of nuts, seeds, and fruit. Martin dove into the delicious dish.

"Martin, so we're just going to get right into it." Foggy spoke as he sipped his latte, leaving a thin layer of foam resting on his upper lip. "In the last two months, Roshi and I have been thinking things over. I know I said to you that the role as my assistant was fairly uncertain and perhaps just for the summer but…" He looked at Roshi.

Roshi continued for him. "Basically, Martini, when we met you at South by Southwest, we both thought you were adorable."

"And the fact that you called me every week since the festival was downright annoying but shows a strong persistence that reminds me of when I started in the industry." Foggy still had the thin, white moustache but Martin was too engrossed in what they were saying to care about telling him. "We want you to be a full-fledged part of our team, indefinitely. Things are really on the up-and-up for us right now. Lodgepole Pine's debut album has achieved the right kind of success for a debut and we've got a lot of offers and opportunities coming up that I honestly can't deal with on my own."

"I'd help but I'm too busy making sure I look good for the photos," Roshi smiled at Martin, pretending to pose for a photo. Martin noticed that this comment was half-serious and half-joking.

"I want you here basically every day to help me organize the tours, book flights, and manage the team. Along with this, you'll come with me to every meeting, party, and show that we deem necessary for us to go to. How does that sound?"

Although Martin had tried to ask Foggy every question about what this job would entail in his weekly calls, Foggy had been hesitant to reveal any details about what was going to happen. He would always say "let's just figure it out when you get here". This was much larger than anything that Martin was expecting and he had no way to hide his enthusiasm.

"Seriously?!" He looked at both of them skeptically. Roshi nodded earnestly with his flashy grin. "Yes! Wow. This is so cool. I mean, you guys actually want me to be a part of this whole thing full-time?"

"We sure do, little muffin." Roshi rubbed his right arm as if it were a little cat. Martin realized that both the excitement and the fur coat were causing him to perspire a little more than he wanted to.

"It's not all fun and games, though," Foggy said, adopting a more serious tone. "Some parts of this industry can be... difficult, to say the least. Furthermore, since we're basically just a start-up, we don't really have the funds to pay you enough to survive in this pricey city so you're probably going to have to get a job in a restaurant as well."

"Yes, anything!" Martin said excitedly without hesitation. His first job was at a grease-covered Outback Steakhouse and since then, he had had significant experience working in restaurants. Besides, he was willing to do whatever it took to help his dreams come to life.

"Okay then, welcome to the world of Lodgepole Pine," Foggy smiled as he said this and reached out his hand. Martin shook it with jubilance. Roshi gave three hugs in a row.

They spent the rest of the day getting more acquainted with each other, which started with Foggy and Roshi telling Martin the story of how they had met. "It all started in a power plant in Northwest Japan..." Roshi had started. The story was astounding, about as dramatic as the film Titanic, and it sounded like they had told it many times. Afterwards, they took Martin around the neighbourhood, showing him their favourite bars and restaurants, telling him that they would take him into all of these places eventually. During their walk, they fed him more details about their current position in the music industry as well as a myriad of offers that they had received in the last few months.

"So, next week we've got two shows here, one in Brooklyn, one in Manhattan, then the following day we're off to play a festival in Montreal. You'll be coming with us. The month after that, you and I are going to be going to a slew of meetings in the city, as well as a plethora of parties, while Roshi gets to work on designing the posters for four different music festivals that we're playing in the fall, as well as writing and recording a hit EP. After that, in the fall, we'll be going on tour with Ponton the Performer."

Martin had to stop him here. All of this was overwhelming him with anticipation but this last statement was beyond belief.

"What do you mean 'we're going on tour with Ponton the Performer'? You mean, **THE** Ponton?"

"Who else would I mean? They offered us to open for them on this big statewide college tour. This is a big deal for us."

"No kidding!!!" Martin started wondering if this would ever feel normal. Everything that these two were saying seemed like it was coming directly out of Martin's "unrealistic dreams for the future" section of his journal. Ponton the Performer was currently his absolute favourite artist. He was a young guy about the same age as Martin, who had been making huge waves throughout the hip-hop scene with his first two mixtapes. He was different from many of the other hip-hop artists out there, incorporating orchestral sounds, melodies that sounded like they could be from Disney movies, and a fresh type of enthusiasm fueled by his variety of psychedelic experiences, about which he was very open. Martin had been following his career ever since the most recent mixtape had come out, sharing it with anyone he met while proclaiming that Ponton would be the most influential musician of the 21st century. *And now he was going to go on tour with him?!*

For the rest of the day, Martin found himself floating in the clouds, bouncing from rainbow to rainbow with childlike joy. Whenever they would stop somewhere, he would slyly retreat to the bathroom to text Rose everything that had happened. She would respond with emojis, which suggested that she was very excited for him. However, when he sent her the message "I can't wait for you to get here and experience this with me!!!" she did not respond. He shrugged it off and went back to his dreamland with Foggy and Roshi.

The evening hurried towards them so Martin went back to his small apartment to get ready for the party. According to Foggy, there were going to be lots of "people" there. He had done air quotations with his fingers when he said that. Martin had guessed that "people" translated to "bigwigs, hotshots, and VIPs". Isaac was waiting on his doorstep when he arrived home, wearing a baseball cap that said "Cool Dog" on it and his favourite blue and green button up. Martin had always admired the way Isaac dressed. It was as if he just didn't care about dressing up in whatever was the fashion at the time but, by doing so, he managed to look more fashionable than most. Martin wished that he had that kind of self-assurance but alas, he did not, which caused him to spend a significant amount of time trying to find the shirt that would make him look like one of these "people". He settled on a black-and-white button up that was a little too loose, which caused the top button to subtly unbutton itself every so often, which was why he liked it. He would often look down at a party and notice a significant percentage of his chest hair had started to show, without him having any choice in the matter. If he was feeling brave, he would leave it like this. He tucked the shirt into slim white pants, threw Roshi's heavy fur coat over his shoulders, and stared into the mirror for over a minute, his thoughts dissociating into judgments and doubts. He slipped the coat off, deciding to save it for a time when he felt braver. Half-satisfied with his outfit, he met Isaac outside and they went off into the night.

Their eyes were bright as they entered the subway, making their faces a stark contrast to the majority of the other passengers', whose eyes were fatally fixed upon their miniature screens. As the train reached another station, Martin felt a buzzing in his pocket and quickly became just like the rest of the passengers. The message was from Foggy and read,

"The password is Jungle Cruise."

"What do you think this means?" He showed the phone to Isaac whose shiny eyes immediately got three times bigger.

"Dude, I know exactly what that means. Leave it to me."

Martin wanted to ask more but some obtrusive beats sounded from the other end of the carriage. Many passengers looked away from their phones for just enough time to shoot a glare of disgust at the direction from which the music played. Isaac grinned, his eyes now as big as dinner plates.

"Ooo, Martin, I've seen this before with my uncle. Check it out."

The kids at the end of the carriage were getting ready for something. As the music started to crescendo, a young boy started dancing, and as the beat dropped he began to spin and flip, using all of the poles in the carriage. Two girls were behind him, one with thick black curly hair that reached her waist, wearing darkened sunglasses and the other, who looked quite strong, wore a shirt that said "Dance Yrself Dirty". As the boy continued his moves, they moved in front of him, doing a sort of tag-team dance that looked like some sort of Cirque du Soleil performance. It ended with the boy plastered up against the roof like Spider-Man while the two girls finished with one lifting the other in such a beautiful way that it would be at home in an international figure skating competition. As soon as they were done, Martin and Isaac clapped with amazement. There was nothing like this back in South Carolina. This was a serious performance, but on a subway! No one else was clapping. In fact, as Martin looked around, he saw that no one else had even looked at them and he couldn't believe it. He would have paid good money to see a performance like that back home. After the show, they came around to collect change, of which they received very little. Once they reached Martin and Isaac, the boys deposited a fair amount of money into the hat, and Isaac said,

"That was *real cool.*" He said this in a way that made him also sound *real cool*, and the girl with the curly hair smiled at him.

"You ain't from here, are ya?" She said in a subtly flirtatious manner. She looked at Martin and saw that he was curious as to how she could know they were not from New York. "We don't get applauded from New Yorkers."

"Keep on doing your thing," Isaac said in a manner that James Dean would have been proud of.

The girl smiled at him, pulled out a piece of paper, and wrote down something on it. It was an address and phone number.

"Here's where we practice most afternoons. Come by sometime."

The carriage stopped and Martin rapidly realized that it was their stop. Isaac flashed a winning smile at his new friend and they exited the train.

"Isaac! How did you do that? I've never seen you act so cool."

"No one knows me here, Marty. I can be whoever I like."

The boys grinned, laughed and sang all the way up the street, creating a subtle warm surround-glow which a few passing squirrels were mesmerized by. They found their way to the address for the party, which was a tall, dark building with a large line of people standing out front. Many of those in line looked bored, as if they had been waiting for hours, and most of them were on their phones.

"Aw, dude, do you think we have to wait in this line? I'm never going to get to meet the 'people' if we're out here forever!" Martin started to panic a little bit as he did not want to blow it on his first night out in New York.

"Watch this," Isaac said with a sly smile. He rolled a cigarette with meticulous perfection and put it in the right side of his mouth, leaving it unlit. He strolled straight towards the front of the lineup with Martin at his heels. There were two burly bouncers standing on both sides of the door and it seemed as if they were not letting anyone in.

"Come on, guys, I've been waiting here for two hours," complained one of the guys at the front of the lineup. His hair was slicked back with so much moisture that Martin thought he could see it dripping down the back of his shirt. "Do you know who I am?! I work for Spotify *and* Google."

He was completely ignored by the bouncers. Martin wasn't sure what they were going to do about getting in, but he followed Isaac's confidence right up to the bouncer on the left. He was seriously tattooed and bearded, wearing a leather jacket with no sleeves and one bandana on his forehead and another around his neck. He saw Isaac heading towards him and gave him a glare that could kill a grizzly bear on the spot. Isaac wasn't fazed and made his way directly to the bouncer's left ear. He whispered something and immediately the bouncer lifted a red velvet rope that was blocking another smaller entrance to the left of the main one, allowing Martin and Isaac to pass through. There was a small foyer that led to an open elevator with only one floor button on it. Isaac pressed it with a satisfied look upon his face.

"What did you say to him?" Martin was incredulous.

"Jungle cruise."

"Ohhhh, of course." 'Jungle cruise' was the password for the party. "Oh my god, Isaac, we're at a party with a password. I thought this only happened in movies!"

"Only in New York." Isaac said wryly out of the left corner of his mouth.

The elevator slid its way up without a noise and softly opened into a large, darkened space full of attractive people, comfortable furniture, and lots of coloured glass. It seemed to Martin to be the perfect place to host a party with a password. The subtle darkness of the whole place made everything seem a little obscured, as if one would also need a password to talk with any of the guests or sit on the chairs. Foggy and Roshi were near the elevator, chatting with a grey-haired man who seemed extremely interested in the two of them. Foggy was deeply invested in the conversation, but Roshi had been observing the rest of the party and yelled with joy when he saw Isaac and Martin.

"MY BOYS! Come here!"

They made their way towards him and were introduced to the man with whom they had been talking. His name was Eric Steen and he was the president of Weather Records. Martin immediately registered that he was definitely a "person" and made an effort to act as relaxed and affable as possible. When Foggy introduced him to Eric as his assistant, he almost melted into his Doc Martens. Roshi and Isaac were already knee deep in a conversation about interstellar travel and decided to go out to the balcony to see if they could see any stars to which they could travel together one day. Foggy went back into his conversation with Eric about the state of the music industry and how difficult it was for artists these days. He wanted to make sure that Roshi would never feel this difficulty but their current situation was making it hard. It was obvious to Martin that he was subtly trying to catch a fish here and was quickly successful.

"Hm, well, we have been looking for a new roster of talent. A few of our current artists are aging a little too quickly." Eric said, pointing with his eyes at someone nearby who Martin recognized.

"That's Prismacolor Scholar," Martin said, mustering up as much confidence as he held in his belly. "Didn't he just release his first album? I thought it was really successful."

"Things change quickly here." Eric said curtly without even looking at Martin, who felt rather uncomfortable and ashamed of himself for even saying anything. He retreated back into a quiet state of observation.

"Foggy!" A beautiful, slender blonde woman made her way towards them with a wide smile and a scent of lavender and roses.

"Selena! Excuse me for a moment, boys." Obviously this Selena was much more important than the record deal that Eric was potentially offering which left Eric and Martin standing quietly together. It was quickly obvious to Martin that Eric wasn't planning on beginning the conversation, though he didn't seem to be leaving either.

"So, how long have you been doing this?" Martin asked nervously.

"Doing what?"

"Oh, uh, the music industry." He tried his best to compose himself despite his anxiety and desire to make a good impression. "For how long have you been in this line of work?"

"A long time." For the first time, he looked directly at Martin who was shocked by what he saw. It was as if he was looking into a deep black pit full of exhaustion and despair. He saw no happiness in this old man's eyes, despite the smile that was plastered on his cheeks. Eric looked away quickly. "Good luck," he said and walked towards the bar.

Martin shivered. He wasn't really sure what he had just seen but it awoke a number of doubts in his mind that proceeded to float their way into the darkness of the surrounding party. Wasn't everyone in the music industry supposed to be happy? Wasn't it the best job that one could possibly have? Helping to make amazing music that would be spread out to millions of people, how could one ever feel exhausted by that? These questions were there and Martin wasn't sure how to answer them as he didn't have enough experience. Besides, that was just one person amidst thousands of others. Maybe he just had problems with his family, or he had just had a busy day.

It was strange to Martin that one person could shake his core so profoundly, but he made an effort to return to the party. He decided to step outside to see if Roshi and Isaac were still star gazing. No one on the small balcony was familiar to him and despite Martin's desire to want to connect with as many people as possible, he felt depleted by that short interaction with Eric Steen. He decided to give Rose a call but she didn't pick up on the first or second try, and as Martin attempted to call a third time, a slender black cat slinked towards him on the railing of the balcony.

"Hey there, kitten," the cat said softly to Martin. "Did you lose your friends?"

Martin looked around to make sure that no one was in earshot.

"No, they're just somewhere else, probably looking for me," he said unconvincingly.

"Mmmhmmmm," she let this draw out, looking Martin up and down calmly. "My name's Sabrina. You can talk with me. How long have you been in the city?"

"Just a couple of days."

"Have all of your expectations been met?"

"I shouldn't be talking to animals here. What if someone sees me?"

"Oh dear, a few days into being here and you're already worrying about your reputation. All you humans are the same." She peered around, scrutinizing the rest of the people on the balcony. Martin found himself severely self-conscious, hoping desperately that no-one would look at them.

"Coming to New York was my ultimate dream and now I'm here at a party with musicians, managers, and the like. But I feel too nervous to talk to any of them! What is wrong with me?"

His voice raised a little with the last sentence, provoking a pretty dark-haired girl in an emerald green dress to give him a look. He put his hand on Sabrina, pretending that he was doing nothing more than stroking the cat who immediately began to purr lavishly.

"Are you sure it's something wrong with you that is the problem?" She suggested mid-purr.

"What do you mean?"

"Many elaborate masks are being worn here tonight and it seems that sometimes you are able to see through these masks."

"I guess so. The eagle down at the river back home used to say that it was because of my empathy."

"Mmm, a beautiful ability to have, Martin. Don't forget that. Your awareness of feelings is what makes you who you are."

The conversation paused for a moment and Martin continued to stroke the black cat as it was soothing him just as much as it was her. They heard the sound of another cat screeching in the distance and Sabrina's ears perked up.

"I must go. It was a pleasure to talk to you, dear child. Remember, what goes up must always come down." She jumped off the balcony to the building below, skillfully landed on her feet and ran off into the night. Martin was feeling rejuvenated and went back into the party. He ended up finding Foggy, who introduced him to his blonde friend, a girl named Selena who ran her own perfume business. Once Isaac and Roshi joined them again ("we made up our 20-year plan for getting to Mars," Isaac had told him, patting his back pocket) Martin was feeling some of his former confidence return and managed to enjoy the rest of the evening. He was introduced to a number of people, many of whom Martin could see had a similar type of deep sadness hidden behind a structured façade. But he did his best to ignore this and attempt a connection with everyone he met. Late into the night, Martin was exhausted from the constant conversation and emotional repression so he suggested to Isaac that they head home. Isaac was happy to go and they made their way back to the apartment, where Isaac literally crashed on the couch. As Martin headed into his room to sleep, Isaac said,

"Hey, Marty. Did you notice anything weird about the people we met tonight?"

"What do you mean?" Though Martin knew exactly what he was talking about.

"I don't know, it just seemed that there was a lot that wasn't being said."

"I thought we had pretty good conversations."

"Stop playing around, you know what I mean. It's like, back home, people are real. We would have conversations about what was actually going on in our heads or issues that we'd been having. Out there, it all felt a little substance-less."

"You're just not used to things here. This place is great." Martin replied with a substance-less response and went into his room. Martin's attitude concerned Isaac but sleep was beckoning him to join her so he succumbed to her call and descended into dreamland.

Chapter 9 - The End and The Beginning

As the days edged further into summer, life in New York started to become more comfortable for Martin. Each day with Foggy was new and exciting as he was enthusiastic about the opportunity to have someone to teach about the industry and Martin was eager to learn every detail. Their friendship fortified rapidly, becoming fully established when Foggy put them on the guestlist for Martin's favourite band, The International. They also happened to be Foggy's favourite so the two of them drank whiskey and sang every song together, both grateful for the companionship and camaraderie. Some of their work days were more exciting than others, such as when Foggy announced to Martin that they were off to Manhattan for a multitude of meetings or to spend the morning schmoozing at the glamorous Soho House. Many of the people that Martin met were powerful names in the industry, either heading up record labels, managing large talent, or working for up-and-coming startups. As time went on, Martin stopped noticing any sadness or exhaustion in these people, and instead found himself captured by their conversations about the state of the industry in the digital era or the current competitive marketing strategies of Weather Records against Bonofide Records.

When he had been back home, Martin had been known amongst his friends for starting and maintaining deep conversations that would lead both himself and others into vulnerable, emotional states, creating a stronger connection between both parties and helping heal any sore wounds. These conversations were few and far between in New York, something which Martin missed at first but soon forgot about. Besides, when he spent time with Isaac he was able to delve into more profound conversations about mind states, space, and invasive plant species effects on the soil beneath them. Having such a friend around became increasingly beneficial as things got busier for Martin. Though he had already made a fair amount of friends through work as well as his serving gig at a local restaurant called The Nest, there was something different about his friendship with Isaac. There was no need to have to try. Ever. Though Isaac was living in the Bronx, he had managed to secure himself an incredible internship with a radio promotion company as well as a job as a camera salesman at a fancy photo store in downtown Manhattan, thus making it more time effective for him to stay over at Martin's apartment most nights.

For the first little while, Martin would invite Isaac to any event that he was going to, and Isaac would always show up. This had always given Martin the opportunity to have someone to retreat to when he was emotionally exhausted from the conversations with the "people" at these events. However, as the summer went on, Martin started to invite him less and less, and when Isaac asked about it, he would say, "oh, I'm not allowed a plus one." The truth was, Martin was starting to feel embarrassed by the way his friend might see him. A transformation had started occurring inside of Martin and he was beginning to look and act in a very similar manner to those in the industry that he was spending his time around. Isaac, on the other hand, was not. Along with this, as he started to develop relationships with successful musicians or actors, he felt that these were the type of people that he needed to be around in order to get somewhere, and time with Isaac wasn't providing him this leg up. Despite the pressures of the city, Isaac had managed to stay more or less the same, at least that is what Martin thought. In fact, Isaac had also changed, but in the opposite direction. His eyes were wide open to the misery of many of the inhabitants of the city due to work schedules that were too full and relationships that were too false, and he had made a concerted effort not to conform to this type of lifestyle. Martin and Isaac were both moving, but in completely divergent directions.

Along with this, Martin continued to hear less from Rose, despite his insistence at sending her long "essay-like" text messages every evening with long descriptions of his daily activities, his unsubsiding love for her, and his desire for her to be up in New York. When they talked on the phone, he spent most of the conversation focusing on his adventures and expectations for their relationship, and forgot to consider where it was that she was coming from. On one call in late July, Martin was gushing about his excitement for her to experience dumplings on the Lower East Side when she stopped him.

"Martin. Stop for a moment."

"What?"

"I'm not coming to New York."

"What do you mean?"

"I'm not moving up there."

"Why not?"

"I... I don't have feelings for you anymore. I'm actually not sure if I ever did."

Martin shattered into a thousand shards of glass, littered the sidewalk with his pieces, which subsequently got stuck in the feet of all those who were passing by. Many of those who stepped on the shards of Martin momentarily complained to whoever was on the other line of their bluetooth headsets. An upwelling of tears rose to what remained of his eyes, but he forced them back down, like a large boulder trying to push down a gushing geyser.

"You don't know what you're talking about," he said quietly with a subliminal edge of anger hovering beneath his words.

"Don't say that. I have been thinking about this for a while now. I'm sorry I didn't talk to you about it before, it's just... you were so excited about me and beginning this amazing journey that I just couldn't bring it up."

"I think it's just that we haven't seen each other for so long. I actually have a week off coming up before we head to Montreal. I'm going to book a flight to come and see you." He was clutching at straws made of dust.

"That's not a good idea, Martin. I don't think it will help. Focus on your life up there." Rose responded unemotionally.

"But you're a part of it. You always have been. I'll see you next week." He hung up the phone and thrust himself out of the ocean current that was swiftly sweeping everyone around him down the sidewalk and paused in an alleyway. He hastily checked the prices of flights, irritated by the one bar of signal that he had, and even more so by the 22 percent of battery life that remained on his phone. Since the flights were the following week, they were costly and he was far from being a rich man, but he knew that he had to do this. As he was proceeding to enter his credit card details, a pigeon flew by and landed on a garbage bin next to him. It had beautiful white feathers on the area below its neck and little bands of green that glistened in the rays of sunlight that had found their way into the alleyway. Martin didn't notice this, in fact, he didn't notice the regal bird until it said,

"Mr. Martin Bushnell." Its voice was just as royal as its look, sporting a slight British accent exuding an air of wealth.

"Huh? What?" He noticed the pigeon but went straight back to entering his card details.

"I am here on behalf of the Scholarly Society of Manhattan Pigeons. We have analyzed your current situation and have come to the conclusion that it is unwise for you to return to your hometown. It would be more beneficial if you remained here and followed the path that you are on."

"Shut up," he said with disdain. He had never treated an animal this way before but his change in personality did not faze him as he was focused on getting to Rose.

"I am only here to warn you. It is time to move on, young Master Bushnell."

"GET OUT OF HERE," he spat at the pigeon, waving his arm violently and forcing the pigeon to fly back up into the sky. His wings flashed red and gold as he took off, confirming the fact that he was a regal pigeon indeed.

*   *   *   *   *   *   *   *   *

The following week, Martin was flying out to his hometown while staring vapidly out the window and reminiscing on his last conversation with Isaac.

"Man, I kinda knew this was coming," Isaac had said to him a few hours after he had booked his plane ticket.

"What do you mean? And you didn't say anything?" Martin was frustrated as he had attempted to call Rose multiple times to tell her that he was coming home, but she had not picked up. He had texted her multiple times and only saw "read at 2:03pm" with no subsequent response.

"I just wasn't sure and honestly, a bit too focused on getting myself settled up here in the city. Even the day we drove here, when you two said goodbye, the look in her eyes seemed to suggest that it was more final that you thought."

"She just doesn't remember me since it has been two months since we've been together. Once she sees me, things will be back to normal and she'll probably come back up here with me afterwards."

"I think it'd be better if you just relaxed and enjoyed what's going on here. Your life is amazing and there are plenty of women for you to fall deeply in love with. At the last party you took me to, I swear I saw Zoe Kravitz eyeing you up."

"Drop it, Isaac. I'm going."

Martin looked down at the dark clouds below him and allowed his mind to turn a similar, brooding colour. He had disguised his trip to himself and anyone who asked by saying that he was taking a trip to visit his family for a week. He was going to be staying with them and they were exuberantly grateful to see him when they picked him up from the airport. His mother sensed the unease that he was feeling, and noticed that he seemed a little different, but decided not to mention anything right away.

For the first five days of his trip, he received no response from Rose. She would not answer any of his messages and he had no idea what to do. He almost drove out to her house but his friend Yadiel convinced him that this would be a mistake. Thus, he spent those days telling his friends and family about his experiences in New York, embellishing the best pieces while subtly skipping over any disconcerting parts. The time he spent with them was surprisingly rejuvenating but he didn't allow himself to dwell on this as he was solely focused on finding a way to see Rose before getting back to his "real life" in New York.

On his last day, he woke up feeling crunchy and dejected, as he had lost all hope of seeing Rose and was already dreading the moment when he would have to tell Isaac that he was right. Panicked thoughts started to swirl in his head about being single again and what that would be like. As the panic started to spread throughout his body, he received a message on his phone from Rose.

"I'm coming over in an hour."

His heart began to beat out of its chest and every emotion he knew he had seemed to be bumping into and around his body like a newly-born, hungry swarm of mosquitoes. He went downstairs and saw that his parents had gone out for breakfast with their friends. He had no idea what was going to happen with Rose and was grateful that nobody was around. He ate a breakfast that his stomach had no appetite for and spent the next forty-five minutes just sitting on the couch, rehearsing in his head a script of what he would say to her while combating endless bouts of anxiety. The doorbell rang and he sprang up instantly, smoothing his hair down, then tousling it back up, then smoothing it down once more.

As he opened the door, he immediately noticed how down she was. For the time they were together, she had been furiously alive, eternally shining brighter than the sun. However, at the present moment, the light that had surrounded her had faded to nothing and she seemed terribly tired.

"Hi, Martin," she said both softly and sadly. She entered the house and he immediately embraced her, imagining that a kiss or his touch would reawaken her and show her how alive he could make her feel. The kiss was awkward and she only half-returned it. They walked over to the living room and Martin sat on the couch, hoping that she would sit down next to him so that he could nurse her back to life but she stayed standing still.

"I didn't want to do this but Yadiel called me and told me that it was necessary. I've already said what I wanted to say to you and it hurts me to have to say it again."

"Well, Rose, I didn't have an opportunity to speak when he talked and if you sit down, I can share with you my side of things."

She breathed out strongly and sat down next to him. He put his arm around her to invite her to cuddle up closer. She didn't move his arm away but also didn't move any closer to him.

"I think you have forgotten what it was like with us." He began his practiced speech, already stumbling the first sentence. "The energy that we felt when we were together, the sensations that arose when we kissed, the laughter that we constantly shared. We were like one being that felt the same emotions, thought the same thoughts, it was..."

She interrupted him. "Martin, this may be true what you are saying, but it was on your end and not always on mine."

"What do you mean? No it wasn't. You felt the same as me."

"How do you know that?"

"I don't know, we were just connected. I could feel you."

"Sure, maybe at times it was like that for me, but most often it seemed unbalanced. I felt as if you were deeply in love with me and I was just happily enjoying our time. I don't think that's right."

Martin's voice rose as his agitation grew stronger. "But you're wrong! You are just forgetting! It has been two months and we haven't been able to see each other! If you just come to New York, we can fix this!"

With that outburst having entered the room, she now moved his arm away from her. He was beginning to feel unpleasant sensations arise in all parts of his body, from places that he didn't even know existed. He felt as if black tar was oozing out of a well deep below his stomach, causing his body to twitch with desperation.

"I am not coming to New York and I am not doing this anymore. We were only together for two weeks and you act as if we were married. I can't handle that. I can't handle the loving essays you send me every night. I can't handle the constant need for communication. I can't handle having to uproot myself completely just to appease your desires. I'm sorry. I am going to go now."

She got up and walked towards the door. Martin noticed that the tears that plastered on her face glistened in the sunlight that protruded through the windows and all at once he found her more beautiful than ever before. As she went to open the door, he stopped her.

"Wait."

She turned around but as he looked at her he found that he had nothing to say. The script that he had written had been set on fire and reduced to black ash that settled at the bottom of his mind. He felt as if he was a wind-up music box that had lost its ability to make noise. She looked at him with a deep, apologetic sadness and stepped out into the humid air. He watched her get into her car, noticing she made an effort not to look at him, and soon after, she was gone. Now he felt like a frayed rope, whose ends were beginning to unravel and split him into nothing but tiny strings. As the fountain of feelings arose, he held his breath and pushed them down as far as he possibly could, using every atom of strength that he had to remove himself from them. When his parents returned, he didn't tell them what had happened and the next day on a flight to New York, not allowing himself to even think about her for a single moment.

Chapter 10 - A Fire In The Heart

Suddenly, Martin was sobbing loudly, unable to stop the sounds that were emanating from his throat and hating himself for beginning to try. Although this excruciating sadness was agonizing, no tears would come from his eyes, and he noticed this with a terrified curiosity. He felt sick and ashamed of himself for even thinking about Rose. He opened his eyes, thinking that he could distract himself with something out of the plane's window and hoped to God that no one had heard his cries. As his eyelids opened, he saw that he wasn't on the plane but was on top of a grassy knoll surrounded by forest. A smell of smoke entered his nostrils and a soft touch caressed his shoulder. He looked around with eyes wanting to expel tears but not knowing how and pain residing in his stomach and chest, and saw the most comforting face he had ever seen.

"Martin, I apologize, but we're going to have to end this session here. It's time to go," Dr. Spruce said with considerable compassion.

"Dr. Spruce? What is going on? I was in New York. I was with Rose. I... oh my god."

"Yes, Martin, this can be hard. Especially the first go around. You have repressed this stuff for a long time now and the only way to get it out of there is to look at it directly."

"Did I... Did it come out?" Martin's voice was soft.

"A good chunk of it definitely came up, yep. But that's enough for now. You can't get it all out at once as it would make you crazy. Also, there seems to be a fire burning nearby."

Dr. Spruce gestured calmly towards the column of smoke that was rising fairly close to them. The fire looked as if it was a significant burn, given the thick, dark grey plume that it was causing. Martin looked over towards it, noticing the sound of helicopters in the distance, and his stomach dropped into his feet.

"I think... I'm pretty sure... That's where my house is." He looked at Dr. Spruce for some kind of affirmation or answer. He was still feeling raw from the foray into his mind and was not ready to accept that a fire was actually burning down his house.

Dr. Spruce just looked at him with those beady, compassionate eyes and said,

"Well, if it is, we better start walking over there."

"Walk?! We've gotta run over there! No, I know! I read a book once where the main character got to ride a polar bear through the Arctic north so that she could save her father and eventually the whole universe! I've got to ride on your back!"

Martin moved closer towards Dr. Spruce who stood up on his hind legs and held out his hands to stop him.

"Whoa, hold up, mister. That's not how this works. No fantasy stories here. We're going to walk over there, nice and slowly. Fires can be fast and dangerous, and we don't want to get caught up in it."

"I guess you're right." Martin conceded as they started to walk in the direction of the smoke.

"Besides, I think it's best that we have a chat about what you just went through. How are you feeling right now?"

The excitement and fear caused by the fire had caused Martin to forget about all that he had just seen. It was if he had been fully inside of that Martin of the past, without any recollection of his future self. He was just there, living the past again; that terrible, traumatic past.

"To be honest, I'm pretty shaken up. I had forgotten about that whole experience, it was just gone from my memory."

"Sometimes we repress our traumas because we think that's the only way we can deal with them."

"I can't remember what happened after... after Rose."

"Ah, we'll leave the future of the past alone for now. Focus on your feet on the ground, right here in the present moment, and tell me how your body feels."

Martin took a moment to do exactly what Dr. Spruce said. For some reason, he no longer had the same adverse reaction to the things that the bear said to him. He scanned his body and was amazed by what he felt.

"I feel... significantly lighter as if there was this anvil pressing down on my chest that has lifted. It's still there, I think, but not as heavy. Also, the pain of my wounds seems to feel a little better. Not completely healed, but it seems much easier to deal with it all. Wow."

"The weight of your past is lifting and the wounds of your mind are healing, thus lessening the strength of your present woes."

They walked slowly in the forest for a few minutes and Martin began to notice how alive the forest floor was. In fact, it looked more like the bottom of the ocean as if it were an above ground coral reef. There were orange, coral-like fungi protruding out of spaces between thick, fluffy mossy mats, which surrounded the gargantuan roots of thick trees that lined the path. He was taken aback. How could he have not seen this beauty before? Of course, he had noticed certain things when he was out picking mushrooms, but he was usually so focused on finding something edible and taking as much of it as possible that he never noticed the rest. It was as if he was seeing for the first time. How was this real? Suddenly, he stopped in the path, shocked by another memory from the session.

"I had forgotten that I could talk to animals. That idea was completely absent from my mind. Why did I stop? Why would I ever stop? They were always there for me when I was growing up when I felt as if no one else cared. I don't know how I could have even thought about blocking out that part of my life. Is that why I don't talk to my brother anymore? Because he's the only one who knows? Oh my god, what is going on?"

Martin brought his hands to his face and let the anxiety rise up and bubble in his chest, setting the stage for a full-on panic attack. Dr. Spruce came close to him, sat on the ground, and looked Martin straight in the eyes.

"Come back to me, Martin. Find the forest floor again. Notice your feet on the ground and be here, with me. Observe your breath, the natural flow of breath coming in and going out."

Despite the overwhelming flood of feelings, he managed to follow Dr. Spruce's directions, letting these simple observations calm his nervous system, bringing him to feel slightly more balanced. He sat down on the ground.

"This is just a lot, Spruce."

"Yes. That's how it goes when you start to realize all the damage you have caused yourself and others and when you come face-to-face with the answers to a simple question that you have been avoiding for years."

"What's the question?"

"Who are you?"

Martin sat quietly. Obviously he knew the answer to that question. He was Martin Bushnell. He lived in the forest near Richmond Lake, British Columbia, Canada. He liked to... what did he like to do? He started to think about the ways that he would spend his days and it caused him a severely unpleasant sensation as if a stone were lodged in his intestines. He ignored this, as it didn't feel like something he was ready for, and started to think about how, after seven years, he had remembered a huge chapter of his past that had been completely removed from his mind. What else was in there? Perhaps he didn't know who he was. This terrified him and made him tense up, painting uneven lines across his forehead. If so, how was he supposed to figure out who he was? How could he even answer that question?

"Yes, it's a rather difficult question to face," Dr. Spruce said. "People don't get asked enough and if they do, they don't think about it enough. But, don't feel like you have to answer that question right here right now. I'm just planting the seed." He grabbed a pinecone from a nearby tree, cracked it open and showed Martin three oval seeds that lay inside. "Take one, they're delicious."

Martin, still a bit woozy from the whirlwind of life, slowly took one of the seeds and popped it in his mouth. Dr. Spruce did the same. As he chewed on the little pine nut, the taste spread throughout his mouth, instantly making him feel more alive and present. It was as if he had taken a bite of nature itself. He swallowed and reached out to grab the last nut in the cone, but Dr. Spruce pulled his hand back.

"Nuh uh. Rules of the forest say never to take everything. Leave some for whoever comes next, or for a new growth to occur." He took the little seed, used his large, furry finger to dig a small, round hole in the ground, and plopped it in, putting delicate effort into firmly patting the soil down on top. He stood up and held out his hand to Martin.

"Shall we?"

Martin grabbed his hand and they went on their way. As they talked more, Martin discovered that Dr. Spruce had not been able to see what he was seeing when he was in his memories of the past. He said he had just been there to "hold the space". Since they still seemed to be far from the smoke, he made an effort to recount what he had seen to Dr. Spruce, who only interrupted him to go further in depth into certain situations. He reached the end of the story and, as silence began to form, Martin realized that there were wisps of smoke passing around them, filling up his nostrils with the strong, tingly scent of fire.

"Thank you for sharing that with me, Martin. You did a very good job today. I'm proud of you and grateful to be a part of this experience with you."

Martin was shocked by how that simple statement made him feel. He couldn't remember the last time that someone had said they were proud of him. Tears welled up in his eyes and he looked down at the ground, hoping that this outburst had not been seen.

The bear continued, "now, I must leave you for now. I will see you for our next session."

"What? You're not coming with me?"

Dr. Spruce sniffed the air. "It seems as if they managed to put the fire out quickly, but I must go and check on the inhabitants in this area of the forest. I may need to find some new homes for the birds and rabbits." Noticing Martin's wide-eyed fearful stare, he added, "you'll be fine. Go and face whatever it is that you have to face."

His smile was a glimmering showcase of little white teeth and the image lingered in Martin's mind as Dr. Spruce wandered into the trees. Martin was frozen still for some time until he heard voices close by. As he looked around, he realized how close he was to his own house and began to run towards it, hearing the voices getting louder as he got closer. Part of him was already prepared for what he was going to see. The distinct smell of burnt wood in the air, the sound of anxious voices, and the ash floating all around him suggested the massive blow that he was about to receive. Though, still, when he saw the skeleton of his home, charred and black, looking more like a pile of garbage than a home, he was completely devastated. He burst out of the trees and ran towards it, unaware of the sweaty, exhausted police and firefighters that were congregated nearby. As he got closer, he saw that everything had burnt down. Most of the solar panel had melted, a lone stalk of kale had survived in his charred garden, and there was no house to be seen. Somehow, the only thing that had managed to survive the fire was his mattress, which lay there peacefully, half-covered in rubble like an oasis of eggshell white amidst total darkness. Before he could get too close, he was grabbed from behind by a rough hand.

"Whoa there, buddy, you ain't goin' any closer." It was a firefighter with a bushy moustache and ash covering the right side of his face. Despite his own despair, he noticed that the man had a pair of very kind green eyes.

"That's my home! Or... that was my home."

"I'm really sorry to hear that, friend. Looks like it was a nice home. Probably pretty peaceful out here, eh?"

"Sometimes..." As he said this, he sadly realized that he actually couldn't remember any time when he felt peaceful living there. "Who am I?" he thought.

The policewoman who had been standing with the rest of them had heard Martin's claim to the home and was moving swiftly towards them with a notebook in hand.

"Was there anyone in the house while you were gone?" She had already started writing as she was walking.

"No, I just lived on my own." He noticed that this comment made him feel melancholy, a different reaction from what he was used to. If this were the Martin of just a couple of days ago, he probably would have been screaming at all of them for not being able to save his house. At the moment though, he was just feeling tiny and troubled. The policewoman continued.

"That's good to hear, Mr.?"

"Bushnell, uh, Martin Bushnell."

She wrote for a lot longer than it seemed like it would take to write down his name. Perhaps she could see how sad he was and was writing about that. As she was writing, he took a look over to where his truck was usually parked and noticed that it too had been charred by the fire. However, it looked like it hadn't exploded and he thought that perhaps the engine could be salvaged. That thought formed a knot in the pit of his stomach as he was exhausted and could not imagine mustering the energy for any type of work for the time being. For a moment, he wished he was back in his memories of New York with his carefree, ignorant self who did not own a house or a truck.

"Well, neither do I anymore," he thought somberly.

"I'd say we've all experienced a dose of good luck here today." The policewoman said after finishing the thesis that she had been writing.

Martin looked questioningly at her and then at the house. "Sure doesn't look like it," he said in a surprisingly calm voice.

"Well, of course, your house being destroyed is a shame, but we did manage to stop the fire before it hit your propane tank. That would have been a total disaster."

He noticed the shiny white propane tank sitting intact a few metres from the house. A mattress, a propane tank, and the engine of a truck was all he had remaining. An image suddenly formed in his head of a flying mattress, using the propane and engine to propel it through the air and fly him out of this blackened mess to... where? Where would he even go? Where else was there to go? He didn't want to think about this right now. Luckily, the policewoman continued her analysis of the situation.

"Do you know how this fire was started, Martin?"

"No, I was up in the hills back there through the forest and came back when I saw the column and smelt the smoke."

"What were you doing up in the hills?"

He neither wanted to lie to the woman nor tell her what had actually happened, so he settled for somewhere in the middle. "Uh... spending time with wildlife and reflecting on my past."

"Mmhmm." She began her writing again with a slight smile, leaving Martin to sit with the flux of sensations and emotions that were flowing through him. He realized that he was actually very angry that he had had that extremely transformative experience with Dr. Spruce and then had to be thrust immediately into this terrible situation. Suddenly, he remembered the black cat that he had met at the party in New York.

"What goes up must come down." She had said to him.

His first reaction to remembering her advice was "that's pathetically cliché" but upon closer observation he saw that there was a lot of truth there. Perhaps all the stupid sayings that floated below pictures of tiny cats had some merit to them. He tended to ignore those types of things in favour of more complex philosophical quotes that he would never admit that he actually didn't understand. The policewoman started again.

"Mr. Bushnell, did you crash an ATV on the side of the road yesterday?"

Up until now, he had forgotten completely about the events of the previous day. He looked down at himself and noticed that he still had the bandages on him that Evaline had so carefully dressed him with. As the thought of Evaline crossed his mind he immediately felt a bout of shame for having walked out of her apartment without even so much as a goodbye. "Who am I?" he thought. "A truly miserable man," something within him replied. He looked at the policewoman and made the decision not to lie to her, despite the majority of his mind pointing him in that direction. If he was arrested, so what? He had nowhere else to go.

"Yes. I was out by Large Lake and…"

"Large Lake?" Her eyebrows raised.

"Oh, um, that's just what I named it. There's a large lake a few kilometres down the road over there and I thought that was an apt name." He looked at her for some kind of approval but she just kept writing. After some more silence, she looked back up.

"Continue with the events of your accident yesterday."

"Oh, sorry. I was out by the lake and I ran into a large bear."

"A large bear at a large lake?" She interrupted. It seemed as if a little smile curled up the sides of her cheeks and just for a moment he had a pretty thought about her pretty face. The thought and her smile disappeared quickly as her pen furiously ran across her miniature journal. Martin started to get slightly anxious as he noticed that she was going to run out of paper fairly soon.

"Yes. And… well, I got pretty spooked."

"You live out here in the middle of the forest and were spooked by a bear?" She seemed to be attempting to be serious and having a laugh at the same time.

"This one was different. Bigger and more… vocal. After a brief interaction, I recognized that it was time for me to get out of there, especially as this huge thunderstorm had suddenly formed overhead. It was crazy… blue, untouched sky flipped to being completely covered in these huge anvil-shaped cumulonimbus clouds in less than a second." He hadn't wanted to share this last part as it made him seem a little crazy, but he was starting to trust this woman, despite the fact that she seemed to both want to arrest him and write a novel about him.

"Perhaps the bear snapped its fingers and created a thunderstorm?" She remarked out of the side of her mouth while continuing to write. Once again, was she being rude, or playing around? He decided to say something.

"Hey, listen, Ms..."

"Ah, Detective Orchid Magnolia, but go ahead and call me Orchid."

"Detective Orchid Magnolia, I'm feeling a bit sensitive at the moment due to the fact that my house just got completely burnt down and the last two days have been ridiculously intense. I'm getting a bit confused about the way you're speaking to me. I'm not sure if you are going to arrest me and I'm freaked out about the amount of words you have written about me so far." To say all of this took a significant amount of energy but he noticed that it also made his jaw loosen up a little, as if all those words had been stuck inside. Normally, he could never have said something like that to anyone, let alone a police officer.

"I apologize for your confusion, *Mister Martin Bushnell*. The fact is, I am a police detective and have to be as diligent about my work as I possibly can. I would only arrest you if there was a true cause to arrest you... which we will get to promptly. Furthermore, I moonlight as a fiction writer and base a lot of my stories off my experiences on the field. Thus, the notable number of notes. As your story is fictionally plump like a greased-up turkey, I was hoping to ask you if you wouldn't mind if I use some of this in the story, barring your true identity, of course." The way she floated between her two realities struck Martin along with the honesty with which she conducted herself, especially compared to those one-sided "people" he had seen in his visions of New York.

"Uh, sure, go ahead."

"Thanks." She flashed him a brief smile and his knees shivered momentarily, confusing his already flustered mind. "So, this thunderstorm appeared and then what? You bucked off down the road in your ATV like a mad race car driver?"

"Well, yes, and the rain was pouring down hard. It was as if all the waterfalls in the world had begun pouring out of the little cloud above my head. You can put that metaphor in your story." He was starting to enjoy himself a little. A little scream from inside came to him as if his old secretive self was fighting for control, though this new forthcoming part of him was strong now and wasn't giving in. "I missed the road to my house, the one you took, and went careening towards the highway with no idea where I was going. I could see about five feet in front of me and when I saw the headlights of the truck, it was too late. I smashed into her right headlight and flew off into the nearest tree." He used his hands considerably while he recounted the story, moving his body slightly to add a tinge more drama to the whole event.

"Jeez, man. We've definitely got a good story here, both for a detective and for an author. Now, I've got to tell you something that may hurt you."

He looked at her and saw kindness and pity in her eyes, also noticing that they were a powerful shade of green like the colour of the trees that used to surround his house. He snapped out of this minor trance as she began to speak in a more forlorn voice.

"The fire we dealt with today was, in the grand scheme of things, not so bad. Despite the fact that your house and a small part of the forest was destroyed, there was no damage to any other properties. This is another reason to be grateful, especially since you may have been the cause of the fire."

He was shocked. How could he have been the cause of the fire? He had been traveling through his own mind with a large bear as a babysitter! There was no way he started a fire! Orchid continued.

"What we call a Farm Equipment Fire can be a myriad of things, including a spark caused by friction from a tractor driving along a roadway. It seems as if this is what happened today and what that spark happened to land on was a small trail of oil that had leaked out of your ATV, which then quickly spread out to the surrounding trees."

"How could you know that?"

"I'm a detective, Martin."

"Fair enough. So, I'm the one to blame for burning down my own house? Can I be arrested for that?"

"If I were one of those nasty coppers, I could find a way to bring you in for arson or something along those lines. But the fact is, you weren't *really* the cause. The spark that flew off the tractor was the instigator, though it would be a bit difficult for me to figure out exactly whose tractor was the culprit. Then there's the problem of, do I arrest the tractor or the driver?" She smiled at this and wrote it down. "Hm, there's a good story about artificial intelligence in there," she winked at him and he just stood there, incredulous. He had never had any kind of experience like this with a cop. As the silence lingered, he noticed that the tenderness in his sternum was leaking into his heart space. He didn't like the feeling and ran his mind away from it.

"There is a whole lot of grey area here because you probably shouldn't have been driving like a wild man in a thunderstorm, or leaving your busted ATV on the side of the road, but I'm going to choose to let it go. It looks like most everything you own is destroyed and, to me, it seems that nature has already punished you for your bad decisions, so who am I to do anything more?"

"Wow. Thank you. Thank you for being an honest cop."

She smiled at him, and said, "so who was in the truck that you hit?"

"Well, I guess I was lucky, because it was actually a friend... or not really a friend... or I don't know, just someone that I knew from my town. Her name's Evaline."

"Evaline Parker?"

"I'm not sure, I don't know her last name."

"White truck, short brown hair, doctor?"

"Yeah, that's her!" The excitement in his voice betrayed an emotion that he didn't even know he had.

"Well, the plot thickens. Evaline is an old friend of mine. It's been a while since I've seen her, writing the seventh novel of this series and all, but it seems like now is the time. In order for me to get a better understanding of the whole picture here, it's best if I talk to her about this. You want a ride over there?"

With a pit plunging in the depths of his stomach, he realized that he had no plan of where he was going next. Though the conversation had been mostly about the fire and his house, he had forgotten that his whole life was *actually* destroyed. It seemed that the only thing he could do was to go with this detective to see Evaline. He could see that this was really what he wanted to do, but what would he do when he saw her? Apologize? Act as if nothing ever happened?

"Yes, I do." The decision had been made though he was petrified of his uncertain future.

"Good. Can you give me ten minutes to wrap it up with the firefighters?" She walked off towards the group who were discussing something funny amongst themselves. Martin was grateful for this splash of time so that he could have a closer look at the damage that had been done to his former home. He sighed as he walked past the ravaged truck and the half-melted solar panel, recognizing these strange feelings that had started to be introduced to him. Everything had seemed to happen all at once, crashing him not only into a tree but a whole new chapter of his life. The experience with Dr. Spruce, the destruction of his home, and all the new people who he had interacted with. He was so used to being on his own and had completely convinced himself that he could do without anyone else. He used to imagine himself as one of the monks who retreated to caves for their whole life in order to find enlightenment. He had pushed this ideal so far down his mind that it had caused him considerable psychological damage, and he was just becoming aware of this fact.

He reached the crumpled building and stepped slowly around the rubble, seeing that none of his possessions, beside the mattress, were salvageable in any capacity. He saw something that piqued his interest and crouched down to have a closer look. It was a fragment of his calendar. It said:

2pm: Clean The Gutters

2:15pm: Clean All The Tools
2:25pm: Sweep Up Everything

Seeing the schedule made him feel suddenly sick to his stomach. How could he have done that to himself? There was no time to breathe amidst all that work but the routines were what he had relied on for so long and he didn't know anything different. He was seeing now that it had been a tool for him so that he wouldn't be distracted. But distracted by what? His memories of the past? In his session with Dr. Spruce he had seen a number of traumatic experiences that still lingered. Is this what he had been avoiding by all of this busy work? What else was he hiding? He shuddered and looked away, afraid to go any further into these questions. His mind was busier than it had ever been, as if a self-created dam had burst open, releasing a torrent of confusion, fear, and many other difficult emotions, including significant fatigue. He needed a break. He looked back at Orchid, who seemed very busy writing in two notepads at once, then he stumbled towards the mattress. He flopped down upon it and let out a breath of relief.

The comfort of his bed was soothing as it had always been a safe space for him. Though every night he had struggled to get himself to sleep, those half-dreaming moments when he woke up in the middle of the night were always something he relished. In that space, he was nothing but a brief moment of consciousness sandwiched between two layers of sleep. There was nothing on the to-do list but to return to sleep. As he thought about this, he allowed his eyes to close and a brief moment of fear passed through him with the thought that he would get another glimpse of some terrible event from his past, but no such thing happened. There were no images but the glittery behind-eyelid lights that perpetually existed in the strange darkness. He felt his body begin to relax, noticing that the typical stress that would overcome him when he laid down to rest had diminished, and he slowly settled into a state of slumber.

The dream of Rose began as soon as he closed his eyes. She was clutching a baby close to her breast and when she saw him she whispered,

"This is not my baby. It's hers."

With the hand that was not holding the baby she pointed out of a ceiling-to-floor glass window behind which was a woman in an all-in-one leopard print bathing suit posing in a hot tub, while a stylish young man filmed her eagerly.

"Her name is Rose as well." Rose had dark bags under her eyes that were getting darker with every moment.

"You look exhausted, Rose. Is it the baby? I can hold it for a while if you need a break." Something was causing Martin significant levels of fear and it resonated in his voice. He got closer to her and started to take the baby gently from her. It felt like it was attached to her by strong velcro and there was a slight ripping sound as he removed it. She breathed out deeply as if she had been holding her breath for the last month. The baby felt heavier than he would imagine a baby to be and as he looked down at it, he was shocked to see that the baby had Rose's face, dark eye bags and all. It stared at him with an awful glare and then, in a maniacal voice, it cackled,

"No one loves you, Mister Martin Bushnell. And no one ever will."

Then it opened its mouth as if it were a snake unlocking its jaw and clamped sharp teeth straight into his chest. He screamed with pain as the baby's teeth penetrated his skin, made their way down to his heart, and ripped the entire thing right out. It swallowed the heart whole and laughed. He suddenly felt sharp pains throughout each and every part of his body.

"Martin Bushnell, wake up!" A familiar voice echoed throughout his pain and he felt a slight breeze ripple over his body. He attempted to open his eyes but had difficulty with the left one as it felt as if there was something stuck in the corner.

Detective Orchid was standing over top of him, creating light gusts of winds through a constant waving of her notebooks. "Am I on fire?" he thought.

"Martin, you are completely covered in mosquitoes. Get up, run fast, and hopefully the wind will throw them off you. The smoke has started clearing and the bugs have noticed the feast of large mammals that we have provided them today. Once they've left your body, let's get out of here, but don't you dare bring any of them in the car."

Still affected by the terrifying dream, he moved groggily, affirming with his eyes that he was indeed carpeted by a thin layer of small, black creatures who were filling themselves up with his blood. This horror-movie image got him up quickly as he truly hated mosquitoes. He sprinted round his disintegrated house until it seemed as if the majority of the mosquitoes were knocked off. Still running, he brushed off other areas where some still lingered, including the one on the corner of his eye, and saw Orchid quickly opening the door to her small police car. He ran towards it, examining himself to make sure that none of the opportunistic insects were upon him, quickly opened the door, slammed it tight, and breathed. Orchid looked at him for a moment then broke out into a charming fit of laughter.

She caught her breath. "Were you asleep?"

He nodded shyly.

"Martin on a mattress in the middle of the rubble like a quiet island amidst a poisoned ocean. Man oh man, this day has given me so much good material to work with! You really don't mind if I write about this?"

"Whatever you want." He was distracted and still panicky from the mixture of mosquitoes and the nightmare as Orchid began driving towards the road that ran perpendicular to his driveway.

"You okay? All of that was probably pretty hard for you." She flashed a caring glance over in his direction.

"Yeah, it wasn't really the house, it's just…" He wanted to tell her about his dream but was afraid. The thought of opening up to someone about this was scary, but keeping it inside was even more horrifying. "While I was asleep there, I had a nightmare. Like, a really bad nightmare."

Even just saying this made Martin feel like he could breathe a little easier. "Who am I?" He thought about this again for a moment, noticing that he really had no idea who he was. For as long as he could remember, he had not allowed himself to open up to anyone whatsoever, as he had the idea that he should be able to deal with any difficult situations by himself, through diligent routine and compartmentalization. But now something was telling him that this is not how he had always been. He remembered that young, carefree version of himself who had wandered ignorantly up into New York, unafraid of being emotional or sharing his feelings. Was that who he was?

"Oh?" Orchid said, provoking him to elaborate further on the dream.

"It was about an ex-girlfriend. She had a baby but the baby also had her face and it bit down on my chest and ripped out my heart."

Orchid snorted a little with laughter, but quickly noticed Martin's serious attitude towards it and stifled the snort, reentering with a more understanding tone.

"I've been there. Those ones are tough."

"You mean, you've had a dream baby with your ex-partner's face rip out your heart?"

"No, not exactly that, but listen to this one. I was having this really peaceful dream where I was just out in the forest in a regular outfit, no cop uniform or anything. I didn't have any notebooks or even any thoughts about writing as I was just out in nature completely enjoying my surroundings. There was this massive fir tree with tons of beautiful pinecones that I was staring at. All of sudden, the little pinecones transformed into tiny faces of my ex until there were hundreds of his stupid face hanging off of the tree looking right at me. They all started falling off of the tree and due to the fact that I was directly underneath they were hitting me on the head, the shoulders, and eventually started piling up around my feet until I couldn't move. I was screaming until one landed in my mouth and I could no longer make any sound. I woke up right after being completely buried alive by tiny laughing pinecones with my ex-boyfriend's face on them."

A laugh rose up from his belly, escaping his lips before he had the chance to stuff it back down.

"Oh, I'm sorry. I don't usually..."

Laugh? He couldn't remember the last time that he actually laughed. The fact that something had made him feel the type of wholesome, pleasant sensation that comes with an unforced laugh was astounding. "Who am I?"

Orchid laughed a little. "It's okay, I wrote a short story about it, which helped me process the whole thing. If it hadn't had happened to me, I would have found it funny as well."

Martin sat with himself for a moment, astounded by his actions, as well as confounded by the feelings of familiarity that were emerging towards being around Orchid. He hadn't allowed himself to feel anything like this since... since Rose? These somewhat suggestive thoughts pushed him a little too far over the edge and his body began to shake slightly. Luckily, Orchid began a new thread of the conversation.

"So, Martin. I have another question for you, both for my own curiosity and to flesh out the character in this newly forming novel. Excuse me if it's a bit deep or discomforting. But, who are you, really?"

How could she know that this had been the question that had been flying around his mind like a whirlwind of mosquitoes all day? How was he supposed to answer that?

"I'm not sure how to answer that." He said, trying to avoid this discussion. Was he afraid of who he was?

"You could try." She nudged him gently with her words. Like a true detective/writer, she had developed the skill of noticing when someone had a lot more to say than the words that came out of their mouth. It was an art that could veer into negative manipulation if it fell into the wrong hands, but she had made an effort to use it only if she could see it might benefit another.

He breathed in, noticing that the stress of answering the question was causing his nostrils to tighten, making the sound of his breath more pronounced than usual. He listened to this sound for some time, trying to allow himself to relax so that he could find the answer to this troubling question.

"Well, um, I guess I'm Martin Bushnell..."

"That's a good start."

"I live... well, I lived out in the forest for the past three years, I think, and um... I'm not sure what else to say."

"What did you do when you were living out in the forest?" The way she asked questions was reminding him of Dr. Spruce as she had that same type of compassion that lay behind her words. His trust for her began to grow just a little bit stronger, inspiring him to move past the stress of this conversation.

"Well, I had a garden but the rabbits always got in, I repaired my solar panel because it was always broken, I cleaned the house as it always seemed to be dirty, I mowed the lawn due to the annoyingly fast-growing grass, I..."

Orchid stopped him there. "Did you enjoy any of these things? It sounds like you were doing them because you felt like you had to."

His thin line of defence let its guard go up at this statement. "Of course I did. It was my life. I have to enjoy my life, that's the point!" The words crescendo-ed hysterically as they came out of his mouth.

"Mmhmm. So you're saying that you *have to* enjoy your life, despite the fact that you have been choosing to do things that you don't enjoy. Sounds like you've been a bit rough on yourself."

"You don't know me. I don't want to answer any more of your questions." As he said this, a wave of agitation spread throughout his body and he breathed out forcefully. The tension was overwhelming. Where was it coming from? He had never felt this type of tension before, he thought, or perhaps he just hadn't been aware of it. What was going on? It was strange, the awareness of the torpid tension in his body was actually helping alleviate it in some way, though he was finding it quite alarming just noticing that it was all there. He felt as if he was having the best and worst experience of his life simultaneously. He looked at Orchid, whose face had darkened solemnly and he felt a pang of guilt stab through the carousel of emotions.

"I'm sorry. There is a lot going on inside of me right now and I'm finding everything hard." The honest apology slipped out of his vocal cords and he looked away, embarrassed about how much he had revealed.

Orchid looked at him with another gentle smile. "That's the stuff I'm asking about! There *you* are. Are you willing to talk about what's going on inside you? Why are you finding everything so hard?"

He looked out the window for a moment and realized that he had been so distracted that he hadn't even thought to look out for the remains of his ATV, though it was too late at this point as they were already past the crash site. In his light reflection on the window, he glimpsed a glimmer of gratitude for Orchid Magnolia, who did not point it out when they had passed it, perhaps to not cause him any further pain. Despite his best efforts at stopping himself, he decided to try and explain to her what was going on with him.

"There is a part of this that I want to purposefully leave out, ok? I'm not ready to talk about some specifics." He was referring to his session with Dr. Spruce as he wasn't ready to tell anyone else about his talks with the bear. "When I was out in the forest as the fire was happening, some piece of my past revealed itself to me out of nowhere. A memory, or series of memories, had been buried so deep that I had forgotten completely about this significant chapter of my life. Some of it came up to the surface and it was as if I was reliving it again, and by doing so, I think I was dealing with the trauma that I could never have faced when I was younger."

He paused, momentarily amazed with himself for allowing these words to pour forth from inside.

"After this, I was shaken to the core and as I was attempting to process what had happened I came out to see the devastating sight of my home burnt to the ground. So, as you can imagine, there is a lot going on in my mind right now. Who am I? What do I do now? Where do I go?"

To be this open about anything was a huge milestone for Martin. In fact, he couldn't remember the last time that he had even had a conversation this long and through this thought pattern, he started to wonder why this had all happened. The boy who had moved up to New York had been different. Sure, he had still been full of fear, stress, and anxiety, but he hadn't held them back like he had been doing out here. He had spoken to others about it and welcomed their advice, especially with Yadiel, Isaac, and Rose, who had all been there for him whenever things felt a bit troubling. Why did he stop that? How did he get here? He was not ready to answer that question and moved quickly away. Luckily, Orchid was ready to respond.

"Martin, thank you for sharing that with me. Sometimes it's easier to block things out than to face them but I think you are very brave for doing what you did. Though I can't give you any answers to the questions that you need to figure out for yourself, just know that you have my support if you ever need it. However, I can suggest that you try writing a novel about what you're going through as it might help you process some of those difficult questions. I have started to discover who I am through my writing. I'm happy to help you."

"What have your stories been about?" Martin was suddenly eager to move away from all of this talk about him as the depth of this conversation was tiring him out.

The creases around her eyes formed as her smile lifted her face into an expression of gratitude. She loved when people asked her about her writing, since many of the police force avoided this question due to skepticism about the fact that she was fictionalizing the cases that they dealt with. She spent the majority of the car ride telling Martin about two of her most cherished novels. One was about a man who had been arrested, but all throughout his arrest and time in prison, he had been determined to convince any who would listen that he was not from this planet. The second focused on a young girl who went to the police as she believed that the trees in the forest were following her and trying to take her. The force mostly ignored her as they were busy trying to find a notorious serial killer, who they eventually found out had a large tree costume in his garage. The stories seemed fascinating to Martin and he wondered if these things had actually happened, but she was unwilling to tell him due to the rules around confidentiality.

"Oh, I think we're here," she said suddenly, as Martin noticed they had reached the familiar apartment complex where he had been taken care of the night before. *Was it only the night before?* Time seemed to be twisting on him.

They stepped out of the car, though Martin took a lot longer than Detective Orchid. He had remembered once again how he had disappeared from Evaline's apartment after she had cared for him so thoughtfully. Was she going to yell at him? Would she even want to see him? He walked behind Orchid to the door, slightly diverted by the way her dark hair shimmered in the sun, but not enough to let his panic subside. She rang the buzzer and waited.

Chapter 11 - Softness and Despair

That morning, Evaline had woken up after a complicated dream in which she had been asked to perform seven different emergency surgeries at the same time. She had been confused as to how they had been scheduled all for her, all at once, but she could do nothing but try her best to fulfill them. She sprang from room to room, making important incisions here and stitchings there, but mostly trying to delegate the tasks to the rest of the staff in the rooms. She had managed to complete her duties for six of the surgeries but when she got to the seventh, she noticed the details on the patient report solely said "Mask Removal". She had never heard of a mask removal surgery so she asked the other doctor in the room what was going on.

"Ah, this patient seems to be wearing a mask that needs removing. You're going to have to peel it off. I started it for you but you're the only one who can go any further."

As she looked down at the patient she noticed that it was Martin. Wasn't he asleep in her guest room? Why was he in the hospital? She saw that there was a little flap of skin under his left ear that seemed to have been peeled back slightly. She put on a new pair of gloves and began to peel it back. Martin's face started to be removed like a sticker coming off of a window and to her surprise, there was another face underneath. It was the face of a young, chubby boy who actually had a slight resemblance to Martin.

"As you can see, this is but another mask that needs to be removed." The female doctor, who seemed to resemble Evaline's old police detective friend, said to her, pointing to the other flap of skin that lay below his chin. She pulled this skin off and saw that her own face was underneath it. She was horrified, but the doctor whispered to her,

"Keep going. There's another one."

She pulled off her own face from the patient and saw her father, but there was yet another flap to be pulled so she kept going. Her mother came next, followed by Mr. Rogers, who was her childhood hero, then it was the face of her old dog, her grandmother, the prime minister but with a moustache, and many other faces that she didn't recognize, including a kind bear with glasses. The pulling continued until there was nothing there. The body remained but there was just darkness where the head should have been. Out of the darkness a voice said,

"Underneath all the layers, this is what you are."

She woke with a start, crashing her hand upon her bedside table to grasp her notebook and pen. The dream erupted onto the page as quickly as it could possibly be written. She didn't want to forget this one as it seemed suffused in meaning, though she wasn't sure exactly what that meaning was. She decided to run a quick analysis to try and figure it out.

"Is Martin a ghost?" She wrote on the page then immediately crossed this out.

"I am Mr. Rogers." She liked this conclusion but knew this wasn't right and crossed this out as well.

"We are conditioned by all the people that we meet and the experiences that we have. In fact, we are mostly made up of pieces of all the others that we interact with in our lives."

She put a big check mark on this one and smiled as she loved finding meaning in things. She looked at her clock and saw that it was still early. Reminding herself that she had a guest in the house, she quietly tiptoed to the bathroom, pushing down the handle and lightly shutting the door. She looked at herself in the mirror, hoping that there was nowhere on her face for her to peel off her mask, but fortunately she was fully intact. Looking in the mirror for a little longer than usual, her mind was moving her through a round of "who am I?"

The questioning had been provoked by a major event that had occurred concurrently with her father passing away. About an hour away from Richmond Lake, there had been protests taking place against a pipeline being built on indigenous land, with the majority of the town's indigenous peoples standing up for their rights to maintain that land. Her father had been indigenous, though she had always maintained a distance from that side of her family, feeling a sense of embarrassment that she never really understood. Her father had passed away a few months prior and this, along with the protests, had brought her to start an attempt to understand these feelings inside of her. She was beginning to see that shunning her heritage stemmed from the hidden judgements that had lain below the surface of the majority of her classmates and their families and was now trying to understand more about her father's background so that she could rid herself of these feelings.

As this thought bumped around like a billiard ball on the pool table of her mind, she heard her front door open and close momentarily. A brief bout of fear filled her chest as she started to imagine potentially disturbing scenarios that could unfold between her and a thief, when she remembered that she had definitely locked both the locks on the door the night before. Could it be Martin? Why would he leave so early without saying anything? She quietly re-opened the bathroom door and peered out into the hallway, confirming Martin's departure by registering the lack of his large, dirty steel-toed boots by the shoe rack. A sudden anger overcame her when she thought of how well she had taken care of him only for him to leave abruptly without even a goodbye. She barely knew the guy, but was still upset about the fact that he had smashed her car, slept in her house, and left without even a word of gratitude. In her profession, she had tried to work on not expecting words of thanks, but it still hurt when it didn't happen.

"People need to learn how to love more," she said to herself sadly in the mirror.

When she went back to her bedroom, she still had negative feelings towards Martin lingering within, so she decided to do an intensive hour and a half kickboxing routine, which brought her back down to a more level head. As she got ready for work, she wondered if she would ever see the strange man again. She was curious to know whether his dream-mumblings about the speaking bear had any foot in reality. When she was younger, she had heard her father tell stories about his ancestors speaking with and learning from the animals in the forest, but always thought that he was just making things up for a fun story. However, she had no time to dwell on this as she knew it would be a busy day at work. As she left her apartment, the sky was a radiant blue and she breathed it in, letting go of Martin's mistreatment and moving forward with her day.

*   *   *   *   *   *   *   *   *

After a few minutes of waiting, Martin said,

"I don't think she's here. Maybe we should just go."

As soon as the doorbell had been rung he had started to feel all kinds of guilt and shame running throughout his body. In the past, when Evaline had struck up conversations with him in the grocery store, he had never felt anything like this when he had ducked out of the store with some pathetic excuse. Or had he always felt this but was unaware of what had actually been happening? God, why did everything have to be so difficult and confusing? He was starting to want to be fully out of all of this. He had half a mind to get on the next bus to wherever he could, book himself a room in a hotel, and get away from Dr. Spruce, Orchid, and himself. He still had his wallet as he always kept that on him. As this plan started to force itself into his mind, he noticed a little black and blue dragonfly sitting on his shoulder. He heard it whisper,

"When you run, make sure you run to something and not away from."

He brushed it off and it flew away with what he thought was a slight giggle. He was a little taken aback by this as he wasn't sure when was the last time any animal had talked to him other than Dr. Spruce. He was uncertain if he was pleased by this or not as he felt that things were changing a little too fast for him without any control on his end and he absolutely hated that feeling.

"Martin? What's going on?" A familiar voice came from nearby and soon after Connor was beside him, panting slightly and wearing an outfit that could do nothing but suggest that he had been out for a run. Martin found it a little excessive, with the arm, leg, and head bands all in full effect. He shuddered as this judgment came up in him, but something about it felt more familiar than all of these new things that he had been feeling.

Orchid smiled at him. "Do you know Mr. Bushnell?"

"Yes! Well, sort of. Well, yes. Do I know him? Why? Is he in trouble?" Connor said nervously.

"No, nothing of that sort. He has just had his house burn down to the ground and I'm both doing some research as well as helping him find his way back to things."

"What!? Your house got burnt down? No, man. That's not good, that place was awesome. Do you need a place to stay?" Connor's nerves subsided slightly and compassion took over.

"Uh, no, I'm okay." Martin knew that he wasn't really okay but was stubborn about the changes occurring.

"If I were you, I'd take him up on that offer, Mister Martin Bushnell. It's okay to accept help when it's offered, you know?"

The sensitivity and trust that Martin felt with Orchid was subsiding as a result of the introduction to a new person to the group. He really just wasn't ready to be this open with the world and started to close off significantly. However, staying with Connor didn't mean that he had to be his best friend. It would just be until he could sort things out and get a new house built. The thought of a job like that made his chest ache and he shook a little.

"...Connor, I'll think about it, but yeah, probably, I might need a place to stay for a night or two while I figure it out, but..."

"Amazing! You will have your own bedroom and bathroom and if you want to stay for longer we can talk about you paying a bit of rent but it really won't be much, I think it'll just be great to hang out more and get to know each other better and who knows perhaps we could end up building a sweet house out in the forest where we could be roommates." Connor was obviously energized by all of this though Martin could not understand why.

"Write down your number on my notepad and I'll bring him by after we're done here. Your kindness is much appreciated. This guy's had a pretty rough day." Orchid handed him the pen and paper and he wrote down his phone number. Though his stress levels were still running high, Martin quietly recognized that the interaction between these two was all based on helping him out. He really wasn't used to this. He liked to be the one to be able to solve all of his own problems, but at this moment, this just didn't seem plausible. His mind was flip-flopping like a caught tuna on a fisherman's deck and his body was still dully throbbing, so perhaps (and he hated to think this) he had to relinquish control momentarily to his new "friends".

Connor went to give Martin a high five but then remembered that both his hands were still fairly injured, so he lightly touched his elbow instead. Martin gave a little shudder when he was touched, which Connor recognized and smiled at him gently.

"See you later, bud. I'm gonna finish off my run. What a beautiful day!" He made a grand arm gesture towards the sky and Martin noticed, for the first time that day, how nice the sky was looking. The clouds were a mixture of all types, but they weren't making any effort to block out the sun or the light blue sky and were just floating around peacefully. He felt a sudden burst of emotion in his chest that he recognized once more as gratitude. He was starting to become a little more familiar with this sensation and was even starting to enjoy it. He turned to Orchid, and all of a sudden he felt ready to thank her and share his whole story with her.

"Detective Orchid,"

"You don't have to keep calling me that. You can call me Orchid. Or Orca. Or Orc. I've had a few nicknames over the years."

"OK, Orchid, I just wanted to say that…"

"Martin? Orchidacea?"

Evaline's car had pulled up without his noticing and he immediately felt a lurch of terror when he saw her coming out of her car. He wanted to hide behind Orchid and have her explain everything to Evaline, making up the perfect excuse for Martin that would redeem him for his bad actions earlier that morning. It was a bit late to hide behind her, especially since she was moving towards Evaline for a warm hug. They hugged for a length of time that suggested that they were old friends who hadn't seen each other for quite a while, during which Martin tried to distract himself by staring up at a nearby tree, though it wasn't nearly as alluring as the fearful thoughts in his mind. As Evaline pulled away, she looked at Martin with a mix of kindness and disdain.

"Hey Martin." She said weakly. He noticed that her fist clenched a little when she said this. How was he to proceed? Should he just apologize? He didn't have much experience with this but was about to try his luck when Orchid started.

"Evie, I apologize for how long it has been. You'd think in a small town like this it would be a given that we would run into each other, but besides my police work, I've been keeping myself pretty isolated, working on the seventh novel in the 'Arthur Mississauga' series."

"You're finally working on it? I've been anxiously awaiting the final chapter to that series since you ended the sixth one with Arthur losing all of his limbs and eyesight after falling off the world's tallest building. How could he even catch the Hero Killer in a state like that? You've gotta tell me what happens."

"I'll let you read the first draft as soon as I'm done. I think the outcome will surprise you as it's definitely surprising me!"

There was a brief silence and Martin wondered if it were the right opportunity for him to say something but he couldn't muster up enough courage.

"So, Orca, why are you here? It seems like it's not just a friendly visit, especially since you have *him* with you."

"Let's go upstairs and we can discuss it."

They made their way up to Evaline's comfortable apartment and Martin followed a few feet behind. He allowed himself once more to get lost in the confusion as to why he was here, or why any of this was happening. As they settled onto the sofa, Evaline pulled out some more of her "Billion-Dollar Brownie" as well as some cool iced peppermint tea, both of which Martin devoured ravenously. The last time he had ingested anything was the peanut butter sandwich that Connor had offered him that morning, though it now seemed like one hundred mornings ago.

"What do you call these again, Evie?"

"Billion-Dollar Brownie!" Martin answered without even thinking. He had a little buzz from the sugary treats and was feeling his mood improve.

"You're pretty chipper," said Evaline. "I'm surprised, given how early you were up."

Ouch. Her words were a sharp knife ripping up his chest from top to bottom.

"Listen, Evaline," he started. "It was really good of you to take care of me after what had happened. I had a disturbing dream that night that brought up all these feelings from my past and I just had to go. Everything is such a mess right now for me, I feel like I'm changing too fast and I don't know where it's going, especially since my house is now burnt down."

"What?! Your house?" Her anger seemed to subside and that familiar sense of care that she had provided him before started to return, softening her slightly plump, light-brown face.

"Yeah, Evie, that's actually why I'm here, 'officially.'" Orchid used air quotes when she said this. "Although I was really just looking forward to having some more of your treats." She winked at Evaline who gave a little blush. "It seems that the vehicle that Martin was driving may have been the cause of a wildfire today, though none of that has been fully confirmed, and perhaps never will. However, I just wanted to get the details down of yesterday's incident, just so we can close this case. As long as you're not going to press any charges against him, that is."

Martin's heart beat loudly in his chest. Would she? Despite his honest apology, she probably still hated him. Why wouldn't she? He had always been so rude to her and didn't deserve anything other than that.

"Of course I'm not." She looked at him. "Seems like the universe has already punished you enough."

"That's exactly what I said!" Orchid exclaimed with half a brownie in her mouth and her pen on the pad. "Oh, by the way, Evie, I'm planning to fictionalize a lot of this content for the final Arthur Mississauga book and I just wanted to make sure that you're good with me using anything that we talk about."

"I get to be a character in the book?" Her eyes were wide.

"Well, no, I didn't say that, except, hm, perhaps..." She started writing vigorously, using up six or seven pages of her pad before she murmured "the limbless leprechaun?" She looked at Martin with an air of scrutiny, which made him want to retreat inside himself.

"So, Evie, tell me everything that happened yesterday."

Martin sipped his cup of peppermint tea and pondered snatching a third brownie while Evaline recounted the events of the previous day. It was interesting to hear what had happened from the perspective of another as, the way she told it, the weather was to blame for the crash, although everyone present was acutely aware of Martin's reckless driving. Embarrassment and shame struck him when she reached the part where he left without a semblance of thanks. After the story was recounted, Orchid said,

"So, I'm thinking that Martin will end up being a serial killer." She had a serious face on with her pen gripped tightly between her teeth. He looked back at her, shocked, and began to attempt a response, though nothing but a brief stuttering sound came out of his mouth. She seemed to snap out of her trance upon hearing this, and noticing Martin's despair, she exclaimed, "in the book, in the book! I don't think you're a killer *in real life.*"

Martin breathed out the rest of the air that had conglomerated within his chest, befuddled by the rollercoaster that his mind was taking him on. Any mention of anything slightly agitating was throwing him completely helter-skelter. He hated feeling this sensitive as it made him feel weak and embarrassed. However, there was still part of him that was attempting to embrace this sensitivity; that it was helpful and wouldn't last forever. He felt stuck in between two worlds and, as if she could see into him, Evaline asked,

"Are you okay, Martin?"

He wanted to shrug it off, say "I'm fine" and walk out the door but instead he grabbed that third brownie he had been undressing with his eyes and said "no" in a meek voice. The two looked at him as if they were his closest friends. He shied away, not wishing for their pity, but maybe it wasn't pity, maybe they just cared about him although they didn't even know him. Orchid's phone rang and she answered it quickly.

"Hello Constable... Yes, I'm just wrapping up this case... OK, see you soon."

She hung up the phone and looked at the two of them.

"Constable Foldback wants me back at the station pronto." She ripped off Connor's number from the notepad and gave it to Evaline. "A friend of Martin's ran by and offered him a room indefinitely. Do you mind giving him a lift there?"

"No problem." Evaline smiled and Orchid collected her notebooks. Before she left, she gave Evaline another warm hug and then to his surprise, she embraced Martin as well. He responded rather uncomfortably by patting her on the back with one of his arms, while a collection of confusing feelings crowded his held body. His memory harkened back to that time in New York when he considered social skills his most important ally. So much had changed since then, but he still couldn't really get an understanding of *why*. There was something big that he was missing that might help him fill in the gaps. His body gave a little shudder as he thought about having to go back into another session with Dr. Spruce. As Orchid left, she said to him,

"Hey, it'd be cool if you came by the station sometime and helped me flesh out your character in more detail. Make sure to grab us a couple of slices of the Creamy Carrot Cake from Sunflower Café next door. It has been fun to meet you and I truly hope that no more babies rip out your poor heart." A toothy grin emerged and she made her exit, leaving Martin in the apartment that he had desperately escaped from just that morning.

"I didn't get a chance to say this, but it's okay that you left like that this morning. It just brought up some bad feelings as it hurts not to feel respected." Evaline spurted this out as soon as the door had closed. Martin felt comforted by what she said and settled back down into the cosy sofa, allowing his body to loosen up a little.

"It was just... I had this dream that made me feel disturbed. Everything that has happened the last two days has made me feel as if an asteroid slammed into the side of my head and I don't know if I'm going crazy or becoming sane." He took a moment, remarking to himself how honest he had been with both Orchid and Evaline that day. Was this because of the session with Dr. Spruce?

"I wanna hear more about it, I do. I know this is bad timing and you may not be into it, given what you've been through, but my band is actually playing a show in a couple of hours here in town and I've gotta get over there pretty soon. I'm happy to drop you off at Connor's on the way... unless you want to come."

A show? He hadn't been to a show since... he didn't know. Since New York? It couldn't be. Though he was having trouble remembering any details other than those memories of New York recently unearthed, he knew that he had adored music back in the day. Perhaps he had even played in a band himself? He had no idea but had this sudden urge to experience something like that again. He recognized the same feelings of curiosity and wonder in him as when he first went up to New York.

"Yes!" This word shot out of him like a gust of wind and even Evaline was surprised.

"Really?! OK, let me get changed. Maybe your friend Connor would want to come? I'll leave my phone if you want to give him a call."

She hurried off to the bedroom, leaving Martin alone with his rapidly changing sense of self. He sat there for some time, arguing with himself about his decision to go to this show. One part of him was suggesting that concerts were childish and meaningless, while another side of him was retorting that maybe it's okay to be a child again once in a while. After he got sick of this discussion, he shook his head furiously to dislodge the annoying thoughts and then remembered that Evaline's phone was sitting next to him. Although Connor still annoyed him with his enthusiastic kindness and fascination with Martin's lifestyle, the thoughts about being at a concert alone were more overwhelming. Since Evaline would be actually playing in the band, he couldn't rely on her to provide him with any comfort. He felt sickened momentarily by the fact that he actually thought he might need comfort but once again the tenderness that lay stuck to his sternum arose and he gave Connor a call. He got his voicemail although it was not Connor's voice, but rather the voice of a posh elderly gentleman.

"You have reached Master Connor Balsam. He is most likely performing Shakespeare or competing in Wimbledon at the time being. He shall return your call imminently."

The phone beeped but Martin was still a little taken aback by that strange greeting. It took him a few seconds to remember that he had to record a message.

"Oh, sorry, I forgot to... Uh, hi Connor, this is Marlin... uh, Martin Bushnell. From the... the solar panel guy." He winced at the thought of his melted solar panel. "My friend here, uh, Evaline, is in a band so a concert she is performing. I mean, she is playing a show and maybe you want to go. I'm going, I think, so maybe you want to go." As he hung up the phone he chastised himself for such an awkward message. He would have never accepted such a pathetic offer like that and all of a sudden felt paralyzingly nervous, worrying that Connor may reject him and take back his offer to have him stay. Why was he worried about that? He didn't even want to stay there. Though the thought of another delicious peanut butter and banana sandwich crossed his stomach and eased these troubled thoughts. A few minutes later, Evaline's phone rang and he saw that it was Connor's number. He fumbled with the phone for a few seconds then answered.

"Hello? This is Evaline's phone." Why did he say that? He knew that it was Connor calling for him.

"Marty McFly?"

"Uh, no, this is Martin."

"I know dude, I'm just playing around. So, where's this show? What do I wear? When are you picking me up?"

"Oh, um, you want to come?"

"Of course I want to! That's why I asked those questions."

"I don't know the answers but I guess we'll come pick you up in half an hour?"

"Rad. I'll wear my vampire costume."

"What? No, don't do that." But it was too late for this as Connor had already hung up the phone. He wondered if he had been joking around or not. It was hard to tell as he didn't really know Connor that well. He felt embarrassed by the thought of being at a show with someone dressed up in a vampire costume. Then the fear of going out in public started to set in. In the past three years, he had just popped in and out of town to buy whatever he needed that week, making desperate attempts to avoid socialization at all costs. Now he was going to a show? He started to regret this rash decision and was about to call Connor back to call it off when Evaline came out of her room.

"You think this is a good outfit?" She asked, though he couldn't imagine why she would ask *him* for fashion advice. He had worn the same run-down clothes every day for as long as he could remember. Though, he did have a flair for fashion back in the day. He started to remember the fur coat that he was given by Roshi, but he seemed not to have any memories of actually wearing it. He remembered that Evaline was waiting for an answer and turned around to look at her. She looked ***Cool***.

"You look Cool with a capital C." He said innocently, then looked away. What a terrible thing to say! But then again, her outfit *was* pretty amazing. She wore a floral headband that had a large white and grey feather sticking out one side of it. At the other end of her body, she sported serious cowboy boots that looked like they had actual spurs on them. In between, she had put on a well-fitting floral dress with a ropey belt that seemed to wrap down her right leg like a man made snake. In the past, whenever they ran into each other, she had typically been wearing her doctor's outfit and Martin had been in too much of a rush to dart out of the store to even give her a second glance. Something inside him seemed to find her very pretty though he was terribly afraid of that feeling. It was unfamiliar but reminded him of Rose, which caused him to shut down slightly, turning fully back around and putting his hands in his lap.

Evaline seemed to be content with his response and grabbed the rest of her things before running into the kitchen.

"I almost forgot! There's no point in us going hungry on a night like this and I have the perfect road food for us. I call it a Sesame Street Stir-Fry and it's just as good cold as it is heated up."

She grabbed a large tupperware container along with two pairs of chopsticks and shoved them into her bag.

"Vamonos, señor."

Her lively mood perked him up a bit. Maybe this night wouldn't be so bad. Besides, it was just a concert. There was no pressure for him to do anything, even talk, since the music would be too loud for proper conversation. He thought about finding a corner to hide away in the venue and this pleased him. He got up, looked down at his dirty outfit self-consciously, and followed Evaline out of the door, who seemed to be bouncing down the stairs.

"I just feel so full of life before I play a show," she remarked as they exited the door of the apartment building. The sun was making its way down for the night and a squirrel darted up a nearby tree to watch it fall but not before giving Martin a good stare-down. It seemed to him as if the squirrel winked at him though he couldn't be sure. Evaline noticed Martin pause momentarily to stare at the squirrel and then seemed to go deep into her own thoughts. She remained quiet until they had started the car and were on their way to Connor's house. Suddenly, she quietly mumbled, but just loud enough for Martin to hear her.

"Long ago when animals could talk, a bear was walking along."

He looked at her. "What was that?"

"My father used to tell me these stories at night. He said that they were true stories passed down from his ancestors and, as a child, I believed every word he was saying. However, as I got older and the stories softly faded away, I put them in a box in my mind labeled 'fantasy'. Something that you mumbled the other night when you fell asleep made me start to remember the stories again. The majority of them are about talking animals that ultimately end in some sort of lesson or wise words."

He remained silent. What had he said in his sleep? Had he talked about Dr. Spruce? Were they actually going to a show or was she taking him to a mental hospital?

"I need to look more into this and go back into some of my father's old stories. I actually think I have some that he had written down as he was afraid that I would forget them. It might help you understand a bit more about yourself."

"I'm not sure what you heard but it's..." He paused, feeling fragile and apprehensive.

"You were going on about a bear who talked to you as if it were a therapist. I believe you said his name was Dr. Spruce."

"Oh god, here it comes." Martin thought. "Here's the part where she tells me I'm a lunatic."

"It just sounded so much like one of my dad's old stories and I am curious to know where you heard it. Where are you originally from, Martin?"

He felt a blast of relief ripple through his crippled body, which got quickly replaced with confused feelings of inadequacy.

"Um... I actually don't remember."

"What do you mean you don't remember?" She shot a concerned look at his darkening face.

Her GPS announced their arrival before he could respond, distracting her concern and bringing them back to the task at hand. Due to this challenging conversation, he had forgotten they were going to Connor's house.

"You go grab your friend. I've gotta give my bandmate a quick call to see if she needs me to pick up anything for the show."

He opened the car door, then turned around to face her.

"Hey, let's not talk about this stuff with anyone else around, okay? Lots of troubling thoughts and questions are floating around me and I struggle to open up about this."

"Of course," she said with a soft smile.

"Thank you... for everything."

He exited the car with warm cheeks of gratitude and headed to Connor's door. There was a note on the door,

"Come in, I'm just gettin' ready."

The door was unlocked so he stepped in.

"Connor?"

There was no answer but suddenly he felt something fuzzy rub against his legs and he jumped backwards. It was Redbird the cat, who seemed to be his biggest fan. He sat himself down on the floor to give the cat a stroke as he felt he needed the comfort. The white cat also sat down and faced him with her great, round eyes.

"Hey Redbird," he said quietly, doubting that he would get a response though slightly hoping for one.

"Hi Martin," she said with a regal purr attached to the words. He jerked back a little.

"You can understand me?" he whispered, hoping that Connor wouldn't enter the room.

"Of course I can. Now, come on, this fur ain't gonna pet itself."

He smiled with amazement as the cat comfortably set herself in his lap. He allowed himself to relax into the purring and petting, wondering why he hadn't ever had a pet before. Well, maybe he had, he thought, as a large chunk of his past was missing. Perhaps he had had tons of pets.

"How come I don't know myself at all?" He said both to himself and the happy white cat.

"That's a lifelong journey, dear Martin," she replied.

"You better run or I'm going to drain your blood," a heavily accented voice whispered into his right ear suddenly. He jumped up, startling the cat to hide underneath the couch, and turned to face his assailant. It was Connor, wearing a full-on vampire costume.

"Connor!" He shouted, still shell-shocked from the scare. "You can't wear that to the show, it would be..." He stopped there, afraid to say "it would be embarrassing for me". Luckily, Connor just laughed.

"I know! I just wanted to freak you out." He tossed off the costume and removed the fake teeth, revealing a more regular outfit that lay underneath. He peered under the couch at the frightened cat. "Sorry 'bird, didn't mean to scare ya." She eased her way out and gave him a slight glare, which melted into googly eyes when he scratched her head.

"Let's go, Jon Snow."

"Um, I'm Martin, I don't know who Jon Snow is."

"I was just making a sweet rhyme. Relax a bit, friend."

They left the house and got into the car. Evaline introduced herself to Connor, though they quickly realized that they had met before at some past event or something, which made for easy conversation that Martin was relieved from. He was grateful for this. Evaline passed him the Sesame Street Stir-Fry and a pair of chopsticks. She had made good work of the food already but there was a healthy amount leftover. He eyed it greedily but then had a nagging thought of offering some to Connor. He wanted it all for himself but the offering of the peanut butter banana sandwich that morning made him feel like he had to. He reluctantly offered Connor his food but fortunately he denied it, saying that he had filled himself up before they had arrived. Martin ate up the delicious meal with appreciation, though mostly grateful for the fact that no one was watching him eat as he could not remember how to use chopsticks. He ended up just poking the vegetables as if with a fork, though the rice and chickpeas proved more difficult. After some tinkering with the sticks, he seemed to have found a way that satisfied him and helped him finish the meal.

He chimed into the conversation just slightly, feeling more grounded due to the nourishing food. However, as they made their way to the back of the venue to park the car, he felt a deep pit of anxiety open up into his stomach, bringing up thoughts of New York and all of the fake "people" that he had met. Then he realized that he might have become one of these people himself. After all, it seemed as if he had been hiding a significant amount that even he didn't know about. Is this who he was? Just a man wearing a mask? If so, he was terrified to find out what lay beneath.

Chapter 12 - The Show

As they parked at the venue, Evaline rushed through the back door, saying a brief goodbye to the two boys and promising to introduce them to the rest of her band after the show. She told them she had put Martin's name on the guest list with a plus one for Connor. Martin felt a little distraught to be left alone with Connor. Though he didn't really feel comfortable with anyone at the moment, he would rather have been with Orchid, or even Evaline, than Connor. There wasn't anything particular that he disliked about Connor, it just felt as if he had to hate him for some reason. He took a large breath in as they made their way to the front of the venue, braving himself for whatever was to come next. There was a lineup full of colourfully dressed individuals, which caused Martin to feel ashamed once again about his ragged, dirty outfit. He and Connor got in the line behind a couple who were talking rather loudly.

"I'm just so excited for the show! I just *need* to dance. It's one hundred percent *necessary.*" The girl in front of Connor said.

"Babe, you're wasted. Don't talk so loudly." The guy next to her replied, just as loudly.

"Yeah, but you're wasted too." She responded accusingly.

"True, but that doesn't mean you're not."

"You're totally right." She laughed. Martin wished he could close his ears and get away from this pathetic excuse for a conversation. The hatred towards them spread through him like snake poison and he was about to tell them to shut their mouths when Connor spoke.

"So, we didn't really get a chance to talk earlier as I was focused on toning up my hams."

"Your hams?" The way Connor spoke constantly brought Martin into a state of confusion.

"My hammies, los hamstrings," he tapped the back of his thighs. "I'll translate what I said a little better. I was running and I missed the opportunity to connect with you."

"I didn't need a connection." Martin was starting to feel rather agitated just by being in the lineup. Sure, most of the day he had been feeling a little off, but this was different. It felt darker and he felt angrier.

"Well, okay," Connor was used to being shrugged off like this. He sometimes felt as if he had been born too enthusiastic for the world he lived in, but had developed the skill of pushing through any sort of judgment. "I just want to check in on you, Marty. Make sure you're okay after you know... everything."

"Um... Yeah, no, I'm fine."

"There was too much hesitation in that statement for me to believe any of that."

Martin looked at him, allowing his tortured feelings to express themselves in his face. He noticed this then quickly tried to make himself look more stoic. He could see that Connor had noticed something, and was about to speak when they heard,

"MAKE SURE YOU HAVE YOUR IDS OUT. IF THEY ARE NOT OUT YOU ARE NOT COMING IN. IF I FIND YOU HAVE A FAKE ID, I WILL SHAVE YOUR HEAD AND THROW YOU IN A DUMPSTER FULL OF DEAD RATS."

Martin went up on his tiptoes to find the source of this ludicrous statement and his eyes landed upon the security guard. He seemed to be one of those people who take their job a little too seriously. He was shorter than average, with bulging muscles and a terse black moustache. His neon yellow shirt read SECURITY on the front, the badge on the left of his chest said "RICHMOND LAKE SECURITY ASSOCIATION" and a patch on his right said "DON'T TOUCH ME".

"Well, at least there's someone else who is just as messed up as I am," Martin thought rather nastily.

The queue began to move more quickly towards the front door, which meant that Connor forgot about asking him about his feelings, for which he was grateful. He was sick of people asking him about his feelings as he just wanted somewhere to hide; where he could finally figure this all out and get back to normal. But what did that even mean? Once they got up to the front of the venue, Connor gave a sneaky smile to Martin who saw that Connor had not taken out his ID. Before the security guard could say anything, Connor looked him in his dark, hairy eyes, and said,

"Can I see your ID, sir?"

The security guard looked at him, baffled and repulsed. Martin felt the same. Why was Connor doing this? The security officer seemed incredibly perplexed as to how to respond. Connor continued,

"I ain't letting you in the show if you don't show me your ID."

"You're the one who needs to be showing the ID," the security said both awkwardly and sternly.

"Sir, I appreciate your words, but let me ask you, who is the one wearing the RICHMOND LAKE SECURITY ASSOCIATION badge here?"

"I am!" However, when the security guard looked down he noticed that the badge was no longer on his chest, and now sat pinned to Connor's right chest pocket.

"How the hell did he do that?" Martin thought. He was slightly impressed but also fearful as to what was going to come next. It happened quickly. The security guard grabbed his shirt and pulled him right up to his face.

"YOU DO NOT WANT TO MESS WITH ME, BOY." Spittle flew from his mouth and showered both Connor and Martin. For a moment, Martin made himself laugh when he imagined himself pulling out a tiny umbrella and putting it in front of the guard's mouth. For some reason, this interaction was actually making him feel better, until he saw that the security guard had noticed him laughing. He let go of Connor and walked right up to Martin until their noses were lightly touching.

"WHY. ARE. YOU. LAUGHING?" Panic swept through Martin's body. He was no longer laughing. Nowhere close. The man's breath smelt like extremely old pizza and loose hairs on his mangy moustache pricked Martin's face. Martin lifted up his left hand to show its contents to the corner of the officer's right eye.

"Here's my ID, sir. We're on the guest list," he muttered meekly. The man was breathing heavily and Martin could feel every warm breath dirty his face a little more each time. He closed his eyes, mortified by what was to come next, but fortunately the man backed away. When he opened his eyes, he saw that the badge had returned to his chest and Connor was showing the man his ID with a euphoric smile. The guard had pulled out his notebook and saw that, indeed, Martin's name was on the list. He stared at them with heavy disdain.

"If you weren't on this list, I would have thrown you down that manhole." The security guard had calmed down slightly but was breathing heavily. "If you do **anything** in this venue other than watching the show, I'm going to eat you alive." He licked his moustache threateningly and let the two boys pass through.

"How... why did you... what did you do that for?!" Martin noticed he was holding both outrage and respect for Connor.

"Security Samson and I go way back. He is always yelling and threatening others, even when he's not on duty so I make an effort to twist his buttons whenever I can." Connor's face was proud and unshaken.

"But, how did you get that badge without him noticing? I didn't even see you do it."

Connor looked at Martin seriously.

"Now that's something I cannot tell you."

They walked into the concert venue, which was quite a large space, unexpected for a small town like Richmond Lake. The lights and sound equipment seemed up-to-date and the place was already filling up with people, causing Martin to feel rather claustrophobic. He noticed that the couple who had been in front of him in the lineup had already managed to buy cups of beer and were squeezing their way to the spot right in front of the stage, spilling three-quarters of their drinks on the people they pushed past. He started to think about how much he despised being at shows and had a sudden flash of memories pop up of multiple drinks being spilt on him at countless shows. He looked around for a dark space to which he could escape, but it seemed that they had found a way to have every nook and cranny be perfectly visible.

"You want a drink or anything?" Connor asked him kindly.

"No, I don't do that."

"Cool, I've stopped recently too. We're gonna be good roommates." Connor added a little nod and wink combo, which Martin didn't really like as, for a moment, he had forgotten that he had to go and stay at Connor's house. For how long would he be there? What was he going to do with himself? At least there was the cat Redbird who seemed to make him feel a little more comfortable with her purry presence.

They found a spot that was close enough to the stage to be able to see, but far enough not to be fully immersed in the crowd for which Martin was grateful. The pre-show music blaring out of the speakers was a bit too loud for Martin's liking but, as he had predicted, it forced Connor to converse only through yelling, which he seemed unmotivated to do. Martin took this moment of time to think about his plans for the future. He had to find a way to rebuild his house. But with what money? For the past three years, he had been spending very little, growing a lot of his own food and only buying things when he really needed it. Though he hated all types of banks and credit unions, he had kept a bank account as he knew it would be difficult to keep bundles of cash in his house. At present, he was very grateful for this as all of the money would have burnt to a crisp in the fire. However, he knew that he didn't have enough in his account for a whole new house as he hadn't worked since he moved to Richmond Lake, focusing solely on maintaining his property. But how had he made the money for that in the first place? Disconcertingly, he couldn't remember at all. This gap in his memory was really starting to bother him. Why had he blocked everything out? Was it really that traumatic?

Okay, so he wouldn't rebuild his house. But then where would he go? Perhaps he could sell the land, but would anyone want to buy burnt land surrounded by a torched forest? He began feeling more trapped as he thought about all of these options and their downfalls and could not think of a viable solution or plan. A fire started to ignite in his stomach, warming up the rest of his body, and flooding his veins with chemicals of fear. He was about to experience a fully-fledged panic attack when the lights went down and the music from the speakers turned off.

* * * * * * * * *

Suddenly, there was nothing but darkness, pain, and a lack of understanding who or where he was. Nothing was making sense, though he knew for certain that he had a searing pain emanating from the bridge of his nose. Why was it so dark? Were his eyes closed? Yes, they were. He tried opening them but the pain exploded and poured through the rest of his body. What the hell had happened? His legs shuddered as he felt something crawling on them. Was he dead? Or being killed?

"Nuffin' in the world is so bad as physical pain. In the face of pain there are no heroes," a strange, rough voice whispered from the location of the thing crawling on him. He had heard those words, in that combination, somewhere else, but could not bring himself to remember where it had come from. The nasty, talking creature was moving closer towards his face. This was it. Whatever it had done, it was about to finish the job. He started to wonder if his whole life would flash before his eyes, as is often said, but if he couldn't even remember his name, that experience would almost certainly not arise. Was he able to speak? He attempted to say something and managed a feeble whisper.

"Just finish it. I can't have more pain."

The crawling voice was closer to his face now.

"Yes, yes, be patient, mate." The voice had a slight thuggish accent, though it seemed to have more kindness than he would have expected from a murderer. This didn't really make him feel any better as the pain was overwhelming. Then, he felt something cold touch the bridge of his nose and knew that it was over. "Well, good riddance," he thought. "What's the use of a human who can't even remember who he is?"

As he braced for the unknown sensation of death, he began to feel a soothing cool feeling that began at the centre of the pain and expanded outwards. Ah yes, the cool sweetness of death. It made sense. His body loosened up significantly and he lost consciousness.

A few hours later, he awoke, but didn't feel dead. The pain was nothing but a cool throb and he was still laying in the same position as he had been before he had slipped into deep sleep.

"Martin." He said to himself. Yes, that was right, his name was Martin.

"Your name?" The kind voice was still around, though it seemed a little sleepier than it had been earlier.

Martin made a hesitating attempt to open his eyes once more. He managed to have them half-open without feeling significant pain, which gave him the confidence to lift them all the way. It felt as if there were 10lb dumbbells attached to each of his eyelashes. Once he managed the incredible feat he noticed that there was a radiant, colour-filled sky above him, nestled between two buildings. Was he in an alleyway? His body told him that he wasn't ready to explore his immediate surroundings so he kept his gaze focused on the sky. It was truly a splendid sky and he felt as if he had never seen anything like it. The night was ending and the sun was clocking in for the day shift. The light from the sun created a gradient of colour, beginning with black then moving to purple, blue then a dazzling combination of orange and pink. He wished that it could always be like this and that he could just lay back looking at this multicoloured ceiling for the rest of his life. No pain, no fear, nothing.

"It's spectacular, isn't it?" The voice seemed to be listening to his thoughts, which was even more apparent when he continued, "nuffin' lasts forever though."

"Who are you?" asked Martin with a semblance of curiosity, though pretending that he didn't really care.

"Yous can call me Buffalo," the voice replied with a proud emphasis on the name. It seemed as if this was not his real name, but that he wished it would be. "And you're Martin."

"Yes, I suppose so."

As Martin said this, he began to have some faint memories. Hadn't he been at a concert? With some... with Connor? He remembered Connor, and with this memory the rest of the previous day flooded back to him. Dr. Spruce, Orchid, Evaline, all of it. He could vaguely remember waiting for the show to start but could remember nothing after that. He also remembered how this seemed to be happening to him way too frequently recently. It was like he was stuck in some ridiculous cycle of forgetting, remembering, forgetting, remembering, endlessly on repeat.

"What brought me here?" He asked himself quietly.

"Ah, you have arrived at the next question." A familiar voice bounced between the two buildings and entered Martin's ears, filling him with a collective feeling of dread and awe.

"Dr. Spruce?"

"Get up, Martin. We have work to do."

Martin cringed as he attempted to move his body, expecting the rest of him to feel the way that his nose had earlier. Surprisingly, his body felt quite limber, and he was able to push himself up by his elbows to observe his surroundings. He was in a strange, dark alleyway, as he had guessed. The street on the end closest to him was beginning to wake up with a few people scuttling by like beetles without a glance at the alleyway, evidently making a beeline for their morning coffee. One car flew by like a dragonfly, hoping to beat the beetle-walkers to the coffee shop. This seemed like a fairly normal thing to Martin but the other end of the alleyway didn't make any sense. About halfway down, vines and other clinging plants hung on the sides of the buildings, starting out sparse but eventually completely taking over the buildings by the end of the alley, with no street at the other end, instead a full-on lively forest. He couldn't remember the town ever being this close to the forest. This is where Dr. Spruce stood, husky and soft, appearing to be conversing with some small creature. Martin realized that he had been laid down on a dirty mattress that had been tossed into the alleyway, which looked and felt quite similar to the one that had been left in his house. There were strange silver hairs littered all over it but he had no time to investigate this as Dr. Spruce looked at him and beckoned him over with a move of his head.

Martin rose shakily, not due to any bodily discomfort, but more from the fear of what was to come. As he walked towards the forested end of the alley, he saw that Dr. Spruce had been talking to a little raccoon with a tiny bowler hat. The raccoon bowed to him as he came close while Martin just stared, slightly incredulous.

"You're not going to thank your rescuer?" Dr. Spruce asked him with a smile.

"Oh, uh, thank you. But what happened?" Martin looked first at Dr. Spruce and then at the raccoon named Buffalo.

"I can't tell you much. I was out here sniffin' around for some grub when I found ya and your busted face laying down at the alley entrance over yonder. Without much difficulty due to these bulgin' biceps o' mine, I pulled yous onto that mattress and let yous rest. I scampered into the forest and got my buddy Celeste to fly over to Doc Spruce to whisper him the situation. I knew yous was something special as not many of yous humans find this alleyway. As I was waiting, I made yous a poultice from willow bark to help soothe summa that pain."

"But how did I get here in the first place?" Martin was beginning to get upset again, mostly with himself this time, for his stupid, blank-filled memory.

"If you follow me, that question shall be answered soon enough."

Martin looked back, with a slight hope of escaping, but to his dismay, he could no longer see the alleyway or the street beyond as the vines had now blocked the way completely, leaving him no choice but to follow Dr. Spruce into the trees. Though a fair amount of curiosity existed inside him, he knew how shaken up he had been by the last session and was afraid that he would be broken apart further. Everything had just been so messed up recently! Was there any way to get things back to normal? Alas, he couldn't see any reasonable option so he just resigned himself to wherever they were going. Buffalo whispered into Dr. Spruce's ear, who gave him a slow nod, and with a cheeky smile that he flashed to Martin, he jumped onto Dr. Spruce's back.

They walked for hours. Martin dragged behind slowly, not close enough to hear the animated conversation that Buffalo was having with Dr. Spruce, though from the way they interacted it was obvious that they were old friends. A few birds and a white-tailed deer passed by them on their way, though they all seemed to be a little afraid of Martin and did not come too close. If he was being honest with himself, he would admit that he was also quite scared of these animals. The realization that he used to be able to converse with all of these creatures, and the sudden revival of this ability, was still a bit frightening to him. In fact, it made him feel more like an outcast than ever before.

With this thought, he stopped short, not noticing the mighty trees that grew around him, or the soft moss that lay below his feet. He could only see a piece of the thought that he had just had.

"Who am I?" He softly said to himself. "I'm an outcast; a lonely, frightened outcast."

"And that's okay." He felt a soft touch on his arm and gave a start. Dr. Spruce had noticed him pausing and had come back by his side without Martin noticing. Despite the bear's size, he seemed to be rather skillful in the art of making little noise.

"But what brought me here?" He asked again, pleading to the bear for an answer. "How did I end up like this? Why can't I remember my past?"

"We're almost there. Trust me, please." The bear's small eyes met his and he felt that same feeling of trust that had been developing with those who had helped him after his house burnt down. Buffalo, who was still on the bear's back, held out his hand for Martin to hold. He allowed himself this comfort, and the three of them walked on.

Chapter 13 - The Fairy Ring

Despite the fact that they had been walking for the majority of the morning, the sun had still not risen fully, leaving the forest shrouded in an eternal misty dusk. As they walked on, Martin's eyes captured a low fluorescent light emanating from behind a patch of trees a few feet up the path.

"Couldn't have arrived at a better time," stated Buffalo. "You see them lights up there? Those are them fairies."

Martin stepped backwards slightly. "You're kidding me. First I get sent into my mind by a talking bear, then a raccoon applies a poultice to my wounds, and now I'm going to meet fairies? This is *inappropriate*."

"I'm not sure what you mean by inappropriate," remarked Dr. Spruce with a quizzical look.

"Oh, um, it's just... this is just getting too much like some of those hokey fantasy novels that spend their lives on thrift store bookshelves."

"Ah, I see. Well, those lights aren't the winged magic-dust fairies that you are imagining. They're much more... grounded," he said with a smile.

To Martin, this sounded like some sort of Gollumesque riddle and he felt a sudden animus as he hated that he did not know what was going on. There had been too much of that lately. He mustered up his courage and barrelled forth towards the lights ahead, budging past Buffalo and Dr. Spruce. When he came to the glowing clearing in the trees, he saw a number of small mushrooms that had formed a ring around the edges of the clearing, exuding a beautiful golden light. He was simultaneously pleased and disappointed. Despite his scornful comment about the inappropriateness of real fairies, he had been silently hoping that the fantasies were true. However, he was also afraid of what else might exist if fairies happened to be real. The two contrasting emotions cancelled each other out and he ended up just disassociating from everything for a minute.

"We call 'em fairies." Buffalo said from his right, shocking Martin out of his stupor. He had gotten off Dr. Spruce's back and was standing close to Martin's leg. The feeling of his silky pelt on Martin's leg was nice and there was a quiet peace that rippled out from the ring of mushrooms and radiated through the three of them. They stood there silently for a few lifetimes. For an inexplicable reason, the sun had now decided to make its way into the sky, moving quicker than usual, perhaps realizing that it was late for its day shift. As the rays of light pierced through the dawn, the glow of the mushrooms began to soften and disappear. As the luminosity faded, Buffalo turned to Martin and looked upwards.

"I'll be seeing you, Marty."

"You're leaving?" Martin had gotten slightly attached to his furry helper and felt a little tremor in his heart.

"Wife's gonna be wondering where I been. I ain't even returning with no food. If I says 'I been busy taking care of a human' she's not gonna be a happy critter."

"I'm sure the mushrooms won't mind if you gather a few. They are the fruits of the forest floor, after all." Dr. Spruce pushed him gently with his large nose towards the fairies and Buffalo gathered a few up. He gave a beatific grin to the two of them and scampered off into the trees.

"Here we are again, Martin. Seems like you've been through a lot since our last session."

A fountain of fear sprang up from within.

"I'm not... I'm not sure I'm ready to go back into that memory again."

"Ah, don't worry. We're going to do it slightly differently this time. I'm not saying it will be easy, but it will be a unique experience and without a doubt you are strong enough for it. Come."

Dr. Spruce walked between the mushrooms into the centre of the circle that they had created. Despite the vegetation growing all around them, the centre of the circle seemed to be perfectly clear of any plant life, leaving a soft soil spot for them to sit upon. Once they were seated, with a small patch of soil in between the two of them, Dr. Spruce began to use his paw and draw on the ground.

"So, Martin, you want to know what brought you here. That's a good question, albeit rather broad. Are you able to go into any more details about what exactly you want to know?"

Martin hesitated as he wasn't actually sure. He searched his mind and subsequently tried to speak but felt insecure about his answer and stopped himself.

"It's okay, say what comes to mind."

"Well, um, why am I always forgetting everything? It seems that not only I have forgotten most of my distant past, but also things that happened yesterday. I'm in this constant, annoying loop of forgetting and I hate it. Also..." He stopped and stayed silent for another moment.

"Yes?"

"Also, why am I even here? Like, this physical place. Why did I move into that house by myself, off-the-grid or whatever, with all of these stupid tasks that I actually hate and without any friends and all this anger and…" This sudden outburst of emotions had come and gone as flickering thoughts in the past few days, but he hadn't actually been willing to put them into words. It felt both terrifying and relieving to be able to say these things.

"Good. Well said. Come over here, look at what I have drawn up."

Martin curiously moved himself over to Dr. Spruce's side and looked down at some sort of map. Actually, it seemed like it was the shape of three separate land masses. The first one was obvious, it was Canada, their present location, but he couldn't place the other two. He realized he couldn't even remember (*"yet again"*) the last time he had looked at a map of the world but the two shapes seemed vaguely familiar.

"Do you like traveling, Martin?"

"Uh, I don't know. I don't really do it."

"Well, today, you are fortunate to have won a trip to three beautiful destinations. The three locations are drawn below and, as the lucky winner, you get to choose where you go first!" Dr. Spruce had adopted the rich, bombastic voice of a game show host. Martin chuckled lightly as it seemed quite uncharacteristic of the bear, but was awfully charming. He quickly jumped up onto his hind legs and Martin looked up at him, slightly amazed.

"In order to get the best benefit of this serious work, we have to make it fun, don't you think?" He winked at Martin and shouted, "drumroll please!"

Dr. Spruce began making the sound of a drumroll on his mighty bared chest and suddenly it sounded as if the rest of the forest had joined him. There was a mighty drumming sound all around him that left Martin incredulous, though he quickly realized that by the end of this drumroll he was to make a choice of where he was going to go. He wondered if all of them related to memories from his past or if he was actually going to be traveling to the present-day versions of these places. He decided not to pick Canada as he was already there, so that might be boring. Though he couldn't place the other two, one of them seemed to be beckoning to him. He waited for the raucous drumroll to end and placed his finger on the drawing in the middle. Dr. Spruce peered down at the choice,

"Ah, I thought this might be the first decision. Enjoy the Lone Star state, cowboy."

*   *   *   *   *   *   *   *   *

Martin was laid flat out on the cool grass. The weather in Austin was profoundly beautiful and the fact that he was buzzing off weed brownies that he had been given backstage only added to the serenity. Foggy, Roshi, and he had arrived in Texas that morning, as Lodgepole Pine was playing back-to-back weekends at the Austin City Limits Festival. The festival gigs were squashed between the numerous college shows that the band was playing with Ponton Low. The first week of that tour had blown Martin's mind. For about a year, he had touted himself as one of Ponton Low's biggest fans and spent every day in blissful disbelief that he had the opportunity to be on tour with him. The night before, he had even managed to have a conversation with him one night by the tour buses. Ponton had been smoking a cigarette by the bus with a few of his tourmates and Martin had shyly made his way into the group. As he joined them, he muttered nervously,

"It's cold and I'm warmer in a group."

He was trying to make some excuse for joining their little circle, but knew this made no sense as soon as he said the words. He hated himself for a moment but luckily no-one acknowledged it and they continued on with their conversation. Martin remained silent, mostly keeping his eyes on Ponton, even when he was not the one talking, but quickly looked away when Ponton's eyes met his own. As Martin stared quietly towards the ground, Ponton offered him a cigarette. He conspicuously pinched himself to make sure he wasn't dreaming. He had never smoked a cigarette before and had promised himself that he never would, but this was a once-in-a-lifetime opportunity. He took the cigarette and a lighter, thanking Ponton in a strange rasp of a voice, and began to smoke his first cigarette. The disgusting feeling of foreign smoke in his lungs was quickly replaced with a strange head-high that made him feel a little more confident. As he sucked more on the cigarette, he began to feel more comfortable in the group, even making a weird joke that made Ponton laugh. They had disbanded soon after, but the day after, Martin was still high off of that experience - and the weed brownies.

The field around him was starting to liven up. It was the morning of the first day of the festival and the eager early morning festival goers were just starting to arrive. He looked at them smugly. Just so that they could be in the front row for their favourite bands, they had to arrive early and camp out all day in the hot sun with barely enough water and food. Martin, on the other hand, had an all-access pass, which meant that he could show up a minute before any show that he wanted and stand on the side of the stage, which made him feel proud and accomplished. He had worked hard to get there and believed he deserved everything that was happening to him. As he was grinning to himself, a little bird landed down beside him, looking as if it were going to say something. He took a little pebble and threw it at the bird, laughing to himself as it flew off in a fright. He was sick of all these animals trying to talk to him. It made him feel different from those around him and his utmost goal was to fit in with this new crowd. He had been rubbing shoulders with all types of people from the entertainment industry and felt as if they were beginning to accept him.

His phone buzzed in his pocket. His heart dropped for a moment and he thought, "Rose?" He scrambled for his phone and saw that it was Isaac calling. Of course it wasn't Rose, he hadn't spoken to her since he left South Carolina. Why would he even be thinking about her? Since he had left, he had managed to force down all his memories of Rose in an attempt to move forward and fully assimilate into his "New Life" in New York. This had been fairly easy for him, especially since he had taken to an addiction of smoking weed every night after he finished his day's work. He answered the phone.

"Isaac. Buddy. What's up?"

"Hey Martin, how's the tour going?"

"It's incredible, my man. Everyone is loving me and I'm pretty sure that Ponton and I are soon to become best friends. I'm guessing they're gonna ask me to join their team anytime soon... of course I'll say no." He let this fantasy play out in his mind, momentarily forgetting that Isaac was on the other end of the phone.

"Cool, dude. I'm glad you're having fun."

"Yeah."

There was a significant amount of silence.

"Uh, so, Martin. I've got something to talk to you about."

"Okay, sweet, but listen, I've only got a few minutes as I've gotta get backstage."

"Well, you know, we haven't really spent a lot of time together since you got back from South Carolina. I guess you've been pretty busy with your job and parties and whatever."

"You're saying it's my fault?" Martin reacted defensively and sat up on the grass.

"Hey, Martin, I'm not accusing you of anything, I'm just saying that it seems like we've moved away from each other a bit. Along with this, I kinda feel like I've done everything I needed to do up here in the city. I got the job, the cool internship, went to some VIP parties. You know, the New York dream."

"There's always more to do in the big city," Martin retorted, uncertain of whether or not he believed what he was saying.

"Sure, sure, maybe for you, but we're different people, you know? I just think I'm ready to go back to South Carolina and start anew back there."

"Back to South Carolina? Why would you do that? Even if you become the Mayor of Columbia, you'll be nothing but a big fish in a little pond."

"Maybe that's all I need."

"You don't make any sense." Martin was angry and the fact that he was still high was not helping as it always seemed to amplify his emotions.

"I'm sorry you think that. It's my choice, man, and it's what I'm going to do. I'm going to be leaving next week."

Martin couldn't understand the plethora of emotions that were swirling around his mind. He was feeling jealousy, anger, sadness and made a strong effort to push these away, going for indifference instead.

"Okay, whatever. I hope you have fun."

There was another silence. Martin could tell that he had hurt Isaac but he couldn't express any emotion, especially if anyone was around who might see him. His reputation was most important and the only thing that was going to get him anywhere.

"Martin. Are you high?" This question seemed to hit Martin in that tender place in his sternum.

"So what if I am, mom?" He snarled.

"Just be careful with that stuff, man. I know it's been pretty hard for you since you and Rose broke up but you can't just…"

Martin interrupted him. "I'm fine! It hasn't been hard. I love my life. All of this is my dream. I'm sorry you don't understand that, but like you said, we're different people."

"Okay, man. Well, listen, I'm gonna go. If you ever want to talk, like *actually* talk, I'm always here."

"Yeah. Enjoy."

"Bye, Martin. Be careful out there."

Martin hung up the phone furiously. Isaac was leaving New York? How pathetic. He didn't even give it a shot. And he was telling him to "be careful"? Who did he think he was? He flung himself up and walked to the backstage entrance nearby, making an effort to ignore any glances he was getting. People tended to look at him when he went backstage. Perhaps they wanted him to bring them with him. He secretly liked this attention but pretended not to notice, trying to look as cool as possible. He wondered if they thought he was one of the musicians performing that day. Imagine that. He started to dream about performing on the mainstage as the sun went down but a deep insecurity welled up in him and told him that this would never be possible and he should instead just focus on doing his management work with Foggy. That was the only way he was going to get anywhere.

*　　*　　*　　*　　*　　*　　*　　*　　*

The next evening, Foggy had been schmoozing a reporter from Rolling Rock, who ended up asking to interview Roshi then and there. However, he was not around so Foggy desperately pleaded to Martin to find him and bring him back within thirty minutes. He had texted Roshi,

"Where are you?"

To which he received the response.

"Big Oak Tree."

He had no idea what this meant but he ran around asking everyone he could to point him into the direction of the 'Big Oak Tree'. Eventually, he ran into a man from another dimension, who took him to the tree. The man seemed to be floating, though perhaps it was something to do with the mushrooms that one of the musicians backstage had given Martin a couple of hours before. As they moved towards the centre of the park in which the festival was being held, Martin saw the majestic tree and, following that, saw Roshi was hanging from one of the branches. A couple of girls were below him taking pictures and giggling. It seemed to Martin that Roshi was unsuccessfully making an attempt to hide from these girls. He hated Lodgepole Pine fans as they were always trying to get in with the band, attempting to make some stupid conversation with Roshi, Foggy, and sometimes even him.

"Get away from him!" He yelled at the girls, imagining that he was Roshi's security guard, puffing his chest up and growing twelve feet in height. As he barrelled towards them, the soft blue and amber lights of the surrounding stages flashed upon their faces and he realized how pretty they were. They had soft, kind faces, and he began to fantasize about spending the evening with them enjoying the festival in the way that he used to, in the crowd, jumping up and down without having any type of responsibility. But no, this isn't how it was now. This was his job. This was his life. He said straight to their faces,

"He doesn't want you here. I don't want you here. Go away."

The way he said this caused a flash of pain to appear on one of the girls' faces, momentarily transforming her into a wounded seal. He felt a pang of guilt but pushed it down into his trash can of repression, which was getting quite full at this point. The girls stomped away and he looked up at Roshi.

"Come on, Rosh, you've got an interview with Rolling Rock in twenty minutes."

Roshi jumped off the branch and landed on his feet like a graceful panther, reminding Martin of the respect that he had for the man. Martin had only managed a few times to get him to settle down and engage in an in-depth conversation and, when he had, he was always taken aback at how soft-spoken and charming he really was. Martin began to get excited about walking back to the interview site with him as he might be able to have another one of these conversations. However, luck was not on his side that evening.

"Well, hopefully they're rolling fast enough to catch me!" Roshi said with bright eyes and a mischievous smile, running off into the trees and catching Martin by surprise. When he realized what had happened he took off after Roshi, managing to catch glimpses of his glittery shirt through the trees every once in a while. Pangs of regret flew through him as he passed into a clearing full of neon lights, glimpsing a girl swallow a sword on fire, but with no time to stop and enjoy. Another time, he glimpsed a ring of golden glowing mushrooms, which seemed to trigger something in his psychedelic-infused mind, but he just kept running. Finally, they reached the end of the trees and came to another side of the festival site. "Thank goodness," he thought as he saw that Roshi had stopped. He had stopped to hug someone dressed up in a giant bear costume with a white t-shirt that read "The Bear Witch Project". Martin drew up beside them and Roshi pulled him in to join in the giant bear hug and, although it felt comforting to be held, he would never admit it..

"I'm only doing the interview if we can bring this bear with us." He looked up at the bear's giant cartoonish head and pleaded, "will you come with us?"

The head of the mascot nodded and they brought him along to the backstage interview area. Foggy laughed when he saw this, but Martin could also see that he was a little upset as this was supposed to be a serious interview. Martin felt ashamed, chastising himself for not being stern enough, filling himself with anxiety and insecurity.

*   *   *   *   *   *   *   *   *

It was the second weekend of the festival. Foggy and Martin had stayed in Austin for the week in between the two events while Roshi and the rest of the Lodgepole Pine band had played a couple of gigs around the area. Foggy thought it was important for him and Martin to stay back and do some more management-style work, which had disappointed Martin but he did his best not show it. They stayed with a friend of Foggy's, a marketing guru who had once tricked Amazon's bestseller list system, managing to get a book that consisted solely of pictures of his knee in the #1 spot for books on Religion and Spirituality. His name was Carlos and something about him was profoundly beautiful to Martin and, after the third day of staying with him, Martin realized that it was because of how honest this man was. He didn't seem to be hiding any parts of himself. Almost everyone that Martin had met during his time in New York seemed to be making a strong effort to conceal their emotions or any details about their personal lives. However, Carlos was different, and his presence got Martin to start missing Isaac and his other friends from South Carolina.

Carlos had taken them out one night to a Brazilian restaurant to meet his friend group in Austin, and had gone out of his way to introduce Martin to one of them; a shy girl in her thirties named Farrah with whom Martin had ended up talking for most of the evening. She had been quiet in the beginning but as the conversation went on she became more animated, especially when they began talking about the possibilities of space travel, which made Martin feel like he was talking to Isaac again. It felt like years since he had talked about anything but the music industry. "Not that anything is wrong with that," he told himself. "That's the point of you being here in New York." But, it would be okay to let that go just for a bit, right? As the night ended, Carlos and Foggy signalled to Martin that it was time to go. As he was leaving and saying farewell, Farrah suggested that they watch Cosmos together the following night to which he agreed and went off with a smile.

The next evening, Martin nervously made his way over to Farrah's house, terribly uncertain of what to expect. Though there were plenty of women who he had met in the past few months that he could have attempted a relationship with, he hadn't made any effort. Since he and Rose had ended their relationship he just hadn't felt like it, focusing solely on his work to propel himself as far to the top as possible. To help himself calm down, he decided that the evening to be spent with Farrah was nothing more than friends watching a TV show about space and that's all it had to be. Besides, she lived in Austin and he lived in New York. Furthermore, he didn't want to get tied down in any way just in case Rose… He stopped himself here as fantasizing about Rose was off-limits to him and he would not allow himself to get anywhere close to thinking about her. He put his headphones in and soothed himself with Ponton Low's new record. After this weekend in Austin, they still had two more weeks of tour with Ponton, during which Martin was fully dedicated to becoming his best friend.

He reached Farrah's quaint bungalow in a nondescript, simple Austin neighbourhood. He took out his headphones, stood by the front door, and took a deep breath, noticing momentarily how quiet it was. It wasn't like New York with its constant sirens, shouting, and pigeon pandemonium. It was just quiet with a little birdsong here and there, and a car or two driving past. He almost slipped into enjoying it but once again held himself back, telling himself that even if he didn't love the way that New York sounded, he *had to* learn how to love it. It was his new home and he *had to* live there. He *had to* enjoy it. The intensity of these pressure-filled statements that his mind was throwing his way was overwhelming but he breathed in again and knocked on the door, looking forward to distracting himself with the beauty of Neil Degrasse Tyson.

Farrah opened the door with a gentle smile and gave Martin a hug. He stiffened up a little but then allowed himself to return the kind gesture, feeling as if he hadn't really been properly hugged in a long time.

He was often hugging Foggy and Roshi, along with others that he met along the way, but this felt more authentic, though he couldn't really understand why. It ended before he had time to figure it all out and she invited him into her small home. She showed him around the house and he smiled at the simplicity of it all. She didn't seem to be too fussed about accruing possessions, which made Martin feel jealous as he had brought everything he owned with him to New York, which was proving to be quite a burden. He had been subletting a new apartment every month or two, as he was afraid of committing to a lease, which meant that he was constantly packing and unpacking all of his things, including a large record collection and far too many shoes. They went into Farrah's room, in which there was a small TV, a bookshelf, and a strange mat on the floor that had protruding rounded spikes all over it. It looked like one of those spiky pits that people tend to fall into in the Indiana Jones films, if the spikes had been rounded and shortened.

"Try it out. It massages the feet. It helps to mollify me when I get awfully stressed."

He took off his socks nervously and placed his feet gingerly on the mat, which was both jarring and alleviating at the same time. He feared that at any moment the spikes may make the bold decision to enter into his feet, leaving him perpetually stuck to the mat.

"Do you get stressed a lot?" He asked with 240 degrees of hesitation.

"Of course. There's a lot in this world to be stressed about. School, work, relationships. All of it causes some type of stress to everyone. What do you do to manage yours?"

She looked at him with her sweet brown eyes, which he avoided and said,

"Oh, I don't really get stressed."

Her look turned from curious to skeptical.

"Sure you don't."

He wasn't used to this kind of conversation and it had been quite some time since he had opened up to anyone. Luckily, Farrah seemed to notice this.

"Wanna watch some Cosmos?"

He agreed and they both settled down on her comfortable bed. She pulled out a joint, lit it and offered it to him before she took any of it herself. Martin got himself nice and tranquilized then settled back down against the wall, allowing himself to notice the room around him. The blanket on the bed was a light green that perfectly matched the lava lamp on top of the bookshelf. He was captivated by this, moving his gaze back and forth between the two, until the voice of Neil Degrasse Tyson emanated gently from the lightbox to his left. He allowed himself to be absorbed into the program and, for the next few hours, he completely forgot about New York, the music industry, and everything else that had been worrying him. His nervous system grew calmer with every minute that passed and nostalgia began to arise, along with an unsettling revelation. Since he had returned to New York after he and Rose broke up, he had not allowed himself to relax whatsoever. Even when he was watching movies with Roshi and Foggy, he was constantly nervous about making sure to laugh at the parts that the other two laughed at and making intellectual comments that would impress them. His new life was still so foreign and he constantly felt as if it could be pulled out from under his feet at any minute. However, as he sat here with Farrah, none of that seemed to matter. It was just so simple and authentic. This word had come to him earlier that evening and he wasn't sure why he was focusing on it so much. Wasn't the rest of his life also authentic? He was working hard, making connections and going to parties. Wasn't that what a real, authentic life was? As he began to question himself once more, Neil Degrasse Tyson began to talk about black holes and he got sucked back in.

*   *   *   *   *   *   *   *   *

Martin was back on the festival grounds for the last day of the event after which, following Lodgepole Pine's final afternoon set on the main stage, they would be off to continue on the Ponton Low tour. Somehow, Martin had managed to convince Foggy to allow his friend Yadiel to join them on tour as they would be passing near South Carolina. Yadiel was as big of a fan of Ponton Low as he was and also one of Martin's closest friends. He was eager to see him again, though rather nervous to see if he would be able to integrate him into his new music industry life. He had been feeling recently as if he was supposed to let go of the people he once knew, in order to fully immerse himself into New York.

"Martin!"

It was Farrah. The previous night he had texted Foggy and asked if he could get her a pass for the last day of the festival. In the magic way that Foggy was able to do things, he texted back two minutes later, "done". Foggy was truly remarkable when it came to the industry. With his long list of connections, he could basically get any number of tickets for any show in any country. He knew about all of the parties in New York that no one else knew about, and often would send Martin to these parties as his "avatar" when he didn't feel like going out. Martin was constantly impressed by him and hoped to be like him when he grew up, despite the fact that Foggy was only three years older than him.

Farrah walked up to him and Martin was immediately grateful to see her. Their Cosmos date the night before had been easy and simple. They had watched a few episodes of Cosmos, talked a little more, and then parted ways. He had noticed that the pressure he had been feeling lately had gone when he had been with Farrah. He stood up and they walked together to the backstage area, so she could meet Roshi and the rest of the band. Once they entered Lodgepole Pine's area, Martin suddenly felt a profound anxiety well up from inside of his belly. It lingered in his chest cavity for the entire time that Farrah was backstage, and after about 10 minutes of this he found himself telling her that he had some work to do. He told her that she should go back out to watch some of the bands and that he would meet up with her later. She looked at him with confusion and disappointment, as the night before he had suggested that they would spend the entire day together, watching some of the biggest bands from the side of the stage and enjoying the delicious catering that was being offered to the VIPs.

He noticed that along with the anxiety there was a strong embarrassment that had arisen in him. He was both embarrassed by Farrah meeting the people he worked for, as well as having them meet Farrah. It felt like two worlds of his were colliding but he wasn't even sure what this meant. Why would he have two worlds? It was just one. His life. New York. There was no difference between the simple, gentle way that Farrah treated him and the shrouded, businesslike manner in which his industry peers interacted. It was all the same, he repeated to himself.

When Farrah went back to the festival grounds he felt a strong desire to be alone. He didn't actually have any work to do that day, other than enjoy the festival until Lodgepole Pine played, so he went off to explore the backstage area. As he walked, he recognized some musicians, and usually would have made an attempt to speak to them but he didn't feel like it. In fact, he felt quite dazed and unsure of himself. As he neared the catering area, he heard a woman's voice.

"Are you interested in a free massage?"

He turned to his left and there was a woman with a massage bed underneath a white tent. Foggy had told him about this. At some festivals, they hired masseuses for the artists. He wasn't sure if he was allowed since he wasn't actually an artist, but he had always wanted to try a massage, and thought that it might calm him down a bit.

"Sure. OK."

He nervously climbed onto the massage bed and the curly brown-haired lady began massaging his head.

"I specialize in cranial massages," she said softly. "Are you interested in that?"

"Sure." He replied, though he wasn't exactly sure what that was.

The massage lasted about twenty minutes and mostly focused on massaging all parts of his head. For the majority of that twenty minutes, he felt sickeningly uncomfortable as a large number of unpleasant thoughts and emotions arose during the experience that he was having significant trouble pushing away. He was usually pretty good at repressing these feelings, but it just didn't seem to be working. Along with this, it felt as if strange, water-like sensations were passing from his head to the rest of the body. After she had finished, he stood up and found that his legs felt like jelly. He didn't want to stick around, so he remarked, "thanks" and slumped away on his jelly legs.

He immediately regretted getting the massage. It was as if all of the bad feelings he had been having before had been amplified by a factor of a hundred. Plus, there were so many people around and he hated it. Why were there so many people? Why couldn't he just be on his own? Hoping that he wouldn't run into anyone he knew, he left the backstage area and went back into the field, searching for a place without people. However, this seemed rather fruitless as he was at one of the country's biggest music festivals so, eventually, he sighed in defeat and sat himself down in a spot in the grass halfway between two of the stages. At one of the stages, there was a flock of people, eagerly awaiting the band that was about to come on. He thought that watching some music might distract him from his feelings.

As the crowd cheered, a woman dressed in flamboyant clothing and a feathered headdress came to the centre of the stage, followed by her less-decorated band.

"It's so great to be here, Austin. My favourite city in the world!"

The crowd went wild at hearing this and the band started. Did she mean those words? Was Austin truly her favourite city? He had heard this so many times at so many different shows in so many different cities and felt like it was all bullshit just like the rest of the music industry. Everyone was just saying things that other people wanted to hear and nothing that they wanted to say themselves. As these thoughts arose, he inwardly punched himself. How could he think like that? He lived and breathed the music industry and to work in it was his dream because it was perfect and real. It had to be. The falsehood he was increasingly noticing was just attributed to his overactive imagination. He was the problem. He just needed to be better and then everything would be better. Was *he* the fake one? Was that why he was afraid of Farrah meeting his peers? Because she would see how he really was? A fake ball of flesh, scared, confused, and pathetic. But no, it was New York that did it. He wasn't the problem. He just had to leave New York and everything would be fine. But how could the city be the issue? It was so big. There was so much variety. He was the issue. Or was it his surroundings?

His mind swam through this spherical waterfall of doubt without anything to distract him out of the cycle. He was terrified of everything that was circling through his head.

"As if you could leave New York. It is everything you have ever wanted. You have dreamed of working in the music industry in New York for years and can't just ditch that because you are afraid like a pathetic little mouse. You have to stay, you loser."

He felt like he had been sucked into the black hole that he had seen on TV the night before for all of a sudden there was nothing around him but darkness. The most panic he had ever felt flooded through every nook and cranny of his body as well as the darkness around him. There was no salvation. He looked down and couldn't even see his own body. He was nothing but darkness and panic and that was all it was ever going to be. He was more scared than he had ever been in his life. He had no idea who he was, no clue why he was here, no understanding of anything at all. Then, the panic and darkness disappeared and there was nothing but nothing.

*　*　*　*　*　*　*　*　*

Martin wasn't sure if he existed anymore. However, he still had some semblance of awareness and he clung to it. Suddenly, from all sides at once, thick clouds of smoke poured in and he became one of them. He began to hear voices and could feel that his lungs were there, filled up with scratchy pot smoke. His surroundings began to brighten and he shielded his eyes from the light, noticing that he held a joint in his right hand. He looked hazily to his left and saw that his friend Yadiel was sitting beside him, looking back at him with a look that said, "are you okay?" Martin nodded slowly. The weed was strong and had hit him hard. Furthermore, he was a nervous wreck but doing his utmost not to betray that to the rest of the people in the tour bus. He looked at Yadiel a while longer in order to ground himself, noticing the curly black hair that seemed to be growing in all directions, the light beard that he was always slightly jealous of, and the eyes that were constantly full of life, no matter the situation. He was grateful that Yadiel was with him at this moment as he didn't think he would have been able to handle it on his own. They were in Ponton Low's tour bus, smoking weed with the 22-year old legend and Bernice, a member of his crew.

It was the last day of the tour, which meant that Yadiel and Martin had set out on a serious mission - to establish fully their relationship with Ponton before they parted ways. Having Yadiel on the tour had been a blessing. Since his panic attack in the middle of Austin City Limits, Martin had been feeling incredibly shaky, but having his buddy beside him for the last two weeks had helped him come back to the present and recognize the beauty of the situation that he was in. He tried his best not to think about returning to New York, a thought that inspired significant misgivings within, and instead focused on making the most of his time on this tour. He and Yadiel had managed to befriend a good number of the team that came along with Ponton Low but Ponton himself had always been slightly elusive. They had managed to have a laugh here and there but Martin wanted more. He wanted this friendship to be real. He secretly had dreams of Ponton inviting him to open for him on his next tour, despite the fact that Martin had no music of his own to showcase. Thus, on the last night after the show, Yadiel and Martin had made an effort to locate Ponton and create a lasting bond. This had proved rather difficult and they were ready to leave when they saw Bernice headed towards one of the buses. He hailed them and said, "hey guys, come with me." They followed him, unaware of where they were going, but when they opened the door of the bus and stepped in they were assailed with a cloud of smoke and the sight of Ponton Low himself.

Now, they were sitting on the seats in the bus, the four of them making jokes and talking about mostly nonsensical things. Martin couldn't believe it. He was the quietest of the group and hated himself for it, but just seemed unable to find the right words to say in order to impress Ponton. He wanted to know how he could become just like Ponton but had no idea how to ask such a silly question. He had watched him perform every night from all angles of the stage and been absolutely astonished by the performance this young man had put on. He spent an unfortunate amount of time comparing himself to the performer, desiring the success that he had and ridiculing himself for still being such a little fish. As they sat in the bus watching Bernice perform his stand-up routine, Martin glanced over at Ponton, who seemed to be making up rhymes to himself on the bench opposite. If only he could hear what he was saying. Ponton noticed he was staring and looked back at him, causing Martin to look away with embarrassment. How could he ever have thought he could be this guy's friend? He was so much better than Martin in every way. More talented, funny, interesting. There was no use. Martin felt the ever-more familiar panic rising within him again.

Yadiel noticed this, as he was somehow constantly aware of Martin's emotional states, and decided to establish a conversation between the two of them himself.

"Hey Ponton," he said confidently, after Bernice had finished his routine. "Did you know that Martin here is a really good rapper too?"

Ponton looked at him with slight curiosity and Martin blushed.

"Well, it's been a while, and I was never really very good, I was just being silly, and..." Martin stammered nervously.

"Don't do that to yourself, Martin. You have a ferocity that I haven't seen in many people." He looked back at Ponton. "You know, once we performed an acoustic version of Kanye's *A Beautiful Dark Twisted Fantasy* in the café of our campus bookstore. The best part was that Martin had ripped off his shirt by the second song, swearing his head off and climbing all over the audience."

Martin looked down at his lap with a small smile.

"After the show, they told us to never play there again." Martin said quietly and laughed a little with Yadiel. To his surprise, Bernice and Ponton joined in on the laughter. He looked up at them and they were both looking at him, which sparked a flash of confidence to run through him.

"I love Kanye," Ponton said. "Any song in particular that you like to perform? We could try to do a version of it right here."

Martin was incredulous and spent the better part of five seconds running through the list of Kanye songs thinking about which would be the best one to perform right there with these guys. He was absolutely frightened at the thought but also knew that he would hate himself even more if he did not go along with it. He was about to suggest 'Power', fantasizing about going back-and-forth on the verses with Ponton, when to his dismay the door of the bus opened and a crowd of others joined them. Martin instantly retreated back into himself, sad that he would no longer have the opportunity to make this special connection with Ponton. He didn't like being in big groups of people. That feeling when he would speak with ten others listening to his words was much too overwhelming for him and he resolved to remain silent the rest of the night.

There was nothing wrong with the rest of the crew who had joined, some of them were now friends of Yadiel and Martin, but it was just much too loud for Martin now and he felt like he wanted to go home. He had failed in establishing a lasting bond with Ponton, was feeling the marijuana-enhanced panic ripple through him, and felt like running away. He couldn't do that though as it would make him look even more pathetic. After some time, Bernice started telling jokes again and Martin had an inkling of an idea.

"Yadiel has a good joke he could tell." Martin said through the noise of the group after Bernice had caused an eruption of laugher with his cutely awkward sense of humour. Yadiel looked at him with disdain. With just a look in his eyes, he knew that Yadiel was saying to him, "how could you put me on the spot like that?" However, he took a deep breath in and said,

"So, there were two fish in a tank..."

He let the silence linger for over seven seconds.

"And one of them said, 'how do you drive this thing?'"

This resulted in a small amount of awkward laughter that made Martin feel like an absolute fool. He had completely blown it. It was over. He was pathetic. He was never going to be like Ponton Low as he was nothing but a loser, bound to be working in some management assistant's role for the rest of his life. Ponton was the same age as him and already so successful that Martin had no time to catch up and no longer any motivation to try.

Suddenly, Yadiel's voice penetrated the noise of conversation that had once again flooded the bus,

"Wait. I've got a good one," he said while pulling up his sleeves.

Martin looked at him with a surprised smile. How brave he was to try again after not managing to get any laughs the first time. This second joke that Yadiel pulled out of his brilliant head was fantastic and got the whole group of them laughing. Yadiel had managed to redeem them in the eyes of everyone and Martin felt as if he had never been so grateful to anyone in his entire life. Yadiel was glowing. The rest of the evening went along smoothly and resulted in a final one-on-one interaction between Ponton and Martin where they ended up exchanging phone numbers. The last thing Martin did was attempt to make Ponton laugh by talking in a strange accent, which was only slightly successful.

Yadiel and Martin remained quiet for the first two hours of their drive away from the show. They listened to their favourite My Chemical Romance album while basking in the glory of their completed mission. However, Martin was still feeling slightly dejected. Despite the fact that he had even managed to get Ponton's phone number, he felt as if this was not good enough. The only way he could really get his respect was if he was as popular and talented as Ponton but he could not see how this was possible. He followed these thoughts up with a whole siege of comparisons between him and others whom he believed to be living a better life than he was. These were dangerous thoughts and spiralled Martin into yet another negative headspace, ending with the final definitive fact that he was never going to be good enough.

Chapter 14 - The Developmental Stage

He was staring down at his lap, feeling this wave of sadness envelop his body. How could he treat himself like that? The fact that he hated himself that much was miserable. Tears welled up in his eyes but he was afraid to let them out as he did not want Yadiel to see him. However, as he listened, he noticed that he could no longer hear the noise of the driving car and loud music, but instead heard a delicate bird sound whistling to him from nearby. He looked up, allowing a few of the tears that had been balancing in his bottom lids to fall onto his shirt, and saw that he was in the forest with Dr. Spruce sitting right in front of him.

"Dr. Spruce," he said tenderly. "There's just... there's so much in there."

Dr. Spruce held up his paw as if to silence Martin and pointed down at the ground. Martin looked and saw that the small map of Texas had been rubbed away, leaving the outline of Canada as well as some country that Martin still could not recognize.

"I... I have to keep going?"

"It's the only way that you can understand what brought you here."

He looked back down reluctantly and didn't know what to do, feeling trapped by the knowledge that the only way out was in. Those last memories seemed so fresh, as if they hadn't existed until just now. He was afraid to go into anything unfamiliar again. Perhaps if he chose the drawing of Canada then he could just stay where he was, with Dr. Spruce, and talk about what he had just seen. He looked up at the bear, allowing the rest of the tears to spill down his cheeks like fallen leaves floating down a rainy gutter, and pointed down to Canada. Dr. Spruce smiled at him.

     *   *   *   *   *   *   *   *   *

Martin looked at himself in the mirror, deciding that he had done all that he could do to make himself look interesting. His hair had been painstakingly straightened to form a swoop that ran down to partially cover his left eye, he was wearing a bright green v-neck shirt that showcased the few chest hairs that had started to come in the day after his fourteenth birthday, and he sported a pair of tight-fitting pink jeans that he had nervously bought with his mother at a woman's clothing store in the mall – the only shop with sufficiently skinny jeans. He thought he looked pretty cool, really. All the bands that he loved were modelling this type of look at the moment and he wanted nothing more than to be just like them. He was heading into the second semester at his new high school in Calgary, Alberta, and was making an effort to impress all the people who walked past him.

He went upstairs to wolf down a breakfast as fast as he possibly could without even noticing what he was eating. His mother had made him a large meal, as she was aware of just how quickly he was growing and wanted to help that process as much as she could. He had finished the meal in under two minutes and got up to go.

"Be careful about eating so quickly, Martin. I don't think that's good for your body." She said to him warily.

"I know what's good for me, you don't." He snapped at her. In the last few months, he had been especially rude to his family. His mother knew that a mixture of puberty and the beginning of high school had caused his anxiety to rise tenfold and he had taken this out on his family. He himself wasn't aware of the reasons for these intense emotions and blamed it on the way his family treated him, despite the fact that they were trying their best to care for and understand him. He stormed off to grab his bag, slammed the off-white front door on his way out and made his way to the bus stop.

When he arrived at the school, he made his way to his locker, and saw Carly opening up her locker close by. She had a similar style to him, with short, choppy bangs that covered up her forehead, and dark, edgy clothing. It was obvious that she liked similar music to him, though they hadn't talked about it.

"Hey Carly," he said nervously. She looked at him with a smile and he was about to return the greeting when her boyfriend came up from behind Martin to make his way to her. She greeted him with a kiss causing Martin to feel a sickening mixture of jealousy and anger. He had never been in a relationship and it seemed that every time that he had any interest in someone, they either had a partner already or were not interested in him.

*   *   *   *   *   *   *   *   *

A week later, Martin was sitting in his favourite hallway, studying while listening to one of his favourite bands on his brand new iPod. He loved this hallway as no one else ever came there and, with this recent influx of new emotions, he tended to need more time alone these days. He was whispering the words of the chorus to himself when he felt a touch on his arm and almost jumped out of his acne-covered skin. He saw Carly standing above him and made a concerted effort to compose himself, pretending that she had not caused him any fright. He took out his headphones and tentatively said,

"Uh, hi Carly. I'll be leaving here soon so no problem if you want a quiet place to study."

"Um, okay." She sat down beside him, making Martin feel anxious. He started to pack up his backpack and make his way to leave.

"Wait, Martin. I have something I want to talk to you about."

"Okay." Martin stayed seated on the bench and faced Carly. She looked back at him with a surprising melancholy pasted across her pale face. Despite this, Martin still found her very pretty and felt a surge of butterflies escape into his belly.

"Martin. Um. I want to be with you."

Martin was so taken aback that his head flung backwards a little bit, causing the hair swoop covering his left eye to settle back behind his left ear.

"What do you mean?"

"I want you to be my boyfriend." She seemed deadly serious.

"But you already have a boyfriend."

"He doesn't treat me well and I'm going to end it with him this weekend. Then we can be together."

"Oh.. okay, sure." Though Martin was attracted to her, he had a slight aversion to the idea but couldn't figure out why. However, the excitement about having a girlfriend for the first time in his life took over and he smiled at her. "That sounds good."

Then she came straight in and kissed him. The butterflies that were floating around his belly seem to each birth another hundred butterflies, releasing these baby butterflies to fly around the rest of his insides. As he returned the kiss, he opened his eyes slightly to make sure that no one was entering the hallway. He couldn't imagine what her boyfriend would think if he walked in. However, the coast was clear and he closed his eyes again, kissing her with all that he had.

*   *   *   *   *   *   *   *   *

Two weeks later, Carly and Martin were walking home together from a concert they had attended downtown. As Martin had guessed from her fashion sense, they liked the same bands and already had plans to go to another five concerts that were coming up in the next month. Since she had ended things with her former partner, they had spent most hours in the day together and, when they were apart, they would communicate either through text messages or over the phone. Martin was new to all of this, and nervous about the entire venture, but grateful for the opportunity to have someone to talk to who seemed to understand him. He loved his friends, but none of them liked the same music as him and, as that was the most important thing in his life, he found that rather difficult. He typically went to concerts on his own, something he didn't really mind, but once Carly entered the picture he was happy to have a companion there to ogle at the musicians with him.

They took the train home and Carly rested her head upon his shoulder, grabbing both of his hands, touching her leg to his, and doing everything else possible to get as many pieces of her body touching his at once. Martin felt slightly insecure about this and glanced around apologetically at the fellow passengers, though they all seemed to be too engrossed in their own worlds to care.

"Hey, Martin." Carly said softly.

"Yeah?"

"I love you."

Martin's heart fell into his stomach. She loved him? Isn't that something that people only said after being together for a long time? What did love feel like anyway? How did he know if he loved her back?

"I think I would probably kill myself if I broke up with you."

His heart, which had previously descended to his stomach, had now fallen into his toes. Her sleeve was pulled up and he once again registered the scars that sat on her wrists like pale white train tracks with no destination. She had said these last words with conviction and he believed her, suddenly feeling her grasping hands like chafing handcuffs. The panic spread through him until he realized that she was now expecting a response.

"Um, I love you too..."

"Good."

*　　　*　　　*　　　*　　　*　　　*　　　*　　　*　　　*

Carly and Martin had been together for six months now. The summer was almost over and they had been with each other as much as was feasibly possible in the time away from school. However, Martin's parents took him and his brother to visit their family in England for about four weeks of that time. The internet in their rental apartment was spotty so he found it difficult to communicate with Carly as much as they usually did, something which felt surprisingly good to him though he couldn't understand why. Carly was constantly upset with him and tried to get him to spend his time in internet cafés so they could speak, though her wish wasn't fulfilled as he ended up being rather busy visiting his relatives.

Upon his return, Carly was distraught, accusing him of being with another woman and spending his time communicating with this mystery girl instead of her. The only way Martin could resolve this issue was to allow her to have access to both his Facebook and MSN accounts. She spent a substantial chunk of time browsing through his conversations making sure that he was faithful. Martin felt weary after all this, believing that this relationship was what it was going to be like for life. He thought he had to settle into it, in some fashion, and unconsciously repressed any negative feelings that he felt towards her and the relationship. Besides, he had nothing else to compare it to, so maybe this was just how all relationships turn out.

Martin's life had made a complete change since he and Carly began dating as she would not permit him to spend any time with his friends because that would take time away from their relationship. Thus, Martin began to be deprived of all of the friendships that he had cultivated over the past years leaving the majority of his interactions to be with Carly or his parents. His anger towards his parents had grown stronger with his outbursts often bringing his mother to tears. It didn't matter what they said to him, he always felt as if they were trying to control his life and he hated it. In reality, they were attempting to offer him love, but he was so trapped in his relationship with Carly that he was unable to register any of this. They were the only people on which he could take out his anger towards his own life. Martin's situation was similar to a mosquito being trapped in a glass. The mosquito is unaware of what has happened, repeatedly butting its head against the side of the glass in desperate attempts to get out, though without proper awareness of its being trapped in a cage.

*   *   *   *   *   *   *   *   *

Both Martin and Carly were heavily involved in the theatre productions in their school. The majority of their elective classes were theatre-based and they had both been in the school's production of Romeo and Juliet earlier that year, though to Carly's dismay they did not receive the title roles. That September, as Grade 11 was beginning, there were auditions held for the school's fall play and the two of them tried out. Martin's mind was a stronghold of insecurity and he believed that he had bombed the audition. However, when the roles were announced, Martin was amazed to see his name next to one of the more prominent roles in the show. He couldn't believe it and ran to tell Carly before he took a look at any of the other names in the show.

As he was rushing towards the theatre wing, he ran into his teacher, Ms. P.

"Congratulations, Martin." She said with a warm smile. She was the coolest teacher he had ever had for she was young, brash, and spent a large part of their classes working with them on ridiculously fun improv games.

"Thanks! I'm so excited!"

"Well, there's more. Those roles aren't exactly final."

"What do you mean?"

"There's a good chance that you're going to get the lead role. I'll let you know by the end of the day."

As she walked away, Martin stood there, shocked, his mouth hung open. The lead role? The Grade 11s never got lead roles! Those were usually saved for the more experienced Grade 12 students. His heart was fluttering, his eyes were wide and he ran even quicker to tell Carly though, when he reached her, she was crying by her locker.

"Carly! Carly... what's wrong?"

She looked at him with mascara running down her face and anger encasing her terse mouth.

"You know what's wrong."

"Um, no I don't."

"I didn't get in. And you did."

"Oh... man..." He settled down beside her and tried to comfort her with a cuddle but it didn't seem to do any good so he attempted to use some words. "It will be okay. We'll still have a lot of time to spend with each other. It will be fine."

She looked at him with a deathly glare.

"You have to drop out."

His breath shortened and he felt his arms go numb. Drop out? How could he drop out? This was his dream! He had already been looking into going to theatre schools after high school and to have been a main role in a production would be a huge boon to his resume.

"But..." He had no idea what to say or how to argue this as he hated conflict and knew that if he ever tried to get his point across with Carly, it would set off a series of storms.

"You're going to drop out. Go to Ms. P's office during her office hours at lunch and tell her you are not going to be in the show."

He sat there silent for a long time, not knowing what to do or say. However, as he looked down he once again noticed the scars on her wrists. She had told him she had not cut since they had been together but the thought of being the cause of a restart of such a terrible action helped him to make up his mind.

"Okay. I will."

At lunchtime, he went to Ms. P's office who noticed his dejection immediately and offered him a seat and a small candy.

"Martin, no need to look so glum. I have good news for you."

"Wait, Ms. P. I have to tell you something. I can't be in the show."

"Why not, Martin?"

"Um, I just have a lot of classes this semester and a lot of after school things and I'm going away with my parents and…" He blubbered through these flimsy excuses, though fully aware that she knew the real reason for his actions.

"I'm disappointed in you, Martin."

His breath shortened again and he wished he could become a mouse and quickly sneak under the door frame.

"You're not leaving the play." She said decisively.

"What?" He didn't expect this from her and wasn't sure if she was allowed to tell him that he couldn't leave.

"You heard me. You're in the play and you're staying in it. Though unfortunately I'm going to have to give the lead role to Parson."

A sickness was passing through his lower body that he couldn't understand while the voices within his mind were loudly divisive. On one hand, he was terrified to tell Carly what was happening here, wishing that Ms. P would have just agreed with him and let him leave the show. On the other hand, he was powerfully grateful for Ms. P as it gave him an excuse that he could bring to Carly, placing all the blame on his teacher rather than him. Furthermore, he could feel a bubbling anger towards Carly for having ruined his chances at getting the lead in the show. However, he pushed this feeling as far down as possible, maintaining the world of ignorance in which he chose to live.

He left Ms. P's office while holding all of these emotions within him, feeling like both an anvil and a feather at the same time. When he told Carly, she was outraged and placed the blame on everyone and everything. Martin held her close and talked her down. It was times like these where Martin felt like the owner of a perpetually wounded animal.

$$* \quad * \quad * \quad * \quad * \quad * \quad * \quad * \quad *$$

The summer between Grade 11 and 12 had arrived. The final summer of their high school years before things were to change dramatically. Martin felt as if a lot had been changing in him recently and things between him and Carly were more terse than ever. Due to his role in the school's production, he had begun to make friends with some of the older students in the school and had even spent time with them outside of school, though he never told this to Carly. Two of them were the prettiest girls he had ever seen and for some reason that Martin couldn't understand, they thoroughly enjoyed spending time with him. Martin had inexplicable feelings towards both of them, but never acted on any of these. Despite all that had happened, he had been faithful to Carly, acting out of a mixture of fear and loyalty. However, sometimes he would complain to them a little about his relationship, something he had not ventured to do since it had started, as was the first time he had had friends other than Carly in over a year.

Once, after rehearsal, they were out for dinner with another of the cast members, a boy the same age as Martin named Giuseppe. While they were eating, Giuseppe had been asking a lot about Carly and after some time he said,

"You're very lucky, Martin. I would give anything to be going out with her."

Martin had noticed over the past year and a half that the majority of people who observed their relationship had no clue of what it was actually like. On the outside, they seemed like the perfect lovey-dovey couple with their constant hand-holding, kissing, and loyalty to one another.

"Maybe you should go out with her, then," Martin said, though he was suddenly horrified when these words came out of his mouth. He had stated it rather matter-of-factly, as if it were a perfectly plausible solution.

"...but she's your girlfriend." He said with confusion.

"Yeah... right."

Since the play had ended, he had not had the opportunity to spend time with these new friends. However, in late July, both Carly and Martin were getting ready to attend a week-long theatre camp and

Giuseppe would be joining them on the trip. The day before they were about to go, Carly attempted to convince them to back out.

"Martin, I don't think we should go."

"What? Why not?" Martin had been extremely excited for this theatre camp since he had signed up for it. Ms. P had recommended that he go and she was even going to be one of the instructors for a daily workshop they would do. He thought that it would be amazing to get to know her outside of a school setting, and was also looking forward to having the opportunity to make a few more friends.

"You just got back from England and we're going to go straight into a camp where we will barely get to spend time together."

"You don't know that. We might be in the same group." He secretly hoped that this would not be the case but would never say something so blasphemous to her face.

"I hope so." She said sternly while crossing her arms.

To Martin's relief and Carly's dismay, they were put in separate groups. He couldn't believe it. A week to himself, with little contact between the two of them, other than during break periods. He was confused about the fact that he felt so joyous about this but did not delve too much into it. Despite the fact that he was feeling less attached to the relationship than ever before, he still wasn't able to imagine a life without it.

In the first workshop of the day, the group in which Martin had been placed sat in a circle for everyone to give a brief introduction. He knew nobody in this group, which was both exciting and nerve wracking.

When the introductions reached around the halfway mark, a slight brunette wearing a comfortable red sweatshirt introduced herself.

"Hi, my name is Henrietta. I live in Banff and love to ski." She smiled at the group and passed the invisible baton to the person next to her. Martin didn't hear the next three or four introductions as he had found himself incredibly enraptured by Henrietta. Her voice had this husky quality to it that had drawn him in immediately and the fact that she was both from Banff and liked skiing excited him. His own family had purchased a condo near Banff so that they could spend the majority of the winter weekends on ski hills. However, as the introductions got closer to him, he realized that he should quit focusing on Henrietta, both due to the fact that his stares might seem a little creepy as well as the fact that Carly was sitting in a room not so far away from this one. Finally, it was his turn to introduce himself.

"Um, hi, I'm Martin, I'm from Calgary, and I like to ski." He gave a tiny smile in the direction of Henrietta but didn't stop long enough to see if she noticed. Suddenly he felt a pang of guilt rush through him. Why did he do that? What was he trying to do here? He wasn't going to allow himself to be unfaithful. If he was going to be with Carly for life, as he had managed to convince himself, then he could not be going around attempting to flirt with hippie girls who liked skiing.

However, as the days went on, he found himself more enticed by Henrietta, and they quickly became fast friends. She was way more relaxed than many of the people he had met before and, once she introduced him to her friends from the same area, he realized that it must be the attitude of those living in a small ski town. He was greatly attracted to this, being a severely anxious person himself, and thought that spending more time around this group might help him relax. When he mentioned that he would be around Banff every weekend during the winter, Henrietta immediately suggested that he come to one of their parties as well as go skiing with her. He couldn't believe it. He didn't know what any of this meant, but was lit up by Henrietta's presence and noticed the exact opposite feeling occur whenever he spent time with Carly.

It seemed that Carly was able to notice a change in Martin's attitude and started to get more agitated and hurt as he grew increasingly carefree and distant. He felt guilty about the whole situation but was unable to help himself. He felt as if for the first time he had found something that felt like actual happiness. Previous to this, he had talked himself into the idea that relationships were supposed to be draining and perpetually painful, hoping that one day happiness would be found within it, but that hope was beginning to fade. His experience at the theatre camp had already changed him drastically, as he not only started to develop strong feelings for Henrietta, but also made some other friends with whom he felt profoundly deep connections. It was reminding him of feelings that he had felt before he and Carly ever began to date, as if his cage had been left open and he was just beginning to peer out.

After the camp, Martin made an effort to keep in touch with Henrietta without being discovered by Carly. As she had access to all of his social media accounts and email, he ended up creating a fake Facebook account under the name Rodney Rockefeller just so he could talk to her. It was through this medium that he revealed for the first time to anyone, including himself, his severe hatred for the situation he was in as well as his desire to come out of it. Henrietta was kind and gentle with him, having recently experienced a similar situation, and helped him understand that things didn't have to be this way.

One day, he attempted to have a conversation with Carly about the way he had been feeling recently. He went over to her house and sat with her on her bed while her parents sat in the living room downstairs. He felt more nervous than he had ever been in his life.

"Carly. I wanted to talk to you about something..."

Carly knew what was coming. She had sensed this for the past few months but had made an effort to ignore it, hoping that Martin would come to his senses.

"Marty..."

"I'm not sure if we should be together anymore."

Her face turned a shade of black.

"What if I told you I was pregnant?" She said with malicious intent.

"I know you're not pregnant, Carly. We haven't even had sex."

"But... but, there are other ways!" She was desperate and clutching at straws. All of a sudden, Martin was furious with her for trying to sucker him into staying with her with something like this. The anger that had been resting in the bottom of his stomach for the past year was starting to show. The rage that had been pushed down with heavy weights, leaving it there to fester and transform itself into a creature far more formidable than any fictional villain out there. This creature was now climbing out, finding its way up through his intestines, causing flashes of pain that made the fury even stronger. As the creature rose, Martin could feel its form within him and it made parts of his body begin to twitch uncontrollably. He was afraid of himself and what this monster might do though he knew he would never hurt the girl physically as he had enough control of himself not to do something like this. However, he knew it needed to be released in some way and so, for the first time in their relationship, he stood up for himself.

"STOP TRYING TO CONTROL ME." He screamed in her face, fully aware that her parents would hear everything he was saying but allowing that fleeting insecurity to pass quickly away. "YOU ARE ALWAYS DOING THIS. MAKING ME FEEL GUILTY. THREATENING TO KILL YOURSELF. FORCING ME AWAY FROM MAKING FRIENDS. YOU HAVE RUINED MY LIFE."

His breath was heavy and he felt like he could keep going for the rest of the year. However, he saw the mountain of pain growing out of her face as these words escaped him and he stopped. He knew if he stayed there he would keep shouting at her, until her parents dragged him out of the room kicking and screaming so he decided that he had to leave. He got up and walked out of the room. It sounded as if Carly was about to say something, but he slammed her door, walked furiously down the stairs without looking at her parents, and left the house, making a point to slam the front door even harder.

That night, after speaking with Henrietta some more and mustering up the confidence he needed, he 'officially' broke up with Carly. It happened over the phone and took about seven hours during which he tried his best not to raise his voice while making all kinds of false promises in order to try to keep her as calm as possible. She was distraught, but after the call, he was confident that she would not fulfil her promise to commit suicide. He knew her enough by now to realize that this comment never had any actual weight to it. Sure, she had harmful tendencies towards herself, but she had other things in life that she loved, and he didn't think that she would be willing to let them go. Still, the break up was one of the hardest things he had ever had to do and he spent the rest of the night crying out his feelings of guilt into his pillow.

For the next few weeks, Carly tried everything to convince Martin to get back together with her. She threatened suicide multiple times but, once again, he knew that she would not do it. She called his mother and tried to get her to convince him to take her back, which she made an attempt at, but Martin's newly discovered sense of confidence allowed him to keep true to his decision. Of course there were periods of extreme doubt but in these moments Henrietta was a huge help to him. Though it was improbable for he and Henrietta to actually get together since they lived too far from one another, she was becoming one of his closest friends and confidantes, giving him all that he needed to maintain his position.

*   *   *   *   *   *   *   *   *

Martin sat down in the hallway by his locker. This newfound sense of freedom was still rather overwhelming to him and the tenderness that had opened up in him since he ended their relationship was as raw as an open wound. It was as if all the pain that he had felt during their time together was showing its face to him now that he had stepped into the light but he felt as if needed a break from all of it. Tiredness struck him quickly and he closed his eyes, resting his head against the locker. As he did so, he noticed his body for a moment. It seemed as if he had a full awareness of how his body was feeling, which was strange and new to him. The feelings were not pleasant. He felt bruised in all of the parts of his body that he was able to feel, some places worse than others. Was this all of the pain that had been pushed down by his relationship with Carly? How come he could feel it so strongly all of a sudden? He then started to see how this traumatic experience had managed to connect itself to every decision he had made from that moment onwards. All of the relationships that he had entered since breaking up with her were all full of the same insecurities and fears that his time with Carly had brought up. He had found himself drawn to partners who were either very similar to Carly and he would allow himself to be controlled once more, or the exact opposite; weak-minded women who were easily controlled. All of his desperate attempts with Rose came from the fact that for the first time he had met someone who hadn't been trying to control him and was also not willing to be controlled. She had been confident and he had been sucked in by this. Perhaps all of his issues with trust had resulted from this early stage in his development, and this was part of why he had chosen to remove himself completely from society. "Oh my god," he thought to himself. "It is connected to everything."

He then realized that something had changed. The understanding flooded through him like a searchlight in a dark fog and he saw that he was back in the present. Back in his own body, not in the memories of his 14-year old self. He was afraid of what he had discovered but also riveted by this new wisdom. He kept his eyes closed, trying to remember the day that he had arrived at Richmond Lake and understand the reasons why he had actually moved there but that part of his memory was still blank, which enraged him once more. After all this exploring, he still had holes in his memory? What else would he have to do? What other traumas were blocking his way? He suddenly realized how exhausted he was and knew that he couldn't go into that third memory that Dr. Spruce had presented him. If only he could have a sleep first. He opened his eyes to explain himself to the doctor, but found himself all alone in the forest.

Chapter 15 - An Interview

"Dr. Spruce?" He spoke softly, feeling incredibly weak and sensing the soft ground of the forest beckoning his back towards it. Normally he would not allow himself to lay down on bare ground, afraid of the bugs and worms that may make attempts to crawl their way into the orifices of his face, but this fear did not emerge and he allowed himself to rest on the cool, muddy floor. He was suddenly struck by the light that was shining from above. Though he was in a clearing, the canopy overhead was still quite dense, due to the gargantuan old-growth trees that grew around it. The breaks in their leaves granted thin bands of light to pierce the clearing, illuminating small specks of dust and insects and creating a sight that Martin thought he could stare at forever. Although he wondered where Dr. Spruce had gone off to, he did not seem to be afraid as nothing seemed scary to him after reliving all that trauma.

He observed the shimmering specks above him, noting a butterfly passing by every now and then, perhaps to snack on the floating dots of light. He felt utterly peaceful, more so than any other time that he could remember. However, he *was* rather doubtful about the veracity of his memory, so perhaps there had been a time where he was more peaceful than this. However, it did not matter much as how he felt now was what was important. By piecing together these traumatic memories, he was starting to catch glimpses of understanding as to how and why he ended up where he currently was. When he was younger, he would never have wanted to live out in solitude, completely isolated from the world, without friends or family to talk with. In fact, he had wanted the opposite. He had wanted to be thrust into the world in full and had an ambitious zeal to meet as many people as he possibly could. It was both amazing and frightening how things could change so dramatically. There was still a gap in his memory between New York and the present day, but he imagined that this would get answered when Dr. Spruce returned. As these thoughts came and went like the butterflies above his head, he allowed his eyes to close, and fell into a deep, comfortable sleep.

He fluttered his eyes open from the dreamless sleep, feeling a tickling sensation on his nose. He observed with wonder as a bright blue butterfly sat perched upon the bridge of his nose, staring right at him.

"Good morning Sunshine." The butterfly spoke to him in a melodic feminine voice. He jumped up in surprise, still getting used to the fact that these creatures could speak to him, which caused the dazzlingly bedecked insect to flutter around in the air before settling down on his hand. Martin was seated now and stared at the butterfly, allowing a warm smile to appear on his face.

"Is it morning?" He wasn't sure how long he had slept but it didn't really matter to him. His sense of time had been flip-flopped around during the last few days.

"Yes, dear human." The wind picked up a little through the trees causing her wings to ripple, showcasing the tinges of silver that were hiding amongst the blues. Martin noticed the sound of the wind in more detail than he ever had, realizing that it sounded as if it wasn't just one instrument but a whole orchestra. There was whistling, humming, and melody all meshed within the sound. The butterfly continued, "morning means it's time for you to go back to your town."

He felt a pang of disappointment upon hearing this as he didn't want to leave while he was feeling so peaceful. He remembered how the last time he had done this with Dr. Spruce, he had been feeling similarly serene, only to be struck with the ferocious fact that his house was burnt down. Besides, he had to stay and wait for Dr. Spruce. Wouldn't he be coming back at some point?

"I have to wait for Dr. Spruce. We're not finished our session." He said, eyes bright with innocence.

"Ah, he sent me here to find you, sleepyhead. He apologizes for his early departure but there was an urgent matter to attend to in the heart of the forest. He sends his regards."

"He sends his regards?" A twinge of irritation punched him in the stomach, but he felt a little more in control of this than before. "What does that mean? I'm just supposed to go?"

"Your reunion will come sooner than you think, allowing your final session to begin and end in due time."

"Final session?" He said with dismay. "How can it be my final session? I'm only just getting started to understand it all."

"I'm only the messenger, sweetness. Now, flutter away to your home, I have some dots of dust to devour." She flew off into the bands of light, glimmering like diamonds and sapphires below the lofty canopy, leaving Martin feeling slightly dejected but strong enough to pass through these negative feelings. He allowed himself to enjoy this peaceful time in the forest as fully as he could, walking slowly back in the direction from which he, Buffalo, and Dr. Spruce had come. As he trotted along, he admired everything he saw: the crusty lichen on the hardwood of the ancient trees, the fungi cups and corals colouring the ground, and the melodies of the birds that echoed from every direction. He felt as if he had nowhere to go, nothing to do, and no-one to be. The intense general whose voice constantly boomed in his head ordering him to do this or that task seemed to be on a much-needed vacation. The tender, mouse-sized part of himself was leading the show providing him with a refreshing perspective on things.

As he walked, deep geysers of gratitude would appear from within every once in a while when he noticed a mushroom he had never seen before or when he heard squirrels chirping in the trees. He didn't know why he was so fortunate to be getting the opportunity to explore the traumas of his past and relieve himself of some of their pain, but he believed that the nature around him had something to do with it. He wondered if other people got the same kind of opportunity, then began to *hope* that all others would experience what he was going through. These feelings of compassion for others felt completely new within him and it was as if he could see his old self on the verge of being mostly eradicated; a thought both exciting and terrifying.

As he went on, he saw something up ahead that looked different from the rest of the forest. He got closer and saw it was the same alleyway that he had found himself in with that unexplained bloody nose and Buffalo the raccoon. He was sad to be leaving the lush forest but knew that it was important to listen to Dr. Spruce's advice and head back into the town. As he passed through the alleyway and out into the street, he noticed the feelings in his body dramatically change. It was as if he could sense every atom of anxiety from the hurried passersby, the rushing cars, and the bustling stores. This was the first time he had noticed this and he wondered if this was the reason why he had been so averse to being around this type of society. Perhaps his body had always felt these unpleasant sensations but he had just been unaware of it, causing him to react by running from any conversation or situation that might bring them up once more.

He suddenly realized he had no idea where he was going. The only destination that seemed to make any sense for him to go to was Connor's house. That was, at least temporarily, his home. He walked through the streets in the direction of the home, observing the faces of the people he passed and attempting to smile at those whose eyes caught his. It was work that made him nervous and he only tried it with a handful of people before deciding it was a bit too much. The city didn't feel as disgusting as it usually did to him but more of a matter of interest. His mind started to mull over the incredible fact that everything he was walking through was an attempt by human beings to create some sort of home; somewhere that they could find comfort. Perhaps they had tried too hard and created something that was a little too false at times. As these curious thoughts floated around him, he was interrupted by a familiar voice.

"Martin!"

A little white cat ran up towards his legs and began to rub herself against them. He picked her up with a smile.

"Redbird!" It was Connor's cat. She was purring and Martin felt as if he were too.

After a moment of stroking, she looked at him with serious eyes.

"Martin, you must go straight to the police station. Detective Orchid has been on a hunt for you ever since Connor and Evaline declared you missing after the concert. The two of them are out looking for you right now but, the last I heard, Orchid is still in her office. Go! Now! I will find Connor."

She scrambled out of his arms and ran in the direction from which Martin had come. Had Connor and Evaline gone to the forest to look for him? As he looked around, he noticed that he was right across the road from the police station, and entered the greying building with a curious apprehension juggling around his lower torso. There were two serious-looking men at the front desk engaged in a heated conversation that seemed to be focused mostly on issues regarding race.

"Look at the statistics, man. It is obvious that there is something very wrong going on down in the States, but if I'm being real, I'd say it's messed up everywhere. If, in a certain state, the African-American population is, say, 28 percent of the population, but the amount of arrests of African-American people is 82 percent of the total arrests, that is absolutely based on discrimination." Martin heard an accent in his voice that seemed to place him from a Spanish-speaking country.

The other man wore a thick moustache and stood there sternly with his arms crossed. "Maybe that just reflects the nature of that population."

"That's the problem right there! See! You are the type of person that just exacerbates the problem." The man was enraged and rightly so, Martin thought. As the stern man was about to respond with another potentially hurtful comment, Orchid stepped into the room without noticing Martin's presence.

"Guys, this is not the time or place for this. It is an important discussion, but you must have restraint when people walk... through... the... door." She said these last four words almost in slow motion, as she had just noticed that it was Martin who had been the one to walk in. She rushed up towards him and embraced him with such love that for a moment he just found himself standing stock still. He shook off his shock and wrapped his arms around her as well. He felt warm and cared for, wanting nothing more than to remain there for as long as possible. They lingered in the gentle hug for some time, until Orchid pulled away and stared at him in the face.

"Where have you been, Martin?" She noticed his nose, which despite having been mostly healed by Buffalo's poultice, was still looking a little crooked. "That's where he punched you, eh?"

"Wait, who punched me?" As she mentioned this, Martin remembered that he still *couldn't* remember the events that led up to him being crashed on a mattress in that alleyway.

"Oh dear, you can't remember? It must have been some sort of punch to knock out your memories like that. I think we need to have a nice, long talk. Follow me to my office."

The two cops at the front desk were staring at the two of them, both with rather amused smiles plastered onto their faces. Martin glanced at them while following Orchid to her office, though he quickly looked down at the floor, focusing on the tenderness that was lingering in his chest. Perhaps he had left the peaceful forest too quickly as he was now feeling rather vulnerable being around all these watchful eyes. He shuffled behind Orchid into her office, feeling grateful when she closed the door behind them as he didn't feel ready to interact with anyone right now, especially those he didn't know at all.

When he dared to look up off of the floor and around the office, he was taken by how comfortable it all was. The two chairs on opposite sides of her desk were padded swivel chairs that had a colourful fabric sewn on them. The floor was carpeted and it was one of those shaggy white carpets that were the most feet-soothing textures in existence. He wanted nothing more than to sink his toes into the furry whiteness. It seemed that Orchid read his mind as she said,

"If you don't mind taking off your shoes before stepping on the carpet, it would be much appreciated."

"Don't mind if I do," he said quietly to himself, though Orchid heard this tiny comment and smiled brightly.

"Tea?" She offered and he nodded in acceptance. She turned on a small induction burner in the corner of the room with a teapot on top of it. There was a window to the left of this that looked over a small grassy area with a few spruce trees dotted around where a little sparrow was hopping around on the grass, sporadically pecking the ground. Martin smiled at this and felt a soothing feeling spread through the tender area in his chest. He looked around the office and noticed a wall on which a few interesting photos hung. The figures in the photos looked like they were important in some way but Martin wasn't sure who they were.

"Who are those people in the photos at the top?" He pointed up to a row of three photos that had caught his eye more than the others.

Orchid looked up from her tea collection and smiled once more, which caused a few butterflies to wake up in his stomach. Everything seemed to be affecting him much more dramatically than ever before.

"Those are my top three inspirations. On the left is Margaret Atwood." She pointed to the photo with a woman wearing a silvery glove that matched her wild grey curls. Next to her was a black-and-white picture of a strong, young man in a football uniform. "That one is Jack Kerouac and seated next to him is the love of my life, Isaac Asimov." The love of her life was sitting at a typewriter flashing a goofy smile at a camera while wearing a significantly large pair of white sideburns. Martin felt slightly jealous when she professed her love for this man but wasn't really sure why though the idea passed through his mind to attempt to grow similar-sized sideburns.

"Do you write here?" Martin coyly asked. He was interested in learning more about this woman, though he was immediately insecure about this inquiry as he thought that she might just want to discuss more official, police business. However, she seemed to be genuinely happy to talk to him in this manner, which was made obvious by the bouncy way that she plopped herself into her chair.

"I write *everywhere*." She said with a slight air of exasperation, though he could tell she also held pride in this statement. "I have to make sure to have all my spaces feel comfortable just in case I get a flash of inspiration. Though, to be honest, it's a little more difficult here as I don't want to be shirking any of my duties with the department. I tend to mostly write notes while on the job."

"Why are you a detective if you like writing so much?" More self-doubt flashed through him once he asked this as he was worried that this could be considered a question that probed a little too far. If someone had asked him a question like this when he was in New York, such as "why are you working in management if you desire so much to be a musician?" it may have sent him into a panicky spiral. However, this didn't seem to faze Orchid, which made him a little envious of how self-assured she was.

"When I was younger, I tried *just* writing, but I never felt inspired. 'Write what you know,' they say, but I didn't know anything. I was bored by everything that was coming out of me so I thought, 'let's make my life more exciting.' I trained to be a police officer, and somehow ended up quickly in the role of detective." She looked around her office as if she was still rather unsure of how she had got there. "I almost have too much to write about these days."

"I admire you," he said shyly. She flashed an appreciative smile at him and her cheeks flushed a rosy pink. He thought that his cheeks were probably the same colour. The whistling of the tea kettle interrupted this precious moment and she poured the boiling water into two mugs that made Martin laugh out loud. They were both faces of animals, with certain features of the face protruding from the mug. The part that made

Martin laugh was the fact that one was a bear and the other was a white cat. She handed him the bear mug and he looked at it, feeling rather excited about the synchronicity of this. As he drew the cup closer to him to observe the bear's face, he smelt a tantalizing mixture of lavender and bergamot emanating from the hot water. He felt the soothing sensations pass over him and was looking forward to the water cooling down so he could put a taste to that delicious smell. Orchid sat back down and pulled out two notebooks.

"So, Missing Martin. You've been gone for three days. Want to tell me what happened?"

He gave a small start and spilt a splash of hot liquid onto his lap. "Three days? How is that possible?"

"...did you forget that as well?"

"It seems I'm in the habit of forgetting things."

"What do you mean by that?" She asked curiously, starting to put her pen to paper.

"Um, well..." Feeling more like confiding than ever, he decided that it was necessary for him to tell Orchid about everything as the entire situation felt too much for one person to handle. "Promise just to listen and not say anything?" She nodded quietly and he suddenly felt tiny and afraid.

He started his story on the morning of the day he met Dr. Spruce, going into painful detail about the excruciating events of the morning that forced him to bust out into the forest on his ATV in search of something to shoot. As he reached the part about his first interaction with Dr. Spruce he felt a tension well up in his chest as if a wall was starting to be built, protecting him from revealing anything that might make him look like a lunatic. However, the tiny, tender mouse who also lived in his chest burrowed under the wall, giving him inspiration to continue. Once he had divulged his first encounter with the bear, he felt a huge wave of relief pass through him, though Orchid was writing furiously and he wondered insecurely what her notes said. In his imagination he saw:

- Martin thinks he talked to a bear
- Martin believes the bear is a therapist
- This man is crazy

However, he tried to shuttle these thoughts away from himself so he could continue with the story. If she was going to arrest him, send him to a mental hospital or whatever else happens to crazy people, so be it. At least he would get this story out to someone. Thus, he continued, telling her about his first glimpse of his memories of New York, Rose, and the like. He jumped over their first meeting at his burnt down house as she had also been there, moving further towards the moments before Evaline's concert, stopping the story just as Evaline's band was about to take the stage.

"For some reason, I have another blank spot in my memory here. All I know is that I ended up on a mattress in an alleyway with a bloody nose."

"Is it okay if I speak?" She said meekly.

He had forgotten that he had asked her to remain quiet and nodded his head up and down while saying, "of course, sorry." The storytelling was making him feel more vulnerable and he was grateful for an opportunity to take a quick break.

"I think I can tell you more or less what happened that night and it makes much more sense now based on what you've been telling me." She seemed more serious than earlier, which once again brought him the worry that she had placed him as a madman. "Connor came here when you had been gone for more than a day and told me that you were missing. He was really worried about you. He really likes you, you know." She looked at him and he looked away, suddenly embarrassed about all the mistreatment that he had given Connor. "As part of the missing person's report we filled out, I had him write down an account of what happened that night from his perspective. Do you mind if I read it?"

"No, of course." He was eager to know what had happened.

She cleared her throat, a little dramatically and he wondered if she had ever tried acting before. She changed her voice for the reading, sounding impressively similar to Connor. "'So, we were at the concert, and before we went in I played a little trick on the security guard. I regret this now. Everything seemed fine when we were there and we quietly waited for the show to start as the music was thumping and we would have had to shout to talk. When the lights went out to signal the show starting I looked over at Martin to maybe have a moment of excitement with him, but I saw that his eyes were bugged out. I mean, very wide. He seemed to have a significant amount of sweat on his forehead and as I looked a little closer I saw that his chest was moving a little too quickly. I yelled, "Martin, are you okay?!" He didn't look at me or respond whatsoever. His wide eyes were fixed on the stage so I thought that maybe he was just really excited. The band came on the stage and Evaline came to the centre. She looked really good.'"

Orchid paused for a moment and looked at him with a smile. "He had crossed that last part out but I thought it was cute so I read it." Martin was glad she did as he found it surprisingly pleasing that Connor might have taken to Evaline. "'A few minutes into the show, I looked back at Martin and he looked worse than ever. He was totally frozen with no colour in his face as if Mr. Freeze had shot him with his ice gun! I grabbed his shoulder and he jumped, looking terribly shocked. He looked at me and said "I have to go now" and he just booked it through the crowd. For a moment, I had no idea what to do and just stood there like an idiot with my mouth hanging open. Lucky no-one pulled out my tongue! Then, I made my way after him out of the front door. That same security guard was standing there and yelling down at Martin, who was literally laying on the ground, breathing heavily. I realized afterwards that he was totally having a panic attack. The security simpleton was saying, "GET OFF THE GROUND YOU SHOULDN'T BE HERE" but as soon as he saw me come out he got even angrier. He grabbed Martin by his shirt and pulled him up, which got me really riled. I tried to separate them but the halfwit just got angrier still and punched Martin in the face! He went to punch me as well but I managed to avoid it and get the idiot in some kind of hold, during which Martin ran off into the night. I tried to go after him but, when I let go of the cretin, he grabbed my arms and said he was going to call the cops. This didn't end up happening, but once I was free of all of this it was too late and I had no idea where to go to find Martin. I thought he may have ran back to my house or something, but I guess not..."

Orchid looked up at Martin and her features softened, signifying her sympathy for him. He felt embarrassed and didn't know what to say as he was sorry that Connor had to do that for him, worried that Evaline might hate him for running out of her show like he had run out of her house, and still thought that Orchid might think he was a psychopath. After some silence, she said,

"Seems like you've been through a lot of trauma, Martin. As we discussed once before, we all have our demons but something's been especially twisted in your mind, causing you to forget certain things, which I think explains the dramatic reaction you had here."

"Does it?"

"Of course. Think about it. From what you have told me so far, it sounds like this experience you had in New York has had a significant impact on you. Was this the first time you had been to a show since then?"

"Um, I don't know, but probably."

"Well, it makes sense that you had a panic attack. All of that trauma was brought up again."

"I guess you're right. Wow." He suddenly felt sad about the fact that he had had to go through all of these things. He wished that he could hug his younger self and make everything better.

"Wanna keep on going with what happened when you regained your consciousness in that alleyway? We can dissect it further once you're all done," she suggested.

"Sure," Martin said, although he felt he had been dissected enough the past few days. He continued recounting the events leading up to his second session with Dr. Spruce. It was difficult for him to explain the memories that he dredged up and, as he spoke of the panic attack at Austin City Limits in more detail, he started to feel some of that panic still residing in his chest. He realized that perhaps he hadn't released it all yet, a thought that greatly disappointed him. He had assumed that by going back into these past memories and experiencing them once again he would have fully rid himself of any of the trauma that still lingered inside of him. The same thing happened as he was telling the stories of Carly, parts of which almost brought him to tears, and when he ended he felt an element of anger bubbling and couldn't just let it sit there.

"I can't believe she told me she was pregnant." He slammed his fist down on the table in front of him, spilling a few drops of his tea, which he had forgotten about. "How could she do that? That is a disgusting way to manipulate someone." His hands were clenching in and out of a fist, and after this outburst he immediately felt guilty. "Sorry…"

Orchid looked up from her notebook and gave him a piercing look. "Never apologize to me for expressing yourself." She looked back down to her page and he felt a ripple of reassurance shudder through him. He was grateful that it was she who he was yelling this to as she held an air of serious maturity around her that was intermingled with a playful curiosity. He admired this and thought that he might attempt to cultivate this attitude himself.

"Thanks, Orchid. Well, that's pretty much the end of it. I opened my eyes after going through the last memory and Dr. Spruce was gone, so I just laid down and fell asleep. I felt so clean, as if I had been put through a washing machine. When I woke up, a butterfly messenger from Dr. Spruce told me to come back to the town, so I did just that. And now I'm here." He shrugged as if suggesting that everything he had just described was nothing to him. However, the truth was that he was feeling raw and insecure about disclosing all of these extremely personal experiences. He grabbed the mug of tea and sipped it slowly, unfortunately not paying too much attention to the delicious tastes that it offered, and instead focused on Orchid, waiting for a reaction. He was bracing himself for being called a nutcase or a freak. The room was quiet as Orchid stared at her notepad, making a few notes here and there, furrowing her brow as if she was trying to solve an extremely difficult Sudoku puzzle. Amidst the silence, Martin registered the background of insects buzzing and looked over to see the window was open slightly. Once again, the sounds of nature brought calm to his mind and he rested in this tranquil space until Orchid broke the silence a minute or so later.

"Martin, I just don't know what to say." She was still looking down at her notepad.

"You think I'm insane, don't you?" His chest tightened and he held his mug of tea with tense fingers.

"Of course I don't," she looked up at him and there were now droplets of water resting on the bottoms of her eyelids. She was crying? Why would she do that? "I just want to... this is... thank you for trusting me."

The same type of butterflies that a rollercoaster causes swooped up and down his esophagus in rapid succession. Tears welled up near his eyes as well but he felt afraid to let them fall so they ended up resting just out of eyesight.

"It's pretty obvious you've been hurt badly."

"It's nothing, really, I was young and have gotten over it by now." He was shocked that he said this as it was not what he actually wanted to say.

"Martin, we both know that's not true. These things from the past, they can linger for a seriously long time. Sometimes experiences like this can haunt people for their whole lives. My father was still struggling to reconcile a relationship from his late teens when he was on his deathbed. He tried his best to avoid any mention of it, but both my mother and I could see that it managed to infect him almost every day." This hurt her to talk about and she removed her gaze from Martin and glanced down at her notepad. "You're a very lucky guy to get to work through these things right now. Perhaps one day you can be free from their control, you know? Free to choose your own path."

"I don't know how it's possible. Like, if I have been affected by these things my whole life but haven't remembered any of them until now, how could they control me?" He felt like he already knew the answer to this but ignorance still lingered.

"The subconscious holds a lot of secrets that it doesn't share with us. Often, when I write characters, I focus a lot on what their subconscious looks like, and how that would drive their actions. It's not something that really gets written on the page often but it helps me create truthful characters."

Martin pondered this for a while as a bird sang a song from an outside tree.

"The thing about what you've told me that I don't really understand is why you have been unable to remember anything whatsoever. It's like you were some sort of strange newborn in a grown man's body, just going along without knowing anything about yourself."

"I knew that I liked peanut butter."

She laughed a little. Upon mention of this, he realized how hungry he was.

"Have I actually been gone three days?" He asked as the hunger grew stronger.

"Yeah, Martin, seems you were really deep in there."

"Well, I need to get something to eat or I won't be able to continue with any of this without slipping into unconsciousness again."

"Great. I'll take you to my favourite café."

The two of them left the office and, as they walked out of the front door, Martin overheard the racially-charged conversation between those two police officers was still going on. However, it seemed that the obstinate officer was being a little less racist than he had before. As they exited the building, he felt the hot sun on his skin and his eyes settled into a squint. Adjusting to the light, he noticed that someone dressed in dark clothing was running towards them. He shielded his eyes from the sun as Orchid threw on a pair of sunglasses. They both saw at the same time that it was Connor running towards them with Redbird at his feet. However, he wasn't the usual bubbly version of himself, in fact, he seemed terribly distraught and, as he ran closer, Martin saw that he had a bleeding gash in his right arm. He was panting as he arrived in front of them and looked straight at Martin.

"Martin, thank god you're okay. I would hug you but I don't want to bleed on you." Without a pause, he then said, "guys, something is very wrong. Evaline... Evaline got taken by a pack of wolves."

Chapter 16 - The Wolf Pack

Evaline felt like a heavy rock laid down on top of another heavy rock. Her eyes were jammed shut and as she moved her body slightly she felt tension in all of her joints. What the hell had happened? Her head was pounding, which pierced her memories like shards of glass. She blearily thrust her eyelids open with as much strength as she could muster, causing the pain in her head to expand. As it happened, opening her eyes did little good as she was surrounded by nothing but darkness. She tried to get her body to follow her commands and it slowly cooperated, bringing her up to a tense seated position. She slowly felt around on the ground with her hands, trying to decipher her location, but all she could feel was crunchy, hard rock. How did she get here? All of a sudden, she remembered, "the wolves!" A stifled cry escaped from her mouth and immediately she heard,

"Shhhh."

It was a soft, gruff sound that resonated with kindness.

"Who... who's there?" She asked hesitantly. Her eyes were beginning to adjust to the darkness, due to a fragment of light coming from far away. She focused on the area from which the sound had come and could see a large, dark lump.

"If you're too loud, our captors will not be happy." It was a whispery, gravelly voice that seemed very inhuman.

"Okay," she whispered. "Um...well, my name's Evaline."

"Call me Spruce."

The name brought up a memory of Martin mumbling about a talking bear. Could this be... could this be him?

"Um, do you happen to be a doctor... and a bear?"

"Why yes, I tend to be both of those things quite often." The murmuring voice was rather jovial, which confused Evaline, for she didn't understand how one could be joyous when trapped in the darkness by wolves.

"My friend... he mumbled some things about you but I wasn't really sure what he was talking about."

"Ah, Martin. He's a hard worker. I'm expecting him here soon."

The wind whistled through the cave and Evaline felt a cool breeze touch her cheeks, which made her notice that her pains were starting to ease slightly. She wasn't sure what he meant by expecting Martin but she didn't think to question it, instead wanting more details about her present situation.

"You mentioned our captors... Are they the wolves that attacked me and Connor when we were searching for Martin?"

"Yes, indeed. The same thing happened to me while I was searching for you."

"You were searching for us? But why?" Suddenly another question crossed her mind. "Wait a second... how am I talking to you?"

"Ah, dear Evaline, nature's abilities have no bounds." A flash of white appeared from his direction; a smile? "I began searching for you after a little bird told me that a pack of foreign wolves had entered into a place where they should not be, hot on the heels of a couple of humans."

"But then how did the wolves manage to get you? You must be pretty powerful yourself. From what I can see through the darkness, you are huge."

The bear made an odd coughing noise and muttered, "and I thought my weight loss regime was going well..."

"Oh, I'm sorry, I didn't mean..."

Dr. Spruce laughed softly, "I was just having a laugh, little one. It's good to laugh, especially in tough times like this. To answer your question, I allowed the wolves to take me."

"But why would you do that?!" Her voice raised in exasperation.

"Quieten down, dear Evaline. To have harmed the wolves would have caused significant damage to the relationships between our territories. There are others where they came from, who would not dare to enter here due to the treaty that was created many years ago. However, it seems that these ones are young, hungry, and reckless."

"If they're hungry, why didn't they eat us already?"

"Of that, I am not sure. Perhaps they want something," he said thoughtfully.

As if on cue, heavy breathing and a rough snarl appeared from the direction of the dim light, now blocked by a huge dark shadow, which Evaline recognized as one of the wolves. It seemed to be speaking, although unlike with Dr. Spruce, Evaline was unable to understand it.

However, when the bear responded with its own version of snarls and grumbles, she was made fully aware that they were communicating. After a short back and forth, the wolf's shadow disappeared from the front of the cave with an angry snap of its teeth.

"Yes, just as I thought." Dr. Spruce spoke once again.

"What did it say?"

"I find it such a shame when things like this occur. They're very cunning, those wolves. Supposedly they only followed you as they knew I would come running to your rescue. Now that they have me, they will only let us go if the rest of the council and I agree to forego the aforementioned treaty, allowing the wolves to hunt freely through this area. According to Sheeba, the wolf whom you just heard, the resources of their territory are depleting due to humans building some sort of pipeline through their land. Once again, it's all such a shame. I would love to allow them in here, but these wolves have a history of going a little wild with their hunting."

"Well, what is there to do?" Starting to see the surreality of this whole situation, Evaline felt suddenly nauseous while her body throbbed with increasing strength as her injuries diminished.

"I'm going to take a nap. You can do whatever you like." The calm and playful nature of his voice bothered Evaline. Take a nap? How would that solve anything? However, before she could protest she heard gentle snores emanating from his direction. She felt a sense of despair ripple through her while she tried to think of a plan. Despite her initial determination, her body and Dr. Spruce's example made her feel otherwise, enticing her to lie on her back once more. She felt a shroud of sleep spread over her like a thick, wooly blanket and, while she tried to throw it off, she had no success. Within minutes, she was fast asleep, though with her last seconds of consciousness she realized that she had not asked about Martin. Where could he be?

*   *   *   *   *   *   *   *   *

Martin narrowly avoided a few jagged shards of newly-broken glass as he stepped gingerly back into the alleyway from which he had emerged just an hour or two earlier.

"Watch your step," he remarked and looked back at Orchid, who was tight on his heels. Connor had been forced to stay back despite his protests, as the gash on his arm had been bleeding rather profusely. Orchid had rushed into the station, grabbed the two policemen at the front desk, and ordered them to drive him directly to the hospital. His protests were mired down by her ferocious determination and, holding his wounded arm, he had plopped down heavily into the police car with Redbird on his lap and the two of them immediately closed their eyes.

Before he had been placed in the car, he had given them a brief account of the events that had happened with the wolves. Rather woozily he explained to them that Evaline and Connor had been searching for him since the morning after the concert. Evaline had rightly assumed that Martin would have been out in the forest, as his curious dreamy mumbles about Dr. Spruce had suggested that this had been his destination during his recent disappearances. After some time, they sensed that they were being followed, and eventually found themselves surrounded by a pack of five nasty wolves, who immediately rounded them up and began to drag them towards some unknown destination. However, (and this was the part that made Martin even more frightened) a large bear who Connor swore had been wearing eyeglasses had come and pulled him away from the wolves, but not before one plunged its pointy teeth into his arm. Wounded, he had attempted to run back to help Evaline, but the bear had pushed him away so powerfully that he had bumped the back of his head on a tree and remained in a state of half-conscious awareness for a while afterwards. As he sat down on the ground and dimly observed the situation, he saw that the bear tried to get Evaline released but the wolves surrounded it as well, leading to its surrender. Both the bear and Evaline were dragged away and Connor had no idea what to do when he regained full consciousness half an hour later. Luckily, Redbird had found him and pulled at his pants with her teeth, implying for him to follow her, which resulted in his arrival at the police station.

Soon after, Orchid and Martin were well on their way to the forest for some kind of desperate rescue attempt. He had no idea what they were going to do if they managed to find the two of them, but was frightened to see that Orchid had brought her sidearm along with her.

She noticed his worry as she clipped it to her belt. "Relax. I've never had to use this on anyone and hope I never will. Perhaps a shot in the air will frighten these wild dogs."

As they moved towards the other side of the alleyway, the forest began to take over the walls, and both of them began feeling rather doubtful about this escapade. Neither wanted to divulge this to the other, so they just walked along in silence, stuck in their disconcerting thoughts until Martin broke the silence.

"Um, so what are we going to do?" He asked nervously.

She breathed out some relief. "Martin, I've really got no idea. This is pretty far out of my realm of comfort."

"Me too. I don't typically tend to fight packs of wolves."

She giggled a little and Martin softened his stance. Then to his surprise, he felt her hand in his. The already-softened Martin suddenly melted into butter, pooling onto the forest floor and seeping into the soil below. The bacteria and fungi living underground had never tasted butter before and were grateful for such a delicious treat. This buttery Martin was suddenly terribly afraid of the hand that was now touching his own. All types of memories and thoughts were barreling into his mind as if it were an extremely busy train station whose trains carried passengers that he was afraid to acknowledge. He saw different versions of Rose, Carly, and other relationships that he had forgotten about until now. They were waving to him but he didn't want to wave back. In fact, he couldn't wave back because his waving hand was being grasped by another. Martin had slipped into some strange daydream and was amazed by the imaginative nature of his mind as he hadn't thought like this in aeons. Sure, things had been newly sensitive and emotional but not creative, which made this feel new and rather exciting. Suddenly, without knowing why, he observed the feeling of his feet on the ground as well as his hand in Orchid's and he started to feel more grounded while the buttery train stories began to fade away. He was back in the forest, holding hands with a person whom he trusted. That was reality and for the first time for a long time - perhaps ever - he was happy with the reality in which he was living.

As he squeezed her hand, he began feeling confident in himself. These last few days had shown him that a lot more was possible than he thought, so maybe the two of them would actually prove quite capable in a battle against five wolves. But, what if there were more of them? His newly inspired mind began to form an idea.

"I just thought of something, Orchid." With the alleyway completely vanished behind them, they were now deep in the forest. "Keep your eyes out for any kind of creature. Well, preferably one who can move quickly. A bird, a butterfly, a squirrel, whatever."

"Yes, sir," she said while removing her hand from his to give him a jaunty salute. He felt a pang of regret when her hand slipped out of his, but fortunately it found its way back soon after. A few minutes later, she said, "there" in a hushed voice and pointed slightly to their left. What she was pointing at was a beautiful creature perched on a branch. It was fluffy and brown, looking almost like a weasel, and it was staring directly at them. Martin let go of her hand reluctantly and approached the animal with a light step, trying his best not to scare it.

Suddenly, he heard, "why are you walking in slow motion?" It was the creature and it had a lilting, comical voice.

"Oh... I didn't want to scare you."

The animal laughed and the sound ringed throughout the trees. The chortle lasted a long time and its following words were interspersed with more laughter. "You.. scare me? That's amazing. Yeah right. I'm the one you should be scared of." It bared some sharp teeth and Martin admitted to himself that yes, it was rather frightening.

"What's your name?" It asked pointedly.

"Uh, Martin."

The animal scowled. "You serious?"

"Serious."

"Well, here's the problem, my name is Marten too."

"Oh," Martin said with a curious inflection in his voice. "But why is that a problem?"

"I'd say too many Martens is two too many."

Martin realized he was being toyed with. He felt slightly impatient, but didn't want to ruin his chances so he went for the first idea that came into his head.

"Ah, but how do you spell your name?" Martin asked.

"Same as you, I'm guessing. M A R T E N."

"Well, I think everything will be okay then. I spell mine M A R T I N. It's different enough for there to be two of us here, don't you think?"

"I suppose so." A smile appeared on Marten's face. "So what are you doing here, Mar-*tin*?" he asked, emphasizing the 'i' in the name.

"I have reason to believe that two of my friends have either been captured...or killed by a pack of wolves. We are here to look for them. In fact, one of them you may know."

"Who, who, who?" The high-pitched voice showed a sign of excitement upon hearing this. Martin liked this Marten as he reminded him of Alice's Cheshire Cat.

"A great bear who goes by the name Dr. Spruce, although I'm not sure if he goes by that name all of the time or just with..."

"I know Spruce Engelmann. He is one of our Protectors. How could he have been taken?"

"This I don't know," Martin said solemnly. "Though I know it to be true. And what I need for you to do now is find the rest of the Protectors, along with a raccoon named Buffalo, and have them meet me in the fairy ring." He assumed that the fairy ring was well-known as it was undoubtedly a gorgeous place.

"You mean I've gotta run all the way to the centre of our territory?! I just had lunch!!!" Marten said coyly then smiled wide. "I'm just playin', see you in the fairy ring." And he was off. Martin turned back around to Orchid who was grinning at him incredulously.

"Wow, you really can talk to animals. I mean, I believed you when you told me, but I think we can only truly believe things when we experience them ourselves. I'm impressed."

She smiled and they walked on while Martin, hoping that he could remember the way to the fairy ring, tried to scour his surroundings for clues. He spotted a large red and white toadstool on his left and had a vague memory of being enraptured by this mushroom on his way into town a few hours earlier. Although those memories were a little foggy due to the drama of the day, he decided to be confident with his direction and keep moving north. There was a subtle mist that was weaving its way through the trees, adding another layer of mystique to the quiet forest.

"I'm curious, what did it sound like to you when I was talking to that marten?" He asked Orchid as they walked side-by-side and hand-in-hand.

"Funny, I was just thinking about that. Basically, you just matched the sounds that the marten was making."

"What?! That's crazy!"

"You're telling me." She said with a warm, dimpled smile. Despite the myriad of fears surrounding the wolves and the unknown state of Evaline, Orchid was feeling especially grateful to be in this situation. It was as if she was living in one of the books she had written. It was nice for her to not be fantasizing for once but, instead, be comfortable and present in reality. Martin was feeling this gratitude as well as being thankful that he was not feeling alone for once. Due to his trapped mind, he hadn't noticed the loneliness that had been welling up inside him for the past few years. Now that he was coming out of that personal prison, he could see how wretched this loneliness had often made him feel. The trees around them seemed to be breathing in this gratitude and breathing out soothing aerosols that made the two feel calmer and more confident.

"I never mentioned this when we were talking in your office, but before I became an asshole in New York, I would actually talk to animals a lot. From childhood, I was the one who could always talk to animals, and he could speak with the wind, the waves, and the earth."

"Who is 'he'?"

"My little brother, Albert." He stopped short in his tracks and suddenly felt a profound sadness rush up from his toes causing his body to shake slightly.

"What is it?" Orchid looked very concerned and stood to face him.

"I... I can't remember the last time I talked to him... or my parents. I just... forgot them too. Oh my god. I can't even imagine where they think I am." This time, the tears slipped upwards through his ducts and dropped delicately onto the soil below where a grateful small ghost pipe seedling sucked them in, causing it to grow half a millimetre in under a second. Orchid put her hands on his arms and had him look at her.

"Martin. As soon as we have figured out a way to rescue Dr. Spruce and Evaline, you can talk to them as there is nothing stopping you any more. Let those tears out as much as you need to and, once you're ready, we'll keep going."

A few more tears descended down his cheeks and he felt embarrassed that she was seeing him cry, but there was no way to stop this miniature waterfall. He found himself staring at her through the watery film and smiled lovingly.

"Thank you." She wiped the tears off his soggy face and, once again, he felt tiny, soft, and delicate. Many flutters of nervousness were floating through his body, passing through his arms, chest, and legs. He knew what he wanted to do, but was terrified of the repercussions. He tried to convince himself that this was not the right time, that there were more serious things to do, but this argument felt weak and immediately dissipated. So, with a disregard for the nerves, he softly kissed Orchid and felt the sensations of his body transform into tingles of joy. She returned the kiss, just as softly, allowing Martin to pass some of the wetness of his face onto hers. They pulled apart and Martin was still crying, though the tears seemed to have a different character. Light smiles passed between them and they stood there for a few seconds until they heard a cacophony of noise traveling to them from the west. Though the sounds could have been wolves rushing towards them, Martin was certain that these were the Protectors, rushing to the fairy ring. He looked up ahead and saw that they were closer than he thought.

"We must go, the fairy ring is up there."

Orchid looked at him amusedly and confusedly and he realized he hadn't actually told her what he had discussed with Marten. As they made their way quickly to the fairy ring, he quickly explained his idea. Busting their way out into the open space encircled by the ring of orange mushrooms, he was struck with profound shock by what he saw. The animals that were standing around the ring seemed larger-than-life.

There were four of them - a moose, an osprey, a lynx and, to Martin's surprise, a wild horse. On the back of the horse sat Buffalo, who gave him a friendly wave. Marten flashed a smile to them from on top of the moose's head.

The moose spoke immediately. She had a gentle but stern voice that resonated through Martin's body. "Martin. It is good to meet you. We are the Protectors of this territory."

Chapter 17 - In Search of Peace

They had Martin and Orchid sit down around the ring, then quickly introduced themselves. The moose's name was Ellian, the osprey called himself Cranberry, the lynx was Adelaide, and the horse was Ta Wee. Without any further ado, they began discussing the situation at hand.

"Marten tells us that you believe our beloved Spruce has been stolen or even murdered by a group of wolves," spoke Ta Wee melodiously.

"Yes, along with our friend - another human," Martin replied.

"The wolves do not enter our territory. They have always respected our treaty," Cranberry retorted fiercely with a brief flap of his wings.

Adelaide was next to contribute. "Those *dogs* have always wanted this land, though. As we discussed in our last council, I witnessed a small pack of them sniffing around the border about a month ago."

"Spruce had many good words to say about our new friend Martin here. I choose to trust him, though even if it's true, we do not know where they could be keeping them prisoner. If they managed to get them over to their own land, it would be very dangerous for us to go there."

"It's also possible that they have already eaten them," Buffalo chimed in hesitatingly, causing a gloom to pass around the circle.

Martin had been translating everything being said to Orchid and she exclaimed, "there must be something that we can do!" Martin quickly translated this back to the animals, who all remained quite silent. All of a sudden, a small, familiar voice emerged from the middle of the ring. As Martin looked closer, he saw it was the same butterfly messenger who he had met previously.

"It is good you are all here together. I have a message from Spruce. He and the human girl, Evaline, are safe. However, they are being kept in the Forgotten Cave, near the edge of our land, to be used as a currency with which the wolves can negotiate with the Protectors for a removal of the treaty."

"Removal of the treaty?!" Marten piped up. "We can't do that! My family and I will be eradicated by them."

"Marten, we shall not allow this." Ta Wee spoke reassuringly. "Come now all, we must go to the Forgotten Cave to speak to the wolves."

Martin, Orchid, and the animals all got up to leave when the butterfly spoke once more.

"Not you, Martin. You are to stay. Your work here is not finished."

This immediately triggered something inside Martin causing him to feel dismayed and betrayed.

"What do you mean? I have to come with them, I am no use here. Those are my friends that are trapped by the wolves! You can't tell me what to do, you stupid little butterfly." He threw a small pebble towards the direction of the butterfly.

Ellian turned back around to face Martin and a tremor of fear passed through his bones. The moose was gargantuan; at least twice the size of any moose he had ever seen, and the look she was giving him accentuated her magnitude.

"If Spruce wants you to stay here, you stay here. You are no help to us if your work is unfinished."

His gusto had drained out of him and he had nothing left in him to argue this point, though he did have something else to question.

"What about Orchid?" He gestured over to her. "What is she to do?"

"Stay with you." Cranberry spoke from Ellian's left.

"And do what? Last time I was in my own head for three whole days."

"It will be different this time," Ellian spoke once more and turned around to leave. Orchid looked at Martin confusedly since he hadn't been translating for her during his outburst. He explained the situation and she nodded satisfactorily.

"Makes sense," she said matter-of-factly.

"What do you mean it 'makes sense'? We should be helping our friends, not sitting around doing nothing in a dumb ring made of mushrooms." He kicked one of the mushrooms but the resilient little thing stayed right in its place.

"Martin, you and I both know that you aren't going to be doing nothing. Besides, I'll be fine. I have a notebook with me and I'm sure that if you're in there too long I can find something to eat around here." She looked around curiously and then back at Martin. "I wrote a book once about a character who was a master of forest foraging, so I had to study it quite in depth myself. All of these mushrooms below us are both edible and quite delicious, though I wouldn't want to ruin the magic of this pretty fairy ring."

The animals had already gone on their way during this brief conversation and Martin looked hesitatingly at their silhouettes through the trees, his body twitching with agitation. He knew that he had to trust Dr. Spruce as he had done him well so far, but it was painstakingly difficult to be left behind like this.

"It hurts to be left behind..." he said shyly to Orchid while kicking around a little rock on the ground. She came close to him.

"Oh, Martin, of course it does. But from what you've told me, I don't think you're really being left behind here. You've got some good, fruitful work to do, and perhaps whatever you discover may help this whole situation get resolved."

Martin breathed out a sigh and reluctantly made his way to the centre of the fairy ring. As he peered at the soil, he noticed that two out of three of the places that Dr. Spruce had drawn in the soil had been swept away. They were the two that he had previously visited and the unknown one that remained now had some writing underneath it. Delicately written into the soil were the words, "what do you want?" Had those been there before? If so, he hadn't noticed them. He supposed this was the next question that he was to attempt to answer so he settled himself down onto the spongy ground and whispered, "what do I want?" Orchid took a seat next to him and looked at the writings in the soil. She smiled but didn't question their meaning, allowing Martin to close his eyes quietly and settle into whatever was to happen. As his consciousness started to slip away from him, he realized with a slight shock the location of that final drawing. With an anxious tightness holding his chest, he slipped into his past once more.

$$*\quad *\quad *\quad *\quad *\quad *\quad *\quad *\quad *$$

"Papaya?" said the man at the fruit stand, pointing to an extremely mouldy yellow and green fruit that rested on top of a large pile. Martin stared at the mould with an uncertain disgust, assuming that this fruit would be particularly unappetizing.

"Yes. We'll take the one on top," said Albert while smacking his lips. He turned to Martin and said, "the best ones are the mouldy ones, you see."

They sat on the side of the busy road and split the papaya in two. The shopkeeper had lent them a knife to cut open the soft skin and reveal the pinkish orange fruit inside. Martin made an effort not to touch any of the mould, though this attempt proved almost impossible. A few of the seeds rolled onto the floor and Martin thought that they looked an awful lot like caviar.

"You can try the seeds if you want but they taste a bit too much like black pepper for my liking," Albert said while chomping into the flesh of the papaya, letting the juices drip stickily down the sides of his mouth.

Martin looked at his share of the fruit once more and picked up one of the seeds. It seemed to have a gelatinous casing over its black centre. He popped it into his mouth and bit on it. Despite the warning, he didn't find it too distasteful, though it definitely had a strong taste of pepper. He ate a few more of them and scraped the rest onto the floor. Perhaps a stray dog would find them to its liking. He allowed a quick glance at Albert to make sure he was doing it right, then bit into the flesh, making an earnest effort not to have any juice spill out of his mouth.

Upon contact with his taste buds, he was floored by the smooth sweetness that excited his senses.

"As well as being mighty delicious, these are sooo good for your digestive system." Albert said, having finished his half of the giant fruit. Albert had only been in India for a week before Martin had arrived but already seemed to be an expert on everything here.

"Even better," Martin said as he had always had problems with his digestive system and knew that this trip to India would not be easy on his gut. Since stepping off of the plane, he had only had one meal, but he was already experiencing the ramifications of the foreign food. He looked at Albert and smiled.

"It's nice to see you, Bert."

Bert returned a smile and nodded. It had been almost a year since Martin had seen his little brother, who had moved up to Canada for university when Martin had moved to New York. However, in an unexpected turn of events, Bert had invited Martin to join him for a couple of months in India. A friend that he had made at university had a brother who lived in India who was having a lavish wedding to which Bert had been invited - along with a plus one. Martin had been back from New York for just a month when he had received the invite and immediately took him up on the offer. Since his sudden departure from the big city, Martin had been feeling depressed and dejected without any clue of what to do next and a trip to the holy land of India seemed like a great idea amidst all of this. After the wedding, the brothers were planning on visiting some of the old Buddhist sites and monasteries in the north of the country.

"You good on the papaya?" Bert asked. "We can always get another, they're ridiculously cheap."

"I'm good. Let's get to the hotel, I need to lay down."

Bert stepped out into the obscenely busy street and hailed an auto rickshaw, threw Martin's large backpack in the back, and stepped in. The driver had a colourful picture of Shiva hanging down from his rear view mirror surrounded by a plethora of beads of all shapes and sizes. He turned towards them and smiled a kind semi-toothless smile.

"Where to, my friends?"

Bert gave him the address and he zoomed off through the streets. Martin couldn't understand how the drivers were able to manoeuvre through these rickety roads without smashing into each other. It seemed as if a regular two-lane road was being occupied by four or five lanes of traffic, including all types of multicoloured vehicles from large honking buses to slim speedy bicycles. He had been here just under twenty-four hours but was already struck by the vast differences between this world and the one from which he came.

"So," Bert began, having to raise his voice slightly over the sound of the world whizzing by. "I understand if you don't really want to talk about this just yet, as I gathered from mum and dad that you had a pretty traumatic time, but how come you left New York? I thought doing all that was your dream."

"I thought so too," Martin looked down at his lap sadly. "Until I didn't. Long story short, I was way too stressed. I tried to become like the rest of the people that surrounded me but I couldn't handle it. I was working seven days a week, never having an honest conversation, and having regular panic attacks, then using weed as a way to bypass all of this pain. Then, all at once, I just changed. Foggy, my boss there, was talking about how this meditation app had suddenly made tons of money, and I thought I'd download it and try it out. I'd never tried meditating but I was pretty hooked right away. The big moment for me was when I was sitting in my apartment, meditating in the morning, and all of a sudden I could just hear police sirens. It was incredible."

"You found police sirens so beautiful that it made you leave New York?" Bert said with a confused smile.

"Uh, no, what I mean is that for the first time in I don't know how long my mind was just quiet. Just for a moment. And I could just hear the world around me. It was amazing, though it didn't last long. Something about that small moment changed me and helped me see how much I was suffering up there. A month later, I was gone. It was a tough decision and I'm still struggling with it, but I think it was good. I just..." He paused momentarily. "I just don't know what I'm going to do now."

"Well, you're about to go to a crazy Indian wedding then visit a bunch of peaceful monks. I'd say that you're stuck with some awesome things to do for the next two months. Why don't you just try not to worry about the future until after this trip?"

"Easier said than done, Bert."

When they arrived at the hotel, Martin was fairly disappointed. Bert had promised a glamorous wedding, rich with gourmet food, elaborate gifts, and the like. However, the hotel was slightly rundown, and there was even talk between Bert and the receptionist that Martin was going to have to sleep in a tent on the roof, due to the lack of space in the hotel. This idea was immediately demolished when Bert offered to share his room with Martin. Bert looked at him apologetically then explained that since they were not actually related to the groom, they didn't get the best digs. The room wasn't that bad and Martin collapsed onto the bed upon arrival, entering a quick and deep slumber.

*   *   *   *   *   *   *   *   *

Martin swatted at yet another mosquito that was fighting its way through the breeze to feed on his blood. He breathed out in exasperation.

"These mosquitoes are so frustrating."

Bert turned to him. "Yeah, I know what you mean. I'm trying to get accustomed to it like everyone else seems to be, but it just irritates me so much when I feel that pin prick on my skin."

"It's not even that it hurts, I just don't like the idea of them taking any of my blood."

"My precious blood!" Bert said with a hint of Gollum in his voice. The brothers laughed and turned a corner. All of a sudden, their view was overwhelmed by one of the biggest hotels that Martin had ever seen. It had a freshly manicured lawn behind its imposing walls. The only entrance to the hotel seemed to be through a security checkpoint where a lone guard was interrogating everyone who attempted to enter. The hotel was at least twenty floors high and painted a dazzling white while grand pillars showcased its lavish entrance. It was a stark contrast to the surrounding area. Just around the corner from which Bert and Martin had come was an extremely impoverished community with nothing but tents for homes, dust and grime covering everything and everyone, as well as a number of small fires dotted around that seemed about to lose control at any moment. Seeing this had made Martin rather uncomfortable and he had done his best to avert his gaze from any of the residents of the tent village.

The ceremony was taking place at this hotel and was poised to be an all-night affair, according to Bert. Martin hoped they wouldn't have to stay all night as the past few days had already exhausted him no end. The wedding had lasted a week so far, with countless events littered through each entire day. They had been carted around on rickshaws, mopeds, and large buses to different locations throughout the city and beyond. Each event had had its own purpose and reason to celebrate, but one thing remained the same: the food. Since Martin had arrived in India, his anxiety had flared up considerably, due to the newness of everything as well as the ever-pervasive uncertainty about his future. Thus, at each event, he would immediately shuffle his way over to the buffet and gorge himself on the piles of palak paneer, mountains of mushroom matar, and delicious dishes of dosa. The invitees were from all over the country, and were quite particular to their regional styles of food, so each event had featured different dishes from all of these regions, and Martin felt he had to try each and every one. As a result, Martin was having significant issues with his digestive systems (despite the papaya) and the bloated feelings, as well as the mosquitoes, were keeping him up for most of the nights.

However, this event was supposed to be the final event of the ceremony, and Martin was determined to attempt to enjoy it in whatever way possible, if only for the sake of Bert. It had been his suggestion for the two to come to this wedding, and the main reason that they were both in India, so he didn't want his brother to have any sort of regretful feelings. He patted his stomach as they walked up to the gate, silently telling it that this was his last day of indulgence and for the rest of the time in the country he would take gentle care of himself. As they approached, the security guard did a full body search of Martin but allowed Bert to pass through with not so much as a second glance. Bert found this hilarious and laughed his way up to the entrance.

This event was the busiest one yet and Martin was envious of the guests who had only come for this one event, saving their energy for the final show. The brothers grabbed heaping plates of food and went out to sit on the sunny, green lawn. Martin's anxiety seemed to settle slightly as the mixtures of spices tickled his tongue and he patiently allowed one lone mosquito to settle down on his right forearm and enjoy a little lunch as well. Bert noticed this and asked,

"Martin, I've been meaning to ask but never found the right time. Are you still communicating with animals?"

Martin felt a deep shame rush through him. He had hoped they wouldn't have to discuss this. "Um… no. I kinda… stopped when I was in New York. I was… I was embarrassed."

A flash of sadness passed over Bert's face, but he made an effort to hide it as soon as it showed. However, Martin had spotted it, causing his feeling of shame to cut deeper. The fact that they were the only two people that they knew who could communicate with the natural world had created a strong bond between them ever since they were young. Neither had felt alone since the other one understood.

"I've tried a bit since I got back. It just… doesn't seem to work anymore. It's like there's some kind of wall that I built up and now I can't break down."

"Maybe with time it'll come back," Bert said hopefully.

"Maybe," Martin said, though he was doubtful. His desperate attempts to become like all those around him in New York had forced him to create impenetrable structures around the more empathetic parts of his mind.

A few minutes later, with their plates half-finished, the brother of the groom rushed towards them and forced them to go to the front of the hotel to join the parade. What then ensued was a three-hour long dance party along the streets, where the entire wedding party danced around the groom sporting a white sultan-like outfit bedazzled with gems, sequins, and bangles while riding a gigantic white horse. Martin attempted to duck out of the party a number of times due to the hot sun and the sweaty dancing, though he was always dragged back in by an unknown uncle or cousin. He and Bert had been attacked with attention by the guests since the beginning of the wedding, due to the fact that they were foreigners. Since he had arrived, Martin had been asked to take countless selfies and answered the question "where are you from?" so many times now that he had started to make up the answer just to make things slightly more interesting. He tried not to get upset with the people who requested these things, as he knew that they were just curious, but he was so worn down by the end of all of it that the distaste for this attention was evident in his voice.

After the dance party, the "show" began on a massive stage behind the hotel. Martin couldn't believe what he was seeing. He had thought that past week's celebrations had been elaborate but this one took it to another level. It was like being at a music festival, with fireworks, song and dance routines by the bride, the groom, and all kinds of relatives, and very long performances designed solely to hype up the audience. All of this was bringing back bad memories for Martin and he began to get quite agitated. Bert noticed this after some time and put his arm around him with a look of guilt. Bert feeling guilty for bringing him here is exactly what Martin didn't want. He began to ridicule himself for his ridiculously sensitive state and wished momentarily that he could just forget everything that had happened in his past and just start afresh.

*   *   *   *   *   *   *   *   *

The ever-changing landscape was whizzing past Martin's eyes, showcasing quick flashes of arid, dry fields, stifled shanty towns and acres of well-tended farms. They had made it through the wedding and were heading up into the northern parts of India in an attempt to find some more peaceful places to dwell. The day after the wedding, the groom's brother had attempted to convince them to stay another week, suggesting more parties and dancing. Bert had almost taken him up on this offer, but declined after noticing Martin's painfully evident look of protest.

"You know, I'm actually really grateful we didn't stay," Bert said from the bunk above Martin. The train journey was over 15 hours so they had been given beds to sleep in during the ride. "I was almost convinced to stay, for as you know, I love a good party, but having left I realize now how exhausted I am. I just wanna go learn to meditate with some chilled-out monks."

Martin smiled upon hearing this and closed his eyes. "I love you, Berty," he said quietly. "I'm glad to be here with you."

"As am I," said Bert, glancing down at Martin with the purest love written all over his face.

They closed their eyes and rested until they were suddenly woken up by a yelling that echoed through the entire train.

"Chai chai chai garam chai chai garam garam chai garam chai."

Martin and Bert woke up with a start causing Martin to bang his head on the bottom of Bert's bunk.

"What the hell is going on?" Martin said groggily, rubbing his eyes and noticing a little cake of dirt which had formed in the corner of the left one.

The answer came quickly as the chai chanter came towards them, offering small cups of milky black tea for the passengers. Bert bought two cups and they sat together on Martin's bunk, sipping the sweet, spiced drink. When they finished, the train slowed and Bert peered out of the window.

"Oh, shoot, Martin, we're here. Get your stuff, let's get outta here."

They had noticed at previous stations that the train often wouldn't stop for very long, so they rushed to gather their things and hopped off the train into the blazing sun. The train station read PATHANKOT on its colourfully-tiled walls and as Martin glanced around he noticed a number of food stalls set up whose vendors were delivering meals through the barred windows of the train to the passengers. He smiled at this, remarking to himself how fascinating this country was. With everything so different from anything he had known previously, he was having some difficulty in adjusting, but was also inspired by such curiosity.

"OK, we gotta get on a bus now that will take us up to the mountains." Bert said, reading the travelling notes that he had carefully created before coming to India. Martin was grateful that he was not the one leading them around, as he felt entirely incapable in this wild country. Bert looked at him with a mighty smile and said, "can you believe it? We're going to the Himalayas!"

Chapter 18 - The Mountains of Madness

Soon after the bus exited the bustling city of Pathankot, the scenery that began to emerge out of the suburbs took Martin's breath away. The first thing that he was struck by was the dazzling green of the leaves, plants, and grass that hugged the sides of the narrow upward-winding roads. As they ascended, the roads got skinnier, fuelling Martin's anxiety as the bus hurtled round corners, honking its horn as it went. He took a look at the bus driver, who seemed like a meek middle-aged man with a tight moustache and no sign of a smile. Martin wondered if he had dreamed of being a race car driver as a child as it sure seemed that way. But then again, most of the drivers he had witnessed in India drove like this. Perhaps they all wanted to be race car drivers.

They were off to Dharamshala, famous for being the home of the Dalai Lama since his exile from Tibet. Bert was especially excited about an event that took place in the gardens of his monastery every afternoon. Supposedly the monks who lived there would settle themselves in the gardens for a few hours and spend the time arguing with fellow monks or any passersby who desired to find themselves in a heated discussion. It was meant to be a wholehearted debate about topics related to their studies, but Martin was imagining the group of monks screaming at each other about all types of things that they weren't allowed to talk about at other times of the day. It sounded like a good way to vent some anger. Dharamshala was quite a tourist destination, as one might expect, but Bert told Martin that it was just a way station on their journey. He was set on the fact that they were going to meet a beautiful monk dressed in red and gold who would invite them to their secret monastery deep in the mountains, and this is where their real adventure would begin. Martin was skeptical about this as his disappointment in his "New York moment" had broken his imagination and he didn't want to have any more lofty expectations that might let him down once more. They climbed higher into the hills and Bert, seated next to Martin on the leathery bench, turned to him.

"All these bushes around us, do you know what they are?"

"No idea," said Martin, noticing now that all of the vegetation around them was the exact same. The bushes were large, green, and seemed to go on for miles.

Suddenly, the head of a young man appeared in between Martin and Bert. He had clambered slightly over the seat behind them with a huge grin on his face. Martin closed his eyes and hoped he wasn't going to ask them for a selfie. Pictures of him must have been on at least a hundred random phones scattered around India by now and it was getting a bit much.

"Tea," was all he said.

"No thanks," Martin said, brushing him off with slight agitation.

"No, all of those bushes are tea."

"Ohhhhhhhh, cool," Bert said with true amazement in his voice.

"Can I join you in your seat?" He said in an accent that made him sound more like he was from England than India.

Martin was already getting pretty warm and knew that adding a third to the seat would only make this worse. He was about to say no when Bert scooted close to Martin and said,

"Definitely!"

The boy was nicely dressed and had a radiant smile. He looked at the two for a little while, then thrust out his hand.

"My name is Vipul."

Bert grabbed his hand with both of his in an expression of warmth. "I'm Bert and this is my brother Martin." Martin shook his hand, though not as warmly as Bert had.

"Where are you going?" Once again, this guy surprised Martin as typically the first question that he had been asked after taking a selfie was "where are you from?"

"Well, we're going to Dharamshala," said Bert with slight embarrassment. "But, we are planning on meeting some cool monks and getting invited to a hidden monastery in the mountains."

Vipul's eyes brightened and he smiled even wider.

"You shouldn't do that."

"Why not?" Martin said with slight irritation as the heat was getting to him and he was also acutely aware of the hunger that was building up within him.

"Because, my friends, I will show you the way."

Martin felt relieved as he felt the bus slowing down and saw it turning off into a small area with a restaurant, a little shop and bathrooms. The bus stopped and Vipul hurriedly got up, saying,

"I will buy you a map and we will meet back here in fifteen minutes."

Martin and Bert got off the bus soon after and headed straight to the restaurant. The food was fairly tasty, though nothing compared to what they had been eating at the wedding. However, Martin found this to be a good thing as he managed not to overindulge himself this time despite the fact he treated himself to a giant deep-fried samosa. As they were eating, Martin spoke to his brother in a hushed voice.

"We can't trust him, we've gotta keep going to Dharamshala."

"What are you talking about?" Bert said incredulously. "This is what we've been waiting for. Sure he's no monk, but if he is going to show us how to get to some secret palace, fortress, or cave then we *have* to follow what he says. It's the classic spiritual journey! Let go, my sweet brother!"

"But what if he's just like one of those other mosquito men that are just trying to trick us into getting our money?!"

Bert laughed a little and said "mosquito men". He knew what Martin was talking about. It seemed that at every turn there was a small group of men who buzzed in their ears about buying some special item or taking a taxi to some fancy location.

"Let's just talk to him a bit more. If you don't feel comfortable after further discussion, we don't have to go."

They got back on the bus and found Vipul against the window on the seat in which they had all been sitting. He was writing in a notebook and circling locations on a small map. When he saw them, he smiled and got up, allowing them back in their places. Martin was grateful for this gesture, as he found it helpful to have the breeze from the window cool his warm head.

"So, boys, I am your trusty travel guide," he said while showing them the map.

Martin's skepticism began to return and he couldn't help but say, "Hey Vipul, we've already got a destination so if you're trying to get some money from us or send us to some trashy hotel in the middle of nowhere that your friends own, we're not having it."

Vipul was a little startled by this but didn't look hurt. He repaid the harsh words with a compassionate smile.

"My friend, I want nothing from you other than to send you on the journey that you have been dreaming of. You see, my older brother took up robes seven years ago. He *lives* in this 'secret' monastery that you have been fantasizing about. It's way up here." He pointed to a location on the map that looked to be very deep in the Himalayas, considerably close to Tibet. "If you make it up there, they will welcome you with open arms, especially if you mention my name." With this, he winked at the two.

"It looks far up there!" Bert exclaimed. "That's awesome. But how do we get there?"

"It is quite a journey. At least four separate bus rides after this one. It may take you four or five days, but the entire journey will astound you."

"Hey Vipul, if you don't mind me asking," Martin started curiously as his doubt had receded slightly and he was willing to be slightly more amiable. "How come you speak *such* good English? I mean, I know English is the second language here, but I haven't met many people who speak it like you do."

"Ah, well, I only live in India for six months of the year. The other half I am an engineer on a ship that travels around the globe. I have had numerous interactions with many native English speakers and have learnt along the way."

"Vipul, you are so cool. If you want to become my best friend, I'd be one hundred percent up for that," Bert said excitedly. "Can't you come with us to the monastery?"

"My friends, I would if I could, but I am actually going to be setting off to sail at the end of this month. I have been visiting a friend down in Pathankot for some time and must return to spend the last few weeks with my family." Then he made a face as if a great idea struck him. "In fact, would you join me at my family's home for dinner this evening?"

Martin started, "Uh, I don't know, if this is going to be a long trip..."

"Marty, you're always in a rush." Bert turned to Vipul. "Absolutely, yes."

"Wonderful. We can discuss your journey in further detail. In fact, the best place to start for your journey is the town in which my parents live."

About an hour later, they disembarked the bus together and were welcomed by another young man, whom Martin assumed to be Vipul's brother. It turned out he was just a good friend named Guri who was a beautifully poetic English speaker. He drove them to Vipul's house and spoke for the majority of the time about the splendours that they would see on their way to the monastery, as well as teaching them about the culture of the area in which they had arrived. As Martin sat in the backseat, he felt a pang of joy that he had not felt in a long time, bringing light to the thought that perhaps good things could happen to him after all. These friends they had made seemed like incredibly honest, trustworthy people, which were qualities that he had not found in many others for a long time.

Before they went to Vipul's home, they pulled off to the side of the road for a refreshing drink of sugar cane juice. Martin watched with fascination as the owner of the cart grabbed massive sugar canes, rested fresh mint and lime gently on their surface and folded them in two. Then he thrust them into a machine, which ground the juices out of this mixture. Martin was slightly nervous to try the drink but when he had a taste he was flummoxed as it was spectacular and fathoms better than any sugary drink that he had ever had. When he was finished he wanted another and without having to mention it, Guri ordered him one and even paid for it. Martin's wounded mind was starting to feel slightly soothed, even more so when they went to a nearby river and splashed around in the cool waters until the sun started to descend. Martin even braved a full submersion into the chilly river, which livened him up and caused him to laugh at most anything anyone was saying.

Soon after, they arrived at Vipul's warm, small home and Guri bid them farewell. Martin was sad to see him go, but he promised he would see them again. Vipul's mother Arya welcomed them with such joy. It seemed that it was no trouble in the slightest for them to be there and, in fact, he learnt as they arrived that they would even be staying the night. Vipul's parents were going to sleep in Vipul's room, he was going to sleep on the sofa, and the brothers were going to take the parent's room. Martin attempted to protest this but Vipul whispered, "don't even try." As his kind mother continued the preparations for what looked to be a large feast, the brothers settled in and sat with Vipul in the living room.

"Vipul, I don't see why we have to take your parents' room," Martin mentioned as soon as they were inside. "I feel uncomfortable getting this kind of treatment."

"Well, they'll feel uncomfortable if you do anything otherwise. Here in India, for many families, guests are God. You will have to get used to being treated this way. It's how we are and it's truly wonderful if you allow yourself to yield it."

Martin attempted to see the beauty in this, which was much easier when they were presented with the evening meal. It was a wide spread of food featuring all kinds of curried vegetables including cauliflower, okra, and potato, which Martin learnt were called gobi, bhindi, and aloo, respectively. Delicious fresh-made rotis were delivered to them throughout the meal as well as endless servings of steaming rice and refreshing raita. Vipul's parents did not sit with them as his mother was the one serving and cooking this food, and his father was settled in the living room in his white tunic watching cricket with a cigarette. It was tough for them not to stuff themselves silly, especially due to the almost-intense encouragement to "eat more" by Arya, but they managed to eat well and even have enough space to go out for ice creams after dinner. Before they left, Martin attempted to offer to clean up the meal but was given a strong, cold look by Arya and Vipul pulled him away, once again reminding him that he *had* to play his role as a guest or he would be in some serious trouble.

*   *   *   *   *   *   *   *   *

The rickety bus clanked into action and Martin and Bert were on their way once more through the mountains. They had ended up spending three nights at Vipul's place, enjoying their days with Vipul and Guri, as well as the continuously impressive food that Arya cooked for them. They had barely talked to his father, who seemed to spend the majority of his time watching cricket, but the mother had opened up to them and had even allowed Martin in the kitchen for a time to teach him a handful of her cooking secrets. The time had been absolutely joyous for the two brothers and they finally felt as if they were experiencing the real India. The largesse of the wedding had left a sour taste sitting in Martin's mouth and he had begun to have strong judgements towards the country as a whole. However, this time out in a small town with real, honest people had lifted his hopes up and given him more of a hop in his step. After a sad goodbye with their new friends, they were off on their long journey up to the monastery, which was near a tiny village called Ribba close to the Tibetan border. Their friends had even suggested they hop into Tibet afterwards, as although it is often restricted to many, they would be able to get special visas that would allow them to cross the Tibetan Himalayas.

Guri had told them that there were two ways to get to the monastery, one would take significantly longer than the other, and this was the one that he highly recommended. The shorter road would mostly consist of passing through similar-looking towns and landscapes, but the longer trip would thrust them straight up into the mountains, where they would visit gorgeous locales where many travellers did not go. He had to do a little more convincing on Martin's end but they had eventually decided they would take this route. They spent the majority of the first three days on buses, transferring in different towns, while quickly grabbing their typical road snacks of samosa, papaya, and fresh glasses of sugar cane juice, then spending their nights in the towns that Guri and Vipul had marked off on the map. The second day was rough for Martin as something he had eaten had transformed his digestive system into a whirlwind of pure madness, causing it to desire a bathroom stop every thirty minutes, something which was impossible on these kinds of buses. He was quiet most of the day, attempting to calm down his angry body, and was grateful when Bert suggested they stay in a closer town than the one they had planned to stay so that Martin could rest and have quicker access to a toilet. The sickness had mostly passed by the next day, and they resumed their travels, though Martin decided to forego the samosas for a less deep-fried option.

The buses themselves were a mixed bag. On some, the boys had to stand up for hours on end due to the small space and amount of passengers and, on others, they had the bus pretty much to themselves. As Martin had realized on their earlier ride, most drivers drove extremely fast, which often gave him nervous lurches in his stomach when they were driving along the sides of mountains with steep drops below them. The drivers seemed to know what they were doing though, and he supposed that after many years of this type of driving it would become rather natural.

On the third day of their trip, they stayed in a small mountain town before making their way the following day to the larger village of Reckong Peo, which would bring them very close to their final destination. Martin even thought that they might make it all the way to the monastery that day as the map on his phone suggested that Reckong Peo was only a short distance away from them. However, when he asked the local bus station how long the bus would take, the bearded man at the office said "around 10 hours". Martin was confused and showed him the map on the phone, which suggested it was just a three hour drive but the driver only shook his head. After the boys had been on the bus for an hour or so, they realized why this was the case. Reckong Peo was literally on the other side of the mountain and there was no tunnel through it or road around it. They were going up and over it on a thin, steep road, on which the bus could only manage 30 km/h at most.

Once they reached the summit of the mountain, the view was stunning with lush green valleys, snake-like purple rivers and majestic trees as far as the eye could see. The sun was shining brightly and the driver allowed the passengers to take a long rest stop here, as there was a quaint restaurant at the top and plenty of sunshine to take advantage of. The boys each grabbed a thali, which was different at every restaurant, but always featured vegetable subzis, dhal, rotis, and raita. They sat out in the sun and enjoyed the delicious food.

"We are so lucky to be here," Bert said. "I feel so full of joy."

"I feel the same," replied Martin, noticing that for the first time in a long time, he really did.

*　　*　　*　　*　　*　　*　　*　　*　　*

The map from Reckong Peo to the monastery suggested that it would only take them two hours to get to their destination but Martin chose to ignore this prediction due to the previous day's experience. The one thing he did know, and had been quite worried about from the start, was something that Vipul had said to them before they left.

"Have you heard of a show called World's Most Dangerous Roads?" He asked the boys.

"I've heard of it, but never watched it." Martin replied.

"I think our dad's friend worked on that show," Bert said with a pondering look on his face.

"Well, the road from Reckong Peo that goes to the monastery and beyond was featured on there!" He said excitedly, though Martin wasn't sure this was something to be excited about.

Some of the roads so far had already been quite terrifying and featured myriad potholes, steep drop offs, and narrow curves, so Martin was quite unsure of what to expect for this next one. He saw now why it was considered so dangerous, as the road only had one lane and this lane was just about as narrow as the bus they were on. Furthermore, the drop off on the left side was significantly steep, as they were literally winding themselves through a passage that had been cut into the side of a mountain. To Martin's discomfort, the bus driver drove just as fast as any other, honking his horn loudly when racing around a corner to warn anyone on the other side of his location. There were lots of blind spots and many occasions where another bus or car happened to be directly on the other side of the curve and both drivers would stop suddenly. Then, the vehicles would remain there, perfectly still and facing one another, until one would start backing up until it found enough space to turn off slightly and allow the other to pass. It was the most frightening game of chicken in the world. It seemed that their bus driver was not fond of these backing up manoeuvres and would often be the one to sit still the longest until the other backed away. Martin had his hands gripped sharply onto the seat for most of the bus ride, and at one point Bert noticed this and held his hand for some time, calming Martin down slightly.

Despite the treacherous journey, the landscape around them featured some of the most gorgeous vistas he had ever seen. Tiny villages sprinkled themselves on the sides of mountains with extremely limited road access and Martin wondered what the people there were like. To live in such a way - so isolated - must change a person significantly. Vipul had told them that some of these villages were more like a mix of a village and tribe, hearkening back to long ago when humans lived in more tribal states. Martin had began to present his thoughts to Bert when he heard a thud and a crunch on the right side of the bus and all of a sudden the vehicle began to tip over on its left side. Panic flooded every pore of his body and he looked around with dismay, not knowing what to do. Was this actually happening? Oh my god, this was actually happening. He grabbed Bert's hand hard and looked at him in the eyes. He managed to say, "I love you" before the bus toppled completely over to the side and tumbled down the steep cliffs.

*   *   *   *   *   *   *   *   *

Martin's body was pounding like a thousand drums, pinning him down with immense pain. He could barely open his eyes but when he managed to squeak them open a bit he saw nothing but a thin, warm light coming from an unknown direction. Why did his body ache so much? In a flash, everything came back to him and he sat up and opened his eyes wide despite the resulting agony.

"BERT?!" He cried. "BERT."

He looked around and saw that he was in a small cave. The entrance was not far away and he could see that it was either dusk or dawn while a small fire close by burned with vigour. Bert was not there, in fact nobody was. Then how did he get there? He looked down at his hurt body and saw that parts of him were bandaged up with some sort of leaf and there were rags near the fire that were stained with blood. Perhaps Bert had rescued him from the crash, dragged him to a nearby cave, and nursed him. That sounded right - Bert was just out foraging for food. Martin's hopes to see his brother dissipated when a bald-headed man appeared at the mouth of the cave. Martin examined him for a moment, noticing that his skin was light brown, he wore brown rags slightly darker than his skin, and he had delicate wrinkles that had formed next to his almond-shaped eyes. He smiled when he saw Martin but the hurt young man did not return this gesture.

"Where is my brother?" He demanded. "Why did you bring me here?"

Martin's irate questions did not seem to deter the man, who just continued walking slowly towards Martin with a large root in his left hand. The man sat down close to him and attempted to inspect his wounds but Martin pulled away.

"Don't touch me. Tell me where my brother is."

The man looked at him directly in the eyes. His gaze was both penetrating and calming, as if his look pierced some unknown tranquility within Martin's mind.

"Your brother is gone."

Martin didn't register what the man was trying to tell him.

"Where did he go? Why is he not here as well?"

"You were the only survivor. I found you against a tree in the valley."

There was a long silence during which Martin's mind attempted to understand what had happened. Bert was dead. He had died. He was gone. What did that mean? His heart began to hurt with a dull, lifeless pain unrelated to any of the physical pains he had received. The pain felt empty and pointless and following its uprising his forehead began to feel a deep pressure welling upon it. His face scrunched up and he felt empty sensations float around his abdomen. Everything he felt was unpleasant but vapid. He didn't care about any of it, it was just happening. His only brother was gone and it was his fault because he didn't stop them from going on this stupid trip on the world's most dangerous road and because he didn't fulfill his duties as an older brother to protect Bert. He let out a cry of pain as if he finally began to feel all of those empty sensations swimming around him. The pain increased and moved down to his belly while his nose ran and tears flowed uncontrollably out of his bloodshot eyes. His mind became confused and erratic and he lost all sense of what was happening around him. It was all too much. Too overwhelming. The slow rise of feelings then erupted into a cacophony of screams, cries, and tears, which seemed to emanate from every pore of his body. He held himself by his knees and buried his head into his thighs, feeling embarrassed about his outburst, despite the fact that he couldn't control it. This went on for a long time and the man in the cave sat in silence next to him, not making any effort to console or comfort him. Eventually Martin looked at him, his eyes red and wet.

"Bring him back to life." He said with a ferocious snarl. The man just looked at him quizzically. "I know about you monks living in these caves. Bert told me. Supposedly some of you develop these supernatural abilities by meditating too much. So, bring him back to life."

"This I cannot do."

"WHY NOT." Martin screamed and the words echoed around the cave, causing a couple of birds at the mouth to take flight. The man didn't give an answer and Martin didn't need one. He knew that anything he tried would be hopeless. Another silence lingered as Martin silently emoted. Then, the man spoke,

"There is a choice you have to make."

Martin just stared at him blankly with no energy to form a response.

"Martin," he said and a slight shock passed through Martin as he had not told the man his name. "We all suffer. As living beings on this earth, we suffer. The vicissitudes of life push us into all types of negative states where we may linger for hours, days, or even years. You are no different. However, your most recent pains have been significant and I am willing to provide you with two choices."

"OK." Martin said dryly.

"First, you leave the cave once your wounds heal, find your way back up to a road, get a ride from someone, and fly back home to support your family with the loss of your brother. All of the pain that you experience now will be with you for a long time but eventually may drift away, provided you make good choices along your way."

Martin shuddered at the thought of this. He hadn't even begun to reconcile his own feelings towards Bert's death let alone having to tell his family and deal with this pain for the rest of his life.

"What's the second choice?" He asked hesitatingly.

"I do not offer this choice lightly. In fact, I don't even know if it should be offered at all. However, we have come this far. If you choose this route, I will help you construct walls in your mind so that you can forget all of this. You will forget the pain and suffering that you have held onto from *all* of your life's traumas. However, with this you will also forget all of those things too. In fact, you will forget everything that happened before the moment you are put back."

"What do you mean 'put back'?" Martin asked fearfully.

"If you choose this option, you will be placed in a location completely separate from anything you once knew. Your life's goals will be simple and you will have the means to achieve them. Your mind will be manipulated so that you will desire to remain isolated and distracted, so as to keep you from ever getting close to any of the walls in your mind."

"So, you're saying that I wouldn't remember anything at all?"

"That is correct."

"But wouldn't I find that strange or discomforting? I feel like I would be perpetually confused."

"You're not listening. Your mind would choose to avoid any types of thoughts that would ever lead you close to this. However..."

The man sat there silently for some time, pondering on something.

"What?" Martin asked impatiently.

"If you choose this option, know that it is still possible for these walls to get broken somehow. It would take a significant amount of force and effort, most likely by a third party influence, but it could happen and it would not be easy." He paused. "But this is very unlikely."

"What about my family?"

"They would be under the impression that you died along with your brother," the man said solemnly.

With the reminder of his brother, Martin fell into another state of shock and physical discomfort. From the moment that the man had begun to explain this second option, Martin knew he would choose it and he despised himself for it. Was he such a coward that in order for his own pain to be eradicated, he would harm his parents further, and give up all of his memories? Yes, he was. He thought deeper on his pain, remembering the torturous experience in New York that still clouded his every move, the painful relationships with Carly and Rose that had caused him to be distrustful of every woman that he had met since, and the ever-growing dark emptiness caused by the loss of his brother. There was no choice.

"You already know my decision," he said darkly, his voice devoid of any emotion.

"Very well." The man said and put his fingers on Martin's temples. A seething pain ran through him, unlike anything he had experienced so far. He attempted to scream, to tell him to stop, but nothing could come out of his mouth. Moments of his life began to flash before him and then swiftly were pushed away by some foreign force. It felt as if all of his memories were being stuffed into one location of his mind and this other area, which somehow seemed to be located around his sternum, began to feel heavier and heavier. The pain continued but began to lessen as the heaviness grew. Memories that Martin cherished passed by and began to disappear. As this occurred, Martin had a grave realization that this was the most terrible decision he had ever made. Images of his smiling parents flew by and were gone. Bert, Isaac, and everyone else he ever knew were suddenly out of his mind, pushed down into some unknown abyss. Martin still had a sense of awareness of what was going on and wished that he somehow could reverse the decision but knew deep down that it was too late. He started to wonder about the man who was helping him do all this and how he could have trusted him so easily, but these thoughts began to flutter away as well. Soon, most of Martin's mind was empty. It was a strange feeling and he began to question what 'Martin' even was. Without these memories and the collective conditioning of his past experiences what was he? These thoughts were momentarily stimulating but then they dissipated. He felt his body jerk as the area around his sternum began to tighten and he knew that something there was being fortified so as to never be broken, though he couldn't remember what it was that was there.

And then there was nothing.

Chapter 19 - Another Cave

The thick layers of nothingness lingered for an eternity. The awareness that was once known as Martin was still present, though there was very little to be aware of. However, although most of the mind felt completely empty, there were vestiges of thoughts hovering far off in the distance that the awareness was attracted to, and it strained itself in order to hear what these quiet words sounded like, though to no avail. The awareness swam through the murky darkness in an attempt to reach them, as if to find something to hold onto. It swam in circles, exerting huge effort to make the slightest movement. Suddenly, one of those faraway thoughts zoomed close enough for the awareness to catch a glimpse.

"Emptiness sure feels heavier than I expected," the thought said in a familiar tone and dissolved in an instant.

The awareness, hungry for more stimulation, moved faster through the space, using all of its strength to gain momentum when suddenly it bumped into something that felt taut and bouncy. The awareness examined it further and discovered that it was a large sphere of confusion. Every time it prodded the sphere, confused feelings emanated from within and traveled through the infinite space around. As one of these feelings escaped from the sphere, the awareness grabbed onto it and allowed the feeling to carry it farther than it could have gone on its own, in the direction of the only whispering thoughts that could be heard. As it got closer, the whispers grew louder but remained indecipherable. In an instant, both the confusion and the awareness slammed up against a wall, which was thick and fortified. The thoughts that it had heard were behind this wall and still indiscernible. The awareness moved in all directions, attempting to find a way in, but it was impenetrable though, upon closer observation, it noticed a small crack. It sidled up right against the crack and strained its sense faculties to attempt to hear what was inside. It could not understand the words but could hear all types of things - from screaming and crying to laughter and soft sighing. A human-like curiosity arose within the awareness.

"Open your eyes," a massive voice echoed through the chamber of darkness. The voice sounded trustworthy and familiar and the awareness wanted to comply with its orders but had no idea how to do so. It was not aware that it even had eyes and, even if it did, how they were to be opened. The sphere of confusion began to pulse more quickly, flooding the space with chaotic waves of unintelligible noises and the awareness felt fear step in from another location, bringing along doubt and despair. The entire area began to tremble and red light began to flash over everything.

"Martin." The voice said sternly. "What do you want? Tell me now."

There was no awareness of what this 'Martin' was, but there *was* an answer to the question laying just underneath the sphere of confusion so the awareness darted across as quickly as possible to catch it. As it reached it, it heard,

"I want to open my eyes."

The light became purple and flickering, and the darkness faded slightly. The confusion was no longer observable in its spherical form and could only be felt, along with the fear. The wall that it had encountered was nowhere to be found.

"Look at me." The voice bellowed from somewhere to the right. The awareness realized that its eyes *were* open and upon further inspection that it had seemed to have a physical body that existed below the eyes. Was this 'Martin'? It must be. The newly discovered Martin looked to his right. There was a large creature with glistening fur and massive paws - a bear. Memories rushed in from the same space that the fear had come from and along with it came thoughts and feelings, though different from the ones that existed behind the wall.

"Dr. Spruce?" Martin asked in a timid voice and it felt like the first time he had ever spoken. He looked down at his body again, observing his hands, legs, and everything else with scrutiny. Upon finding everything in good order, he observed his surroundings with more detail. He was in a cave. *They* were in a cave. Though it didn't seem real as the fire in the middle was purpley-white and danced around in a twisting fashion that made it seem more alive than the fire of the monk's cave. There was no entrance to be seen. After the metre of light that the fire revealed, there was just darkness. However, when Martin looked up it seemed as if the roof of the cave was covered in multicoloured stars that danced in rhythm with the flames. He looked back at Dr. Spruce who, like everything else, seemed different than ever before. His own fur resembled rippling waves, moving up-and-down and side-to-side. He was looking down at it, with an amused smile on his face.

"Are we..." Martin hesitated. "Are we still in my mind?"

Dr. Spruce smiled and nodded.

"How ever did you get here?" Martin asked incredulously, with a slight smile.

Dr. Spruce laughed and said, "Sometimes it's more interesting to leave certain things unexplained."

"Makes sense. I watched this TV show growing up that would do that often. It would infuriate lots of people but I liked the fact that I didn't know anything. Like, even when it was done there were still some secrets." He paused for a moment as he had startled himself. "That was a memory from my past."

"Yes. They seem to be slipping their way back out."

"A non-traumatic one, too!" Martin said excitedly. "I kind of assumed that all of this work was going to be full of trauma."

"Martin, you made a choice to lock *everything* away. The good, the bad, and the ugly. You're fortunate in this regard, I would say. The positive ones may help you stay grounded as you continue to process the worst."

"Like…" Martin's throat closed up slightly. "Like Bert."

Dr. Spruce nodded. "You have come to another fork in the road, dear Martin. Years ago, a trickster in a cave offered a sensitive boy suffering from the loss of his brother a terrible choice. Choosing his words with quiet manipulation, he made it seem as if you were choosing between a life of pain or a life without."

Martin interrupted him. "What do you mean by a trickster? He saved me from the bus! And he was a monk. Aren't all monks meant to be good guys?"

"No, that is not always the case. One can choose to take the robes with the wrong intentions, and continue to roll in misery for the remainder of one's days. However, I have reason to believe that this was no monk."

"Then who, or what, was he?"

"In order for nature to continue on its flow, there must be balance, as I'm sure you're aware. In some special places, such as the fairy ring where you have been working, there exists an air of purity and a fine lightness. In order for this to exist, there must be the exact opposite and sometimes this opposite force can be embodied as some sort of being. The main function of these beings is to attempt to sway others from achieving any goodness in their time on this Earth."

"It's like Star Wars." Martin said impulsively while laughter escaped from his lips. He couldn't remember the last time he had even seen a television, but all of a sudden these references had been emerging.

"I am not aware of that to which you are referencing, but I'm sure you are right."

"So, let me get this straight. This monk, or not-monk, was manipulating me so that I would move *towards* darkness? But, I had just lost my little brother. I'm sure that would already have brought me to a horribly dark place if I had just let the pain linger."

"Perhaps, but perhaps not. To feel a negative emotion is not wrong in any regard. These emotions continually exist in the body and mind. In fact, to actually feel them is to allow them to dissipate as you have experienced in your work thus far."

"I see, you're right. But..." Martin stopped himself short, slightly embarrassed.

"Go on, Martin, let your thoughts escape your mouth."

"But why would anyone actually choose to feel these horrible feelings? All of them. Anxiety, fear, depression, doubt, despair, and countless others. They're disgusting and if I had the choice I would never feel them!"

"You did have the choice, and you chose not to. Look where it put you."

Martin stopped and thought for a moment, looking back on his time living alone at Richmond Lake where he spent all of his days distracted in some type of miserable task or another without smiling, laughing, or any semblance of joy in his work.

Dr. Spruce looked up at the ceiling and breathed out with a sigh.

"Our time is running out here, unfortunately. Although I would love to discuss these points further with you, it is time for me to offer you another choice."

Martin waited with silence, though he was already certain that he knew what was to be offered.

"In the work we have done together, you have worked hard, and re-lived but a few of your most traumatic memories. By feeling these emotions once more, and bringing your lessons back to the present, you have worked yourself through some of these things that have conditioned your life since. That being said, there is a lot more work to do. This you must recognize. The path to liberation is long and arduous, with no quick fix."

Martin nodded, allowing the fear to bubble up in his chest.

"The work you have done seems to have cracked open an area of the wall that this 'non-monk' created. Your first choice is to allow me to patch that crack back up. However, this would mean that any memories of our work together and anything else you have experienced these last few weeks would also be gone. As your previous choice allowed, this would be another restart. You can go on living without being bothered by any of these difficult emotions or memories, letting them remain within safe confines. There is always the potential for another situation like this one to arise where you may reopen this Pandora's box once more, but this would be less likely the second time around."

Martin felt significant pressure weigh upon him and looked upwards. The lights on the roof of the cave seemed to have dulled.

"And I think you already know the second choice. If you go with this route, I will help you widen the crack, if not break the wall apart completely. Although some of the deeper rooted traumas may remain below for some time, the majority of the memories of your past will return. You will be faced with more traumatic experiences and feelings that may overwhelm you completely. For example, you still have not explored the loss of your dear brother. This will have to be processed immediately and I regret to say that you may not recover from this experience."

There was a deep, soundless length of time that passed between the two. Dr. Spruce was looking rather solemn and Martin's innards mirrored this solemnity. He closed his eyes and began to think. Something felt wrong about all of this but he couldn't quite grasp it. His forehead hurt with a great pressure but upon further observation he realized that it was not pressure related to this decision, it was something else. He moved towards that pressure rather than running away from it. His awareness burst through into the pressure-filled chamber of his mind and he suddenly realized what was happening.

"Where are your glasses, Dr. Spruce?" He asked calmly.

Dr. Spruce looked at him quizzically and Martin felt the pressure stab against his forehead once more. He pushed hard against it, not allowing it to go any further.

"Martin, bears don't wear glasses."

"Sometimes they do. Though, you're not a bear."

"I don't have the faintest idea what you are talking about, Martin. Your mind is a bit raw from all of this memory-hopping you've been doing. The lights are going out, make your choice before it's too late."

"I am not making a choice. Both of those choices are another attempt for you to manipulate me into continuing to be this strange psycho-experiment." The pressure got stronger, but now felt more like a probe trying to force its way into Martin's skull. "Get the hell out of my mind!" Martin yelled this with an intense force and matched it with a focused mental push.

Dr. Spruce's face twisted with pain and for a moment seemed to flicker in and out of existence. Martin attempted to hold onto the focus and keep whatever this was out of his mind. He was already exhausted by this exertion and felt distracting emotions rising and falling in and out of his chest. It seemed as if more memories and feelings were pouring out of the crack in the wall that had been placed there and he was doing his best to remain steadfast and strong amongst the onslaught. All of a sudden, he could hear his brother saying "I love you" with a look of horror plastered across his face. It was the moment just before his death. Martin's focus broke completely and his body began to shake with streams of tears rolling out of his eyes onto the ground below. The pain was immense and unbearable, and along with it he began to feel the pressure-filled probe enter his mind once more.

"Yes," Dr. Spruce said maliciously. "Feel that horrible pain and let it overtake you. Let your mind unravel and fall apart."

The pain was unfathomable and full of every human feeling that Martin knew of. All at once they sliced throughout his body, magnified by the pain in his forehead, and he felt himself shattering. As it all erupted, he saw that underneath it all was some sort of cycle of nonsensical words, repeating over and over in a confusing pattern of psychosis. He felt the probe pushing him towards this space and he attempted to fight back against it but was ravaged by the memories and feelings. He opened his eyes and saw that Dr. Spruce was no longer there and was replaced by the smooth-headed 'monk' that he had met in India. However, there was no calmness on his face, only malicious rage. Martin despised him, whatever he was. He had taken advantage of him and forced him to forget his brother, his family, his life. This anger towards him began to glow within him and seemed to form the question, "what do you want?"

The words began to escape Martin before he even had time to think. "What do I want? I want to be a normal human being with emotions, wishes, and desires. I want to feel pain when I experience it, I want to have joy in my life, and I want to learn how to manage these things in a regular, effective way. Not by repressing it all, and not by feeling it all at once. There is no balance here. You are the most unbalanced creature on this planet and you cannot survive like that. No-one can."

The non-monk began to twitch suddenly and everything else twitched with him. The walls of the cave, the wood on the fire, and everything else was twitching uncontrollably giving Martin the confidence to continue. The pressure had eased up once more and everything inside him seemed to be swirling around much less.

"I have no use for you in my mind. You do not belong here. I once invited you in when I was fragile and afraid, but I have gained some strength and I believe I can force you out of here. In fact, it seems to be happening already. You are not welcome." He added in a soft voice. "May you be happy one day."

These words of compassion surprised Martin, especially since they seemed to rise out on a wave of sensations that emanated from deep within his bones. All of a sudden, illumination began to pour out of him to fill up the space, snuffing out the fire and lights, and revealing the entire space around him. It was a drab, boring cave, with nothing interesting or discernible on the walls, ceiling or floor. It was the cave of his mind in which he had been living for the past seven years and he vowed that he would never return here. The twitching being that sat in front of him seemed to be getting ripped apart by the powerful brightness that had filled up the space.

"You are but one amongst many, Martin. My ways will always continue." He laughed in a glitchy, disjointed manner.

"And I hope that they too can force you out, you poor, lonely thing."

And with that, it was gone. Martin closed his eyes and fell back into himself.

Chapter 20 - Yet Another Cave

"Martin?! Martin!" A voice whispered excitedly from around him. "How did you two get here?"

He felt himself being shaken slightly and let out a weary groan. When he made an effort to open his eyes he saw Evaline's face in front of him. He blinked numerous times and looked around, noticing Orchid sitting next to him in the same crossed-leg position he was in. He grabbed her arm and said,

"Orchid?!"

Her body jumped slightly and she began to open her eyes calmly.

"Best you keep your voices down, my friends," growled Dr. Spruce from nearby.

"Dr. Spruce, is that *actually* you?"

"It's *actually* me," the great bear smiled and pushed up his glasses with his left paw.

"Where are... Martin, you're glowing," Orchid said confusedly.

He looked down at himself and noticed that there was in fact a faint phosphorescence emanating from his body.

"Jesus," he said with surprise.

"I wouldn't go that far," Orchid replied with a slight laugh, looked around herself more seriously, then addressed Dr. Spruce and Evaline. "How long have you been trapped in this cave?"

"Long enough," Evaline said with exasperation. "We're okay though. The wolves haven't even come in here, really. Dr. Spruce says that his council is attempting to have some sort of reasonable discussion with the pack but it doesn't seem to be going well."

"What do you mean?" Martin asked.

"What these wolves hold in ferocity, they lack in compassion." Dr. Spruce said. "They seem to be dissatisfied with any attempt to negotiate. They want to have complete access to all of our land, or they're going to take it by force."

"But surely you must be able to fight them off. Even from what I've seen, you've got some pretty large animals in here."

"We made a strong vow never to fight on this land." Dr. Spruce said wearily.

Martin sat in thought for a moment, realizing once again that he was glowing with a strange light.

"Dr. Spruce, why am I glowing?"

He smiled at Martin, "Perhaps something wants to come out."

Martin stood up with a conviction, his eminent glow inspiring him tremendously. He knew what he needed to do and began to walk towards the mouth of the cave.

"Martin, what are you doing?" Asked Evaline with a tremble of fear quivering upon her lips.

"Let's all go," he said to them. "Come on, things will be okay."

Without hesitation, Orchid came up and stood beside him, holding his hand in a powerful grip that seemed to cause his light to pulse slightly. Evaline looked at Dr. Spruce who got up himself and headed towards Martin, which made her do the same. They walked cautiously towards the soft light coming from outside and began to hear voices in a heated back-and-forth.

"We have told you countless times, you stupid horse, we will not comply with any of your oh-so-wise negotiation tactics." It was a female voice, full of cruelty.

"We are merely trying to find a solution that will make both parties happy," said a calm voice that Martin recognized as Ellian, the moose who he had met in the fairy ring.

"Pshh, happiness. We do not care about your happiness, your well-being, or your survival. We need your land. Our numbers are growing significantly and we are finding less and less to eat due to this human interference. Either you allow us here to feed or we will rip apart the bear and human that we have in this cave."

"I don't think you will," Martin said from behind the pack. The four of them had stepped out from the cave into a clearing where the discussion was taking place. It was nighttime now and there was a full moon in the sky, shining its white light down upon the collection of animals that stood around. Despite the tense situation, it was truly a beautiful sight to behold. The shiny white fur of the wolves glimmered in the light of the moon while the multitude of fantastic woodland creatures stood in a semi-circle around them. As they had emerged, Martin could sense that the wolves were frightened, although they did not betray any hint of it in their voices. He hoped that this would help him with whatever it was that he was about to do. He looked down upon himself, noticing that the colour of light around his body was the same as the moon's. As the wolves heard his voice they turned around quickly while snarling. One of them made a dash for him but Dr. Spruce stood in its way, standing on his hind legs and roaring like the majestic beast that he was.

"SIT DOWN."

His command was so powerful that each of the five wolves sat down immediately, allowing a hint of fright to shake their bodies slightly in the bright moonlight. Martin noticed this and so, feeling more confident than ever, he stood up in front of the animals and began to speak,

"Hello," he said in a proud voice, then paused for some time, clearing his throat loudly. He took a look at each of the animals that were now faced towards him. The female wolf, the alpha, growled at him when he looked at her, which made him step back slightly. "Hello." He said once again then looked down at his glowing body as if expecting it to do something. He realized that he had no idea what he was going to say as he had assumed that the glow would give him supernatural abilities that would allow him to convince the wolves to leave. He had been daydreaming slightly about beginning an epic speech while rising in the air as the wind whipped around him but it didn't seem that this was going to happen. He glanced nervously in the direction of Dr. Spruce, who had a serious smile plastered on his face and his glasses down low as if he were studying something. Evaline was smiling nervously at him and Orchid gave a quick wink as his eyes scanned over her. Well, he had to say something, he was already here.

"Hello." He repeated for the third time. "I am a human being named Martin. To be honest, I really don't know what I'm going to say here to try and convince all of you to stop fighting, but that's what I want to try to do. I've had a pretty insane week so far through which I've dug deep into some strange, uncomfortable repressions that were lying dormant in my mind and I'm still pretty shaky from all of it. I'm not sure if it's the best state to give a masterful speech in, but I *am* glowing, so that means something, eh?" He looked up at the wolves, remembering something an old professor had taught him about making eye contact when making a public speech. He really didn't like looking in their eyes as it was like looking into a dark abyss at the bottom of which were blood-soaked spikes. "For a while, I was a pretty negative dude. Every time anyone would try to speak to me, I would run away with some excuse in an attempt to hide from any kind of conversation or connection. I hope I can change that now." He glanced at the Protectors of the forest when he said this and a few of them gave him comforting smiles, as well as an inspiring thumbs up from Buffalo.

"Human, what is the point of what you are saying? I feel it entirely unnecessary to listen to the ridiculous words coming out of your tiny mouth." The alpha wolf said with malice. "Your kind have destroyed half of our forest with a large pipe filled with oil, and don't get me started on the manipulation of our ancestors into pathetic lap dogs."

"Well, for what it's worth, I've never had a dog as I saw them as kind of a slavery-type thing." Martin said and one of the wolves gave an affirming nod, to which the alpha wolf sent a ferocious stare. He then noticed that the light coming from his body seemed to be a little bit stronger, but it could have been his imagination. "But let me get back on track. I'm talking about connection. I guess, as I've been learning to reconnect with some nice people, it has been difficult, but not as difficult as attempting to connect with those who don't feel as inclined to have a connection. You wolves seem to be angry about a lot of things, which is entirely understandable, and that's not something that can just go away with some incredible speech... Not saying that this is an incredible speech," he added insecurely.

"I think it's pretty good!" Another one of the wolves chimed in and the alpha whacked her over the head with a paw.

"I'm no leader or anything, but if it means something to you, I apologize on behalf of the humans who are messing up your forest and forcing you to cross over to this land to look for food and shelter. Honestly, many humans are ignorant of the impact that they have on nature, as well as each other. That's not going to be an easy fix, but hopefully there's something that I can do, or that we all can do, that can help ease things for you." Although Martin was surprised about the fairly good quality of his words so far, he knew that he was still stalling, trying to find an answer that would resolve the situation. As a small mosquito plopped onto his shoulder and began to suck out 1/16 of a teaspoon of his blood, he had an idea. He felt his body pulse slightly and saw the glow grow even stronger. Was he going to become the moon? This silly thought entered his head and he threw it out immediately. He put his hands outstretched with his palms up in an attempt to look like some kind of peaceful prophet but then realized that this was cheesy and put his hands back by his sides.

"Get on with it so we can eat you." The alpha wolf said, although with less distaste than in the previous statements. It seemed that she was actually rather interested in listening to him continue.

"So, I'm not going to take you through my life story as I've been through that enough the last few days, but I was recently living in a large area of land in which I built a small home, which has now been burnt to the ground. Parts of the surrounding forest got burnt as well, but there is still a lot of that land that flourishes." Some attachment in him tried to stop him from the offer he was about to make but he threw it aside. "If you want, I'm willing to hand over that land to all you wolves so you don't have to bother these guys in their protected area."

"Where's the land?" The alpha demanded.

Martin turned to Dr. Spruce. "Do you mind drawing them a map?"

"I'll never turn down an opportunity for some drawing!" Dr. Spruce said with gruff glee. "Be my light, Martin, and throw me that conk from that rotting log, Buffalo!"

Buffalo struggled to pull off the huge polypore mushroom that was attached to the log but, with some help from Ta Wee, managed to get it off and toss it to Spruce. Martin was curious about what Dr. Spruce was about to do as he had thought that he would do another drawing in the soil. However, he turned over the pretty mushroom to its white underside, grabbed a stick, and began to make an intricate drawing on the surface.

"The Artist's Conk bruises black when any pressure is placed upon it," Dr. Spruce answered Martin's unspoken curiosity, while drawing a map of the surrounding forest, including the treaty lines that had been established with the wolves and the location of Martin's land. It turned out that Martin's stretch of land was directly south of the wolves' current land, which would make it easy for them to incorporate it into their current territory. Once he was done, he handed the conk over to the alpha and the rest of her pack gathered round, making slight noises that suggested interest and agreement. She looked up sharply at Martin.

"How can you be sure that this land won't be torn up by humans like the other parts of the forest?"

"Well, I own it. When it was bought, I signed an agreement that established it as my land and, thus, no-one is allowed to touch it without my permission. If you agree to this, it would be easiest if I remain as the 'owner' of the land on the records, but I am willing to make whatever sort of treaty or agreement with you that will not allow me to step foot on the land from this moment forward."

One of the wolves who hadn't spoken yet looked at him. He had a deep scar over his left eye, which had forced one of his eyes white with blindness.

"If we shall agree, and you choose to return to the land one day, disavowing our treaty, we will be permitted to eat every piece of you, as slowly as we choose."

Martin gulped then nodded slowly and the wolves continued their quiet conversation while analyzing the drawing. As everything was quiet with anticipation, he remarked to himself on how truly incredible the present situation was. Despite the possibility that the wolves would not agree and he and his friends would be torn to shreds, it was still a unique experience. The moon was shining lustrously, there were large animals all around him with which he could communicate, and he was still glowing like a steady flame in a translucent lamp. It seemed that Orchid was experiencing something similar as, when he looked at her, she smiled at him knowingly and he felt a deep orb of soothing peace settle in his sternum. As soon as he felt this, his glow subsided, though he didn't feel disappointed, despite the fact that no superpowers had come from it. As the reverie continued, the alpha wolf began to speak slowly.

"Human Martin, as mentioned, your kind has hurt us considerably and it is difficult for us to reconcile this. However, you have proved reasonable and willing to help us in this time of need. Though I have seen better speeches given, you made up for it in your openness, and for this we are grateful. We will take you up on your offer and leave immediately to find our new home."

It seemed as if the entire forest breathed out a sigh of relief all at once. However, there was something that was weighing on Martin's mind and, though he knew would regret it if he spoke up, it escaped him before he had the chance to stop.

"There is one thing..." he said hesitatingly.

The alpha's lip curled. "What is it?"

"Um... the only thing I have left on the land is a mattress... and I was wondering if I could retrieve it before you settle in."

"Absolutely not." The alpha said with an intense hatred that shook Martin down to the bones.

"OK OK, I'm sorry I mentioned it." He said and looked away with shame.

The treaty ceremony for the giving of the land was rather peculiar as they used a roll of bark from a nearby paper birch tree and filled it with the paw prints of all five wolves as well as Martin's handprint. However, they required this to be in blood, which meant Martin had to ask Dr. Spruce to cut open his palm lightly with a claw so he could smear the blood all over his hand. It hurt a little, but he also thought it was cool to be signing a blood pact. Once the ceremony was over, the wolves howled at the moon in a rather cliché moment and began to leave. As they left, the wolf with the blind eye stopped next to Martin and said,

"This is in regards to that mattress outburst from Alice, our alpha. Just so that you understand, she *loves* mattresses more than anything and they're not an easy thing to find out in the woods. It was probably the worst thing you could have tried to take away."

"Good to know," he nodded at the wolf who returned the nod with a toothy smile and rushed off into the darkness.

Martin breathed out an exhausted sigh and all at once he had realized how tired he was. Craving something as soft as the mattress that he would never see again, he looked around him for a comfortable stretch of ground on which to collapse. Dr. Spruce came by his side.

"Well done, my dear Martin. You have worked arduously today and must be tired. Come with me." He held onto Martin's hand with his large paw and gestured to Evaline and Orchid to follow. The rest of the animals of the forest followed suit, walking quietly through the moonlit forest. Martin's mind fell silent and vacant, though there was a whispering hope that they would not be walking far. Luckily, they stopped at another clearing close by. In the light of the moon, Martin could see that they were on the edge of a large lake, perhaps even Large Lake itself. Dr. Spruce stood on his hind legs upon arrival and addressed the entire party.

"In honour of the full moon and Martin's gracious relinquishing of his land to the wolves, I encourage you all to plunge into the soothing waters of the lake." It was a rather warm night, which meant that the majority of the animals took him up on this and threw themselves into the water, splashing around with laughter and joy. Before stepping in himself, Martin took a moment to stand on the shore and observe once more the beauty of the present moment. All of these unique animals, as a community, were playing around in the water while the moon shone and basked the scene in a delicate white glow. Could anything be more beautiful? He noticed that Evaline had dived in and was attempting to stand on Dr. Spruce's back, which he allowed though he didn't seem too fond of the idea. He felt a hand slip into his and noticed Orchid beside him, looking radiant in the bright glow.

"This day has been precious." She said softly.

"I agree."

She squeezed his hand once more then ran into the water, submerging herself completely in an instant. Despite his fatigue, Martin knew that he had to join them and once he too was bathing in the cool water, his tiredness seemed to subside and be replaced with a lasting peace. Although the night moved on, time seemed to stand still, allowing the momentous occasion to last for what seemed like forever. Eventually, the party grew to a close and everyone involved seemed to have the same idea. As if on cue, the group exited the water and lay down on the sandy shore, closing their eyes and falling into a collective slumber.

Chapter 21 - Martin's Marvellous Morning

Martin's heavy eyelids flickered open despite the fact that he felt as if he could have slept for another 48 hours. However, something seemed to be standing directly on his face and, as his eyes opened to register the world around him, he saw the Buffalo's furry bandit face peering directly into his right eye.

"Sorry bub, jus' making sure that yous alive." He scampered away from Martin's face and onto the ground beside him. Martin slowly rose, allowing all the aches and pains of his body just to be there, stretching himself out patiently until his body was pliant and happy to sit up. He saw that most of the party had gone, leaving only Buffalo, Orchid, and Dr. Spruce on the shore. Buffalo noticed him looking around and said,

"The Protectors had to bounce. Big meeting to tell all them other folks in the forest what happened. Breakfast?" He held out some roasted mushrooms in his hands and handed them to Martin, who ate them with zeal. The mushrooms' warm juices squeezed out as he bit into them, releasing both a satisfying umami flavour as well as a subtle taste of the forest floor causing his stomach to express noises of pure joy.

"We dunt usually cook our foods, but Sprucey told me that's what yous would like so I made up a fire and roasted thems myself." Buffalo said with pride.

"Thank you. They're delicious," he said, while stuffing a couple more into his gob. While eating, he noticed that Dr. Spruce was reciting some sort of monologue while Orchid was writing furiously in her notebook. This surprised him, as he wasn't aware that she too was able to talk to the animals in the forest. As if he read Martin's mind, Buffalo said,

"Theys been talking all morning. Some sort of interview for a new story starring Sprucey and me. My interview's next, how does I look?" He grinned with a flashy smile. "She says that afters yous suddenly appeared in Sprucey's cave, she could hear us as if we was speaking her language."

Orchid proceeded to call Buffalo over for his big interview, and flashed a kind smile at Martin before getting back to work. Dr. Spruce plodded over to Martin and settled down beside him.

"How are you, Martin?"

"I appreciate that you ask me that," he replied with a warm feeling in his chest. "I think I'm good. Pretty raw from all of those deep explorations into my mind but I feel as if at least some of this 100-pound weight that has been resting on me for years has started to ease off."

"Yes, good. You must allow yourself some time to rest after all of this. It can be quite extreme to do all of this work in such a short time, as you have done. Perhaps it will be best to space out future sessions with more time in between."

Martin's eyes widened and he looked at Dr. Spruce. "You mean you're going to continue helping me?"

"Why wouldn't I?" He asked with a smile that seemed to be full of every particle of compassion that existed in the universe.

"Oh, I don't know," Martin said shyly and looked down. "I just kinda thought, since everything was so climactic with that non-monk being and the wolves that it kind of meant that it was the end and I was to go and figure it out all on my own."

"We all need support on this difficult path, Martin. I will be here as long as you need me to be."

"Well, that's a real relief. You see, there was this really weird moment where I kind of completely disappeared and became just this floating awareness where I saw that I had this sort of locked box in my chest, which had become cracked slightly. It seems all these things from my past are going to keep coming out if I encourage them to, which I want to, but yeah... I need your help."

"Sure, Martin." He placed his large paw on Martin's shoulder and gave it a gentle squeeze, which made him feel much closer to the ground. "Do you feel up to telling me about this 'non-monk' creature that you mentioned?"

Martin was grateful to share with him the entire journey that he had been on since he stepped into the fairy ring for the second time. Although he had been through it recently, it helped to process the situation to talk about it and have someone listen. They talked for a long time with Dr. Spruce interrupting at times for further clarification or to discuss parts in more depth. When he came to talking about Bert and his subsequent death, Martin allowed the tears to flow out while Dr. Spruce comforted him gently. Then, as he was wrapping up his recount of the events, Buffalo shouted,

"All done! We's gonna be famous, Sprucey."

Dr. Spruce laughed and nodded in a jovial manner. He looked up at the sun and said,

"Well, it looks like it would be a good time for me and Buffalo to go and be with the rest of our community. They have had a bit of a scare and it will be helpful for us all to be together. Once again, great work,

Martin. The work will always continue but things will get easier for you, I can guarantee that. We will see each other soon." He turned to Orchid and continued, "Dear Orchid, if you would ever like some help to reconcile your own past, please feel free to come and see me."

"I will," she said with a gleam in her eyes. "Thank you."

Buffalo hopped onto Dr. Spruce's back and they waltzed off into the forest as Buffalo sang a song,

"Oo, deep in the forest, the old-growth forest
Lays something that will always know
What you've been hiding, no use in lying
The truth never fails to show

So, step into nature, the oh-so ancient
I know that you won't regret
Your new symbiosis, a piccololiosis
An epiphany you'll not forget."

Dr. Spruce hummed along with him and their voices carried back to the lake for some time. Orchid and Martin sat and listened, enjoying the peace of the moment, then Martin made his way over to her.

"Perhaps we should go to town," Orchid suggested, thrusting her notebook into her pocket, standing up, and brushing the sand off her. "Evaline went off a few hours ago to check on Connor."

"I would love that," Martin said with earnest and they set off in the direction of town.

"So, back in that fairy ring when you went off into wherever you went to," Orchid began as they walked. "I also closed my eyes just to see what would happen."

"And did something happen?"

"Yeah, I guess I went into some of my own past stuff. It was pretty intense to be put right back in those situations without any awareness that it was just some sort of time-traveling mind thing, you know?" She had a bit of trouble explaining her experience but Martin knew what she was talking about.

"Yeah, but I suppose if we *had* the awareness that we were traveling back into our memories, that might also enable us to change something, and from what I saw in that movie with Ashton Kutcher, that can be pretty dangerous."

"You mean the one where he played Steve Jobs?" She asked with a sly smile on her lips.

"Yeah, where he was a time-traveling Steve Jobs who went back to change the past so that Bill Gates never existed."

"My favourite part was when he showed the young Steve Jobs an iPad, but then he immediately got addicted to Angry Birds and never actually invented the Macbook," Orchid bantered while giggling slightly.

"That was good, but nothing compared to the scene when he set all of young Steve Jobs' black turtlenecks on fire with the intention of removing that whole 'black turtleneck image' that everyone got obsessed with. But then, when he got back to the future, he realized that it had just transformed into a beige turtleneck obsession."

"Even worse!"

The chatter continued as they wandered through the forest, stopping here and there to marvel at some of nature's beauties. It seemed as if the whole underground world had popped up to wish them on their way. There were icicle-looking Lion's Mane mushrooms growing from logs, stark white ghost pipe plants showing off their non-chlorophyllic ways, and young spruce tips sprouting out of the ends of their fully grown-selves. It truly was a sight to behold and Martin felt a deep satisfied gratitude living inside of him that seemed to want to spread out to the world around him. He let go of its hold slightly and allowed the pleasant sensations to resonate with love first for those beings around him and then for all others who were not in his presence. It was a beautiful feeling and filled him up with a gentle energy.

"Do you mind if I talk to you about something a bit more serious?" he cautiously asked Orchid as he didn't want to harm the good moods of either of them but still had something weighing him down slightly that needed to be addressed.

Orchid slowed her walk slightly, and said, "of course."

"So, on our way here, I was talking about my brother and how it had been a long time since I had seen him." He stopped for a moment, slightly choking on his words. "Sorry, this is so hard for me even to start to talk about. When I was diving into those memories before we ended up in the cave, I was back with him, with Bert, in India. He had invited me there soon after I left New York as he knew I needed a pick-me-up. He was always so aware of my feelings, even when we were far away. Anyways, we went on this big journey through the Himalayas to a monastery. It was such a beautiful adventure, which really helped me get over some of the depression I had after leaving New York and brought us closer together. However..." He stopped again, both in words and step, and looked down at the ground. Orchid put her arm around him, detecting his sadness immediately.

He spoke the rest of the words between sobs. "However, we got in an accident. The bus driver was driving like a maniac around these ridiculous cliffside roads and all of a sudden we were rolling off of the edge of the cliff. I remember his face as we fell, attempting to say "I love you" before I lost consciousness. I guess I survived but he didn't." Upon these words he fell to the ground on his knees, slamming his fist down on the ground. "And then I forgot it all. I forgot him. His memory didn't even live with me. He just died. I can't even imagine what my parents think, or where they are. Oh my god. It's just so much." He put his hands on his face and cried into them while Orchid knelt down and comforted him silently, allowing his emotions to pour out. Screams and shouts escaped his lips at times, which caused his body to shake. Suddenly, after a big outpour of emotions and trembling, it seemed as if there was not much more that could come out. He looked at Orchid with tears in his eyes and she looked right back at him.

"I don't think anything more wants to come out right now," he said tenderly.

"Thanks for allowing me to be here with you for that," she said. "That was truly brave."

His inner sun shone within when she said that and he hugged her close, grateful for this kind person who had entered his life. He squeezed hard and she returned it, then they slowly rose once more and walked towards town while the outer sun rose over the top of them, bathing the world in its morning glory.

*　　*　　*　　*　　*　　*　　*　　*　　*

When Martin and Orchid returned to town they went immediately to visit Connor and Evaline, stepping into Connor's quaint house to be greeted with joy by Redbird. They found the two of them fast asleep on his bed, heads touching, and they let them rest. They took the liberty of cooking a large, much-needed breakfast for everyone and, once the two awoke, they rejoiced in their reunion. Connor had a large bandage wrapped around his arm and expressed immediately his hope that he would turn into a werewolf upon the next full moon. The four of them shared their stories, released their emotions, and bounced around the banter.

Martin stayed on in Connor's second room for quite some time, which allowed their friendship blossomed. He taught Connor all he wanted to know about what it was like to live off-the-grid and Connor taught him the opposite. Martin enjoyed Connor's company more as the days went on as his exuberant, youthful energy inspired him to move away from his serious mindset and adopt a more curious, open approach to life. They spent some days foraging, others starting a little garden behind the house, and often meditating together. Evaline and Connor became close, which allowed Martin to get to know her better. She encouraged Martin to get back into music, which was tough for him at first, but eventually expanded outwards into a musical project that the two of them worked on together. It was extremely therapeutic for Martin to do this, as he had many negative feelings towards the idea of music in general due to his bad memories from New York.

The sessions with Dr. Spruce continued, though more spread out than the previous ones, as was suggested. They seemed to become more relaxed and easier to reconcile since Martin had already had some experience. Many more memories that Martin had completely forgotten arose and he was able to make an effort to grow more comfortable with these things. The hardest ones were experiences from his childhood that he saw had affected all of his decisions to date. Even the slightest episodes, such as an argument with his parents or a spat with his brother seemed to bring on some seriously intense sensations and emotions that he realized would take time to resolve fully. He had become slightly addicted to these sessions, as each time they occurred he felt slightly more purified and lighter. However, he was making an effort to see the beauty in his day-to-day life outside of the sessions and to forge a balance between the two.

He and Orchid continued developing their relationship, helping each other to deal with any emotions or repressions that arose and working through them as best as they could. He was seeing that despite their many benefits, relationships were difficult work and he found himself sometimes daydreaming about being on his own again. However, he strove hard to flip himself out of these fantasies of the past by reminding himself how ignorant and repressed he had been during these times. Orchid truly was a huge boon to his life, motivating him to take up creative hobbies and to be open and interested in the world around him. She started working with Dr. Spruce as well, which both strengthened her relationship with herself as well as inspired her to no end in her writing. Eventually, she left her role as detective and once again focused solely on her writing, feeling inspired enough by her own inner work and the nature around her to have enough material to write about.

A few weeks after the experience with the wolves, Martin felt confident enough to reach out to his parents. He had no idea where they were or what it would be like, but Orchid helped him in finding their contact information as well as giving him the courage to reach out.

Chapter 22 - Epilogue

"Hello?" A familiar, though wearier male voice answered the phone after a couple of rings. Martin found himself fighting through his emotions before being able to say a single word, and left it slightly too long so as to warrant another, "hello?"

"...dad?"

There was a long, heavy pause.

"Marty?"

"Dad, yes, it's me."

"Oh my... stay on the phone." Martin stayed on the line with butterflies racing around his body and in the distance on the other line he heard. "Lucy, get to the phone right now." Then, after another pause, he heard a faraway yell, "Bert! Bert. Stop whatever you are doing and come here." Martin's heart dropped somewhere that he could not see. Had he heard it right? How could Bert be there?

Suddenly, he heard his mother's voice, and he could easily imagine her face flooded with tears. "Martin?"

"Mom, hi." He had no idea what else he could say. Then his heart shot back into its original spot when he heard his brother's voice shouting, "MARTY?!!?"

"BERTY!!!" He shouted into the phone, allowing the emotion to escape him. "How is that you? I thought you died in the bus crash."

"I could say the same for you, brother."

"I can't believe this," Martin said quietly.

"Neither can we, honey," his mum cried, her voice full of tearful happiness.

The call only lasted minutes as he decided to book a flight immediately to visit them down in the States for that afternoon and ended up at their quiet home in South Carolina by the evening. The reunion was unbelievably joyful and they found themselves soon around the dinner table, allowing the brothers to tell their stories. Martin spoke his version of events with complete truth, despite the fact that it might sound ridiculous to the family. However, all of them seemed to believe and understand what he had said, especially Bert. When it was Bert's turn, he explained that he had survived the bitter fall and was helped to find his way out of the valley by none other than Vipul's monk brother. He had stayed at the monastery for some time, which allowed him to heal, and went out to search for Martin, since there were no traces of his body in the crash. Despite all of his efforts he had been unable to find him, but had held on hope for this whole time that his brother was still alive.

"The wind told me you were still alive," Bert said slightly embarrassed. "Though it was not able to tell me where to find you. Now here you are."

Martin smiled, looking around at his rediscovered family and noticed that he felt truly at ease in his body and mind for the first time in his life.

About The Author

Rupert Hudson is a writer, musician, and improviser living in Vancouver, B.C. He was inspired to write his first novel by an encouraging conversation with his grandfather as well as an inspirational talk by Elizabeth Gilbert. He wrote the book while living for three and a half months in complete isolation while working as a fire lookout in Northern Alberta. To contact the author: rupertarnetthudson@gmail.com

Printed in Great Britain
by Amazon